,8

/2

THE ASSYRIAN
AND OTHER STORIES

THE ASSYRIAN
AND OTHER STORIES

by

WILLIAM SAROYAN

23044

FABER AND FABER LTD
24 Russell Square
London

*First published in mcml
by Faber and Faber Limited
24 Russell Square London W.C.1
Printed in Great Britain by
Purnell and Sons Limited
Paulton (Somerset) and London*

410877-9

For

LUCINTAK

ACKNOWLEDGMENT

Acknowledgment is made to the following periodicals in which some of these stories first appeared: *The Armenian Review*, *The Saturday Evening Post*, *Harper's Bazaar*, *Cosmopolitan*.

CONTENTS

THE WRITER ON THE WRITING

They were written, all eleven of them, in the hope of being sold to magazines for big money because a writer's got to live, but only two of them got big money, though I'll never know why: The Cocktail Party, $5,000, The Pheasant Hunter, $3,000.

I mean I'll never know why they got so much and the others so little or nothing. Less was offered for each of them than I got, but as I had no agent to speak up for me I spoke up for myself. It was awkward to express the opinion that the stories were worth more, or to talk about the matter at all, especially since the editors had offered so much in the first place, but I had been out of touch with such things a good many years and it seemed to me that I ought to put as high a price on my product as possible.

The cost of living had gone up since I had been a whiz in the short story game, selling stories left and right for anywhere from $15 to $125, but even in those days it wasn't fame alone I was after, it was fame with honour, so to speak.

In the year 1938 an editor of a new and tremendously successful magazine, himself a whiz, offered my agent $250 for one of my short stories. The tradition then was for writers to accept all such offers with gladness and a snappy letter of thanks to the editor, most of which would appear free of charge on the page about contributors: "I used to wash dishes, I used to steal money out of cash registers, I used to read Tolstoy, but now I write short

13

stories and sell them. I like to fish and hunt, and one time at a movie when I saw Garbo take off her coat I felt pretty good, quiet-like, I mean, because I knew I had it."

The tradition was also for the boy to send the editor a snapshot of himself and be grateful to the editor for making him famous. The editor and the boys got along fine, the editor picking up stories for $75 or $100 or $150, and the boys picking up their fame every other year from where it had fallen, getting glad and masculine all over again.

So here in 1938 was an offer that looked like a pretty good one: $250 for one little old measly short story, written in one day.

I picked up the latest issue of the magazine off the floor of my workroom and went through it from cover to cover, examining the advertisements. There were a lot of them. Then I found the place in the magazine that said how many subscribers the magazine had. There were a lot of subscribers, too. There were also a lot of news-stand buyers. Then I counted the number of contributors to the magazine and I allowed each of them $250 per item, and the total came to a very small sum, about what two full-page advertisements in the magazine would cost Chesterfield or Coca-Cola. Then I went over my record with the magazine and discovered that my agent had offered the editor about a dozen different short stories over a period of a year and a half, all of which the editor had rejected.

I wrote to the agent and went over these facts and told him to write to the editor and tell him that according to my figures the short story was worth a minimum of $500 and that if he didn't want to pay that much, to send the story back, as I couldn't afford to let him have it for less. The agent wrote something or other to the editor and the editor wrote to me. He pointed out that he had paid a little more for each of my short stories he had accepted, three in all over a period of several years, and that his offer for the present story was $100 more than he had paid for the last one. I wrote back and told him I was aware of the progression involved, but that under the circumstances I still couldn't afford to let him have the story for less than $500. I pointed out that as the circulation of the magazine increased, the advertising rates also increased, and advertisers were not permitted to pay less than the new rate simply because they had advertised before at lower rates. I also told the editor that if he did not pay $500 for the story I wouldn't be interested in offering him any more. He wrote back and suggested that I see a psychiatrist, but in those days medical men weren't going in much for psychiatry and the best I could do was tell my story to a priest at a cocktail party.

He said I was all right.

The agent in the meantime urged me not to put him in bad with the editor insofar as his other writers were concerned and to please let the editor have the story for $250. The editor, it seems, had scheduled the story for a future issue and it would be difficult for him to change that issue. I told the agent to let the editor have the story with my compliments. The agent said he couldn't tell the editor that, so I wrote to the editor and told him.

Several months later the editor sent a cheque for $250 to the agent, the agent deducted ten per cent and sent me a cheque for $225, which I spent in riotous living.

Most of the writers who wrote for that magazine didn't know how to write in the first place and weren't capable of learning. On top of that they couldn't tell the difference between a handout and a payment for work. What they wanted was to be famous and man-like. It was a great trend for awhile there. I haven't looked at the magazine in years, except now and then at the barber's, so I don't know what the trend is these days, but whatever it is it's well hidden away in the advertisements. It's still probably the same school of writers, though. That is, the professional imitators who hold down small jobs on newspapers, or teach English at little colleges, or work in advertising agencies : the stubborn boys who know they'll break through some day because the little woman says so, and inspires them to keep plugging.

The Parsley Garden, to go on with the financial rating of the stories, got small money, $300. I asked for more but didn't get it and let it go because the rent was due.

Three of them got no money at all but came out in a magazine called *The Armenian Review:* The Plot, The Foreigner, and The Theological Student. They were rejected once or twice each before I let them go for nothing. I mean, they looked hopeless anyway.

The Poet at Home and The Cornet Players were rejected two or three times each before I decided not to send them out any more. I must have saved two or three dollars in postage alone.

The Assyrian was started in the hope of having something irresistible to offer to an editor, for I was in Paris at the time and flat broke, and if the story turned out to be about 25,000 words long as well as irresistible, as I hoped it would, I knew I might be paid anywhere from $15,000 to $25,000 for it. The longer I worked on it, however, the more hopeless the possibility of this financial coup became, for the writing would not be cheerful, would not be amusing, would not be something hundreds of thousands of friendly, normal, cheerful people might find in a magazine and know would be nice.

The Writer on the Writing

But only three months earlier I had gone to the trouble of writing something nice and cheerful, The Poet at Home, but this had not proved irresistible, either.

It isn't dishonourable for a writer to write something nice and clean and cheerful. It isn't dishonourable to try to write for money, either, or to try to write something that will appeal to magazine readers.

But if a writer knows he can't write a certain kind of story (not necessarily in itself worthless) but insists on trying to do so because he needs money badly, and then fails, that is foolish.

I have not often written anything *deliberately*. I was generally *impelled* to write, and whatever it turned out to be, it was O.K. as far as I was concerned because it was what I had been helpless not to write. If I saw that it seemed to be something an editor might want, I felt pleased and sent it along.

In other words, a writer's best chance of getting work done and making a living at the same time is apt to be in doing work he can't help doing, no matter how easily it may seem to be resisted by magazine editors.

There are exceptions of course and a lot of skilful writing is achieved and paid for and published because a writer knew how to go out of his way to write something that he was pretty sure would turn out all right. Most of this writing, however, might have been written by any one of two or three dozen meticulous workers who contribute regularly to the popular magazines, including *The New Yorker*. It is all pleasant to read, and now and then even a little moving, but every item seems to have been made by a fine piece of machinery instead of by a human being.

To do good writing is the easiest thing in the world for a writer provided he can get located in himself and among his fellows, but the more a man grows, the more he tries to grow, the more he accepts the responsibility of trying to grow, the less located he becomes and the more difficult it becomes for him to do work that satisfies him. To do good writing is always easy if a writer is willing or able to stay firmly located, or in other words to play safe. Playing safe a whole lifetime can make a writer's reputation. It is a good thing to do if you don't know any better. If you know better, it is still a good thing to do, but a little on the careful side. A man can always go after the tough stuff—the stuff that's so hard to put into the form of the short story or the novel—in his letters to the people he loves, or in his autobiography, or in his private journal. He can easily make a case at the last minute for the way he worked, making known that he knew what he was doing all the time, knew it wasn't much, certainly not enough, certainly a little too skilful and safe, but did it because it was the best he could do effectively with what was left of his will at the time. A man can always go after the tough stuff in his private life, work at it as long as he lives, get nearer and nearer to an understanding of it, and never go after it in his writing, never take a chance on it.

Only one story in this collection takes a real chance: The Assyrian. It is also probably the least effective of the lot as art. Still, I must think of it as the one I most needed to write, and the one most likely to satisfy the reader, not so much by what it achieves, for it achieves nothing, but by what it is unable to neglect.

The Cocktail Party is not an altogether safe story, either, but it is safe enough, I suppose.

The Poet at Home is safe, and cheerful.

The rest of the stories are all safe and sound.

Part of The Foreigner was told to me by one of my

cousins as a joke about a friend of his, and I made up the rest.

The Theological Student I pieced together out of the miscellaneous past, inventing a little here and there when it seemed in order.

The Plot almost happened as I have written it, but not quite. I began to tell the story at parties when I was feeling good about ten years ago, and although I knew no such thing had ever happened, I liked the story, liked telling it, liked watching the effect it had on those who were not able to get away, and so I decided one day to write it in as few words as possible. It is also a spoofing of the preoccupation so many writers have with the idea of getting themselves a good plot to hang a story onto. What actually happened was that a hole was dug in an empty lot by a lot of small boys and covered with boards and dirt so that no one would know there was a cave there. Another group of boys dug a cave into the bank of the same lot and the dirt caved-in over one boy who was almost suffocated before he was dragged out to air and light. The other cave was safe enough, but somebody must have telephoned the police, for they came and lifted the boards and told the boys to fill the hole. This made it necessary for the boys to take to the trees, but here again there was interference and danger. One boy fell out of the tree and hurt his leg. His mother told his father and this man (or somebody) climbed the tree one night and demolished the house. The boy didn't break his leg, he just hurt it a little. We watched him limp home, crying, and expected him back after he had had a slice of bread or a piece of watermelon, but he never came back. The tree was what we used to call a chinaball tree. It was a very small tree, but having a floor in it to stand on, ten feet above the world, six boys at once, some of them almost a hundred pounds in weight, was a very fine thing.

The Parsley Garden is made-up, another item out of the miscellaneous past. Of its kind it is a good story, and a man could spend his lifetime doing writing of this order. The sum of such work might just come to something, too, for the words of such writing only *imply* the real story, which is always an achievement if the real story happens to be something so grave, commonplace, and satisfying.

The Cornet Players is written out of amusement about an assortment of native habits of thinking. I enjoyed writing it, but as I've said no editor who saw it cared to have it for his magazine. The thing it pokes fun at is the crooked use of propaganda when an enormously large error or falsehood or failure has to be made to look to the people like beauty, art, truth and mother. The kindergarten souls who are forever puking this propaganda over the people have always amused me.

It is also about the ease with which any kind of human being can deceive himself as to what he is doing, why, and what's going to come of it. I had to listen to a lot of propagandists of this order for three years, and damned if I didn't finally have doubts about their sincerity. I mean, it got so bad I wasn't sure they *weren't* sincere. But this only made it worse, for if they were sincere, they were all the more hopeless. Famous men I'm thinking of, big men, important men, shapers of history, makers of art, serious men, dynamic men, busy men, men of action, men of thought, men of art. I have often wondered what the hell they think about when they are alone and can be on the level with themselves, when they don't have to work at the job and run with the mob. And what the devil happens to them so suddenly? They seem to fade away so swiftly. Where do they go? What do they do? What do they think when they go back over their big talk and compare it with the miserable truth of things? What do they think when they compare what they said so confidently was going to happen with what *did* happen, *is* happening? Do they think, "I guess I was only kidding"?

The Pheasant Hunter is a tour de force, I suppose, for it is altogether invented and is also not even something out of the miscellaneous past, although the longing for a gun was a pretty steady one. At last I saved up enough from selling papers to buy a second-hand single-barrel 12-gauge shotgun, and went hunting. I got nothing, but got knocked on my ass, as the saying is, and after a few more days put the gun aside and went back to books and Earl Liederman's Body-Building Course. I went hunting in the outskirts of my neighbourhood. I haven't the faintest idea what the game was supposed to be, though I may have believed for a while that I might just come face to face with a stray mountain lion, in which case I wondered if a nonchalant attitude would be more appropriate than a friendly or commanding one. I was pretty sure I wouldn't try to shoot the animal, as I had heard that this irritates them. The people whose houses were in the outskirts where I hunted usually got up quietly from their rocking chairs on their front porches and went inside their houses the minute they saw me coming up the street. I threw a rock at a small bird in a tree once and killed it by accident. I couldn't have felt more disgustingly lucky, for I had slammed hard rocks at such birds for years and had never touched a feather. Many a writer could take an accident like that and work it into something quite impressive. All I remember is that I was afraid of the dead bird and that when I touched its breast with my toe its mouth opened and made a monstrous sound, and that it looked very dead, even though its eyes remained open. I felt ashamed, too, as if I had killed the bird on purpose, which I had not done. I had slammed the rock on purpose, but only because I had done it for years and had never hurt a thing. Since the time of the shotgun I have had a number of other guns and pistols, but they have bored me, for the gun is without a doubt the stupidest invention of man. He really stuck his neck out when he came up with that one, scaring himself half to death and changing the whole attitude of man toward animal and toward himself. He'll never be able to invent a reasonable use for the thing or ever be able to get rid of it.

The Third Day After Christmas is another tour de force, written on the third day after Christmas, 1948.

The Leaf Thief was written in San Francisco in August, 1949, after a long walk.

To sum up the financial score, there would appear to be eight thousand three hundred dollars and no cents' worth of short story writing here, at current rates. It is a rather impressive figure at that, considering that the money was earned by only three of the eleven stories, and that the two long stories, the ones I had hoped would make me rich, earned no money at all. Thus, one must conclude that the short story market is much improved since I was a whiz in the game back in 1934-1939.

During those five years I must have written five hundred short stories, or a mean average of one hundred per annum. Most of them weren't actually short stories of course, but not one of them was written for money, either, so that whatever the hell they were in terms of literary form, they were certainly aloof at least, and they made my name, such as it is.

The Writer on the Writing

I wrote a lot of them because I enjoyed writing and always wanted to know, "What next?" For I always felt that I was as apt to write something fine every time as not, and I believed that what I was trying to prove, what I was by way of demonstrating, was that when it comes to the matter of using words, anything can happen, should be permitted to happen, should be encouraged to happen. I believe I also meant to establish a tradition of carelessness, for it seemed to me from the years of my apprenticeship that the thing that blocked creation was carefulness. The trouble was that after most writers *had* been careful, after they had written stories in spite of the fact that they were creatively blocked, the stories still weren't very good. This seemed a pity, not to say a boring state of affairs for me personally.

What it came to was that either I wrote freely and easily or didn't write at all, and since I had after the age of twenty recognised that I was by nature unfit for any other trade, occupation or profession, I had to make up my mind to write freely and easily and at the same time make whatever I happened to write fairly acceptable, on a percentage basis. That is, one out of ten, one out of five, or one out of two.

The short story form, as such, never appealed to me especially, and for years I couldn't do a thing with it. A bore was always involved in a boring problem and getting out of it in a boring way, and I didn't want to be bothered. I just wanted to say the same words I was saying when I talked.

I didn't want to describe a room or a house or a city or a street or a sky or a hill or a valley or anything else. I wanted to say something about myself, and something about the effect people I happened to run into, including my family, had on me. I wasn't educated enough to write

23

essays like the ones Max Beerbohm or Logan Pearsall Smith or George Santayana wrote, although I hadn't read any of their essays in those days, and besides I didn't like the way essays seemed to go, either. You were supposed to be in possession of certain facts, generally about something so tiresome I couldn't imagine caring to go into the matter at all, and then you were supposed to arrange them nicely and have something written that ought to be nice for an old lady sitting in a rocking-chair on the porch of the Old People's Home to read.

Between the essay and the short story, though, it seemed to me there existed a form or formlessness which would permit me to write. I didn't make a decision about this, however. I didn't need to. I didn't know what I was doing. I was just busy doing the best I could under the circumstances. Everything I wrote seemed hopeless, though, because I couldn't get out of the habit of comparing it with something in a newspaper, a magazine, or a book, and no matter how bad the thing was that I compared my writing with, my writing seemed worse.

At last I decided that either I myself was the beginning and end of the matter, or there was no matter at all. I was interesting or I wasn't. The way I stayed alive was interesting or it wasn't. I just didn't have any other way of solving the problem of literature and getting to work.

I had always felt that I was the beginning and end of any matter, and that I was interesting, but I had been ashamed to make anything of it, for I knew it was the same with everybody else.

The difference appeared to be that I was unfit for any other work but writing and that most other people didn't want to write. I felt that I had to take advantage of this circumstance, and I tried my best for years to do so but got nowhere. At least I believed at the time that I had got nowhere, although in reality I had achieved one or two important things.

At the age of twenty when I stopped trying to make a living at work that bored me and openly declared that I was either a writer or a bum, my family agreed that there was no doubt about it, and pretty much let the matter go at that. This was a great achievement, for I was not obliged after that to prove every day that I was doing my share. I no longer had any share to do. If I worked one day a week or two days a month, the five or ten dollars I earned was spent on paper, clips, postage, envelopes, cigarettes and anything else a writer might need : typewriter ribbons. I had owned a typewriter since August, 1928, from the time I had first gone to New York to make my fame and fortune but had come back to San Francisco, homesick and broke, after six months.

The other thing I achieved was resignation to the loneliness a writer knows all the time ; and the capacity not to need anything irrelevant : not to need good clothes, a fine house with a fine workroom in it in which to work, a big car in which to travel around, a lot of money, or a girl to sit at my feet and sigh because I had just written the word *beautiful* on the typewriter and permitted her to read it.

That is, I achieved *partial* resignation to this loneliness, for total resignation to it does not seem possible for me. I have heard that after years of such resignation, the loneliness that one has been resigned to ceases to be loneliness at all ; but only now and then, for a week or two at a time, have I found this to be the case with me.

I am the best company I know, but only because I *remember* other company. Kids are the best company of all of course, but they grow up, and even before they do you can't spend much time with them because it bores them. They are in fact the only aristocracy of the human race, and after them come those who fail or refuse to wholly relinquish the aristocracy they acquired at birth; that is, the better poets and scientists and other creatively alive people, for the one thing all childhood has in common, as everyone by now knows, is creativeness. And the one thing all adulthood has in common is literalness: the great block to any real achievement of growth. Thus, the so-called adult is for the most part a case of blocked growth, of failure to live all of life at once, from birth to death.

The American writer's preoccupation with earning, with being paid (underpaid or overpaid) for his work, is understandable, for it is simply a fact that unless a writer can count on earning at least a little money, he cannot expect to continue in his profession with comfort, or without embarrassment or bitterness; and these feelings, if they persist long enough, will do something to his work that is not necessarily good, for the cult of failure is as damaging as the cult of success.

Every writer knows that writing of all kinds earns good money for writers of all kinds at all times, including depressions and wars.

The writer who is only a writer is a rare bird these days, most writers having taken posts at universities, gone into the government on a full or part-time basis, or into publishing, play producing, moving picture directing, radio, medicine, agriculture, lecturing, acting, advertising, travel and adventure (to obtain exclusive material), book reviewing, article or interview writing on assignment, or journalism. A number of writers are lawyers or business men.

Pure and simple writing, it would seem, does not pay. The pure and simple writer must get help from the Guggenheim Foundation or from one or another of the annual prize awards, or from friends.

In the days of the old *American Mercury* frequent contributors to the magazine were stickup men in penitentiaries, professional panhandlers, chronic hoboes, and others of this sort with special material to write about. This was undoubtedly for the amusement of H. L. Mencken and his sidekick George Jean Nathan. There was no harm in it, the pieces were interesting, but they tended to divert the attention of the potential writer, trying his best to make a start, from the material native to himself to material that was at best ludicrous. A young writer, getting stories back from editors every day, was apt to feel awkward about not being in a position to write an account of how he cheated, stole, raped, murdered, or felt just before he went to the electric chair.

The profession of pure and simple writing is apt to become a dull one when a writer himself is dull or preoccupied with something else. Consequently, it is in order for the writer, unpublished or famous, to take stock of himself every year or two in order to find out what the score is. For the truth is that if a man is fit for the profession of writing at all, the profession's potential for expansion, enlargement, extension and variety is greater than the potential of any other profession, so that if it *has* become a dull profession, the writer may be sure that it is he himself who has become dull. It is desirable to avoid this, hence a few words on how to do so.

Rules for writers are the same as rules for anybody else whose basic intention is to live creatively: that is, as pleasantly as possible under the circumstances, with honour, integrity, intelligence, humour, decent pride and decent humility. And the making of rules is solely a personal thing, sure to be inadequate for others, or meaningless, or incomplete. Even so, I would put it thus:

A writer should never stop work on the job of creating his own character. He should work at this job every day. It is the best if not the only work he can do for himself as a person, as a writer, and as a social being. No one has yet succeeded in making out a fair case against this seemingly selfish or even self-centred and lifetime task, and there is no evidence that it is not finally the best means by which a writer, or anybody else, may be helpful to others, or useful to society and the world. The creation of character is apt to be even more important than the creation of art, even though it is not likely that a writer will create his own character and not also create works of art.

In the nature of things this is job that is never finished, for no man may believe he has created his character once and for all and is now free to live off of it, as he might say he has made his fortune and is now free to sit on it and live off the interest.

The following would appear to be the means, or some of them, by which the writer may work at the creation of his character:

1. Self-knowledge
2. Health
3. Intelligence
4. Imagination, intuition, collective unconscious
5. Social responsibility
6. Technical skill

The man who does not need to know about himself is not apt to be a writer in the first place, hence we may presume that the writer has self-knowledge to begin with, that in all probability having self-knowledge impelled him to start writing, and that if he is to have self-knowledge at all, the more he has of it the better it will be for him and for his work. The self is not static, therefore must be re-discovered and understood continuously.

A writer in order to live and work (in order to achieve self-knowledge and to create his character) ought to look after his health. His body should be exercised, his appetites satisfied, his lusts frequently disciplined and denied (if doing so does not impair his health : that is, do more harm than good). A writer should bathe as often as he is in need of a bath. He should shave (unless he prefers having a beard) as often as he needs a shave, unless he needs a shave twice a day, in which case once a day will do : in the morning when he gets up, as a clean face frequently improves a writer's work. He should not go in for sports, either actively or to watch, because in all probability he has done both and once or twice is enough for all practical purposes. He also should not do callisthenics, as doing them tends to upset him for not being as young and resilient as he used to be. He should not try to become as young as he used to be.

A writer should think, should be intelligent, but should not throw his intelligence around, as it is bad manners. In company he should be cheerful, courteous, considerate, well-mannered, sincere, affectionate, warm-hearted, but not intelligent in the classic sense, for if he were intelligent in the classic sense he could not be the other things, and if he could not be the other things he ought not to be in company. He should tell jokes, sing, dance, make fun for himself, take part in games, have a good time. If everybody is drinking, he should drink. He should not be above the minor social pleasures, but he should not remain in company which praises Russia and criticizes America, or criticizes Russia and praises America. He should leave such company and go home, as such criticizing and praising is neither intelligent nor a social pleasure. He should not despise people who do it, though. He should kill them on the spot or let them live and enjoy themselves the way they must. If he can convert somebody he happens to like to intelligence and is able to do so quietly, he should do so. He should not try to convert anybody he doesn't like. He is most apt to get along with all kinds of people and to do good work if he doesn't try to convert anybody at all, but if he must try, the best beginning he can make (if it is somebody he likes) is to say cheerfully, "Shut up, just shut up." He should never strike a woman for getting her sexual hunger identified with socialized medicine, and he should not leap to conclusions about socialized medicine because of this identification. He should think about it. He should think about everything. He should think all the time. He should be intelligent all the time, which means that when it is intelligent not to be intelligent he should not be intelligent. He should not be zealous about any conclusions he may reach by the exercise of intelligence, for that is the beginning of the betrayal of intelligence, the transformation of it into something else. He should never argue, except with children, and only in order to please them, and he should always lose such arguments as a matter of principle. He should sharpen and warm his intelligence (and his skill as writer) by observing carefully the intelligence and economic self-expression of children. If he happens to have children, he should spank them if they ask for it, and never apologize for having done so, for doing so is a second punishment, and one they certainly do not deserve.

A writer should learn how to both ignore and encourage his soul: his imagination, intuition, collective unconscious. This is important because an intelligent balance between ignoring and encouraging makes for smoother going, a better quality of self-knowledge, and an easier achievement of help in his work from these powerful and valuable agencies. Too much ignoring is as great a mistake as too much encouraging. A writer should never be astonished by the wonders he is able to achieve from being on cordial relations with these agencies, nor should he permit himself to be shocked by the surprises these agencies are able to present him. He should not permit these agencies to tease him into a pose of being more of a man than he is. Most men are man enough, most writers know there is much of the woman (of creativeness and intuition) in their natures, and all men know half their ancestors have been women. There would not appear to be much necessity in this particular for any writer to go to anxiety extremes in one direction or another.

As for his social responsibility, a writer should meet it at all times and under all circumstances, or at any rate try to do so. If doing so or trying to do so makes his responsibility to himself difficult, he may be sure that he has not yet been responsible enough to himself and that he is not yet ready for full social responsibility. A half-baked man being socially responsible is actually being socially mischievous. A writer should try to avoid this. Being half-baked and socially responsible may be fun for him but at the same time it may cause a lot of agony to a lot of strangers. A writer should not run for public office or permit himself to be appointed to any post in which he is not answerable solely to his conscience, regardless of trends, pressures, expediency. As this is inconceivable, he must not accept any such appointment unless he has decided to abandon the profession of writing and the hope of a creative life. A writer should have as many friends or acquaintances as possible, the more kinds the better. But he should also have available at all times an inviolable privacy, not for work alone but for meditation, recuperation, restoration. He should have enemies and he should be grateful for them, for if he had none, it would in all probability mean that his writing was basically indifferent.

And finally a writer should keep after his skill. He should try to avoid relaxing about it, being satisfied with it, believing it is as developed as he can make it. He should try to avoid imitating himself or repeating himself and should look upon each new work as a new problem to be worked out in a new and perhaps better way. He should write letters, for out of the directness of letter-writing frequently comes a freshening of skill, for in the end every form of writing is essentially a letter to friends, enemies, and strangers. Some of the heaviness of many novels by good writers appears to be the result of their having forgotten what they were doing. A writer should try to remember that anything he writes may have a relatively long life and be read in many different languages by many different races of people. He should recognize this as the greater part of his social responsibility. He should write accordingly. He should think well of himself, so that he may be able to think well of others. He should believe in himself, in his decency, in his devotion to the hope of truth, in his contempt for purposeful, deliberate crudity, vulgarity, crookedness, arrogance, deception, and the degradation, humiliation or corruption of man. He should find it impossible not to love honour and aspire to it at all times. He should avoid martyrdom because work will achieve more than martyrdom will both for his own character and for the decent and unhysterical improvement of others. He should never permit humour to disappear out of his life or writing, for humour is the natural and necessary companion of survival, and there cannot be any survival (of anything) without it. He must survive. He should try to survive pleasantly, meaningfully, productively, and honourably, but if this proves difficult or impossible under his own circumstances, and if it also proves difficult or impossible for him to change his own circumstances because they are so much a part of circumstances in general, then he must try to survive anyway, without these things, or with as much of them as he is able to manage. A writer ought to try to keep himself away from the compulsion (at last) to commit suicide or murder, or to engage in prostitution, or to give false witness, or in any way to befoul or belittle life in any form, or the potential of any form of life to survive. A writer should finally come to the end peacefully and gladly and be thankful for the time he had.

A writer should also avoid being, or trying to be, or allowing others to make him seem to be a messiah, for messiahs are without humour, incapable of it, and they invariably make mischief and impel killing, hysteria, cruelty, mobbishness, and a rejection of intelligence. The only leading that is ever in order for a writer is the leading of his own children when he teaches them to walk and talk, and that would also appear to be the only kind of leadership the human race itself ought to be willing to put up with. The myth of leaders is an unholy one.

The question comes up every year or so (largely among writers themselves) as to whether or not writers are necessary. It has been coming up for many hundreds of years and many good writers have asked it and tried to answer it. Writers are not as necessary for man's body as farmers and physicians are ; they are not as necessary for the easy entertainment of his soul, even, as movies, the stage, radio, television, magazines and newspapers are; and they are not as comforting to *all* of him as the church, baseball, or the horse races are.

Is there, then, any need for serious writers any longer? Any need, that is, for poets?

Language is needed obviously : print is needed, presses are needed, books are needed, magazines and newspapers are needed, writing is needed. But is the poet needed? The statesman must write his memoirs : the scientist must report his findings : the anthropologist, the biologist, the architect, the engineer, the mathematician, the inventor, the astronomer, the soldier, the sailor, the aviator, the explorer, the judge, the lawyer, the millionaire, the manufacturer, the banker and dozens of others must turn in their reports as memoirs, theory, history or general information, but is there any need for the poet, for the writer to turn in his report?

The question seems silly. It would be insulting were it not that poets themselves ask it. This would suggest that the profession is frequently inadequately rewarding, for even Tolstoy gave it up and took up the writing of propaganda, and almost every other great writer finally gave it up, or thought of doing so, and for all any of us knows soon afterwards died, perhaps as a direct result of finding the profession unsatisfying.

Henry James said at last something about his one regret being that he wrote life instead of living it. What did he believe life was? Where had his own, which he had lived with so much quiet style, failed him?

Only a man's own writing may be unnecessary, and it may be unnecessary only when he himself has doubts about its necessity. But every man sooner or later seems to come to the time when he feels his writing is not necessary, and he does not mean the writing he is presently

34

doing or trying to do, he means all of it, the writing he did long ago, that he has probably forgotten how he did.

This does not seem to be a mysterious thing, as I see it. It is something that probably happens to all people and is not so noticeable in them only because they are not writers. This thing that happens is death : that is, death as it happens in the living before they stop altogether. It is exhaustion, or the beginning of it. It is weariness. It is overwhelming indifference about one's self, one's own life, about the whole business of life. It is a natural thing, I suspect. Its natural purpose is to enable men to die, to stop altogether, and thereby to make room for others, for the living, for those who will also die but have a number of good years to go on in which to do whatever it is their living is to express itself by. Every man sooner or later asks of himself if he is necessary, and soon afterwards knows that he isn't. And he forgets that he has been quite necessary, especially to himself.

Nothing is more necessary than writing, no one is more necessary than the poet as long as the writing and the poet are coming, so to say. When the writing and the poet are going, it is probably true that they are no longer very necessary, if at all. By going one must understand that *going dead* is meant and by coming *coming alive* is meant, for a writer, or any human being, may have been *going* physically for years, may have been literally dying of an organic disease, for instance, and still have been coming alive all the time.

The complaint of the writers who have asked the question has been that hardly anyone alive at a given time has been willing to read what the poet has written. This, he feels, proves poetry and poets are not necessary. To this writer, however, it proves no such thing, for no writer has ever complained that only *he* read his writing. Others did read it. Out of the two thousand million people alive in the world more or less constantly perhaps no more than five thousand read it, or fifty thousand, or five hundred thousand, or at the most (in a period of ten years) a million. But how many people who have heard about the Himalayas have climbed them, or even seen them, or even need to? What has the climbing or the seeing of the Himalayas to do with the fact of their being, the fact that they are there, that they have been seen and climbed? How many people have to read a book in order for the book to be necessary?

The complaint has been that multitudes have read newspapers, and that this has been foolish and unkind of them. Has it? I doubt it. As no one asks a writer to be a writer, as no one asks him to write a particular book, it is quite plain that he did so for other reasons, and that they must have been pretty good ones while they lasted, for it is always hard work to write, even to write something immediately recognizable as worthless. He insisted on being a writer and on writing a particular book. (I say book in order to mean simultaneously any kind of writing: poetry, drama, the novel, the short story.) It would seem, then, that the failure implied by the poet is no one's but his own : that he is, in short, unhappy and tired.

This also is something the writer ought to try to avoid, even though it is difficult not to be unhappy and almost impossible for a writer not to become very tired. What may be done about this? Is it desirable for something to be done about it? I think it is, and I think something sensible may be done about it. Certainly about getting tired. Unhappiness is with a man always anyway. It is simply that if he is not too tired he will be able to put up with it better and go about his business.

Writers get tired because they work too hard for too

long, for too many years, but unless they do so they will not get all the work done that they feel they ought to get done.

Now, the question comes up, can a writer get all the work done that he feels he ought to get done and at the same time not get too tired and therefore in the prime of life find himself unbearably weary and sick of his profession? The answer is no, he can't. If he could he would.

What does this suggest? It suggests that writers will do what they must, but it also suggests that if it pleases them to do so they *may* evolve a procedure of living and working that will get *enough* work done and still not make them too tired.

I am interested in looking into the second half of this suggestion.

Anxiety at work is what tires a writer most. Anxiety to do the best it is possible for him to do, anxiety to get it done before his powers fail him, anxiety about size, texture, quality. If a different art of writing comes into being as a result of writing *without* anxiety, it does not necessarily follow that this art will be a lesser art or that it will appeal even less to readers than writing achieved with anxiety. There is no telling. Writing without anxiety is certain to do the writer himself good; which takes me back to what it was I had hoped to achieve for myself when I wrote so many short stories in 1934–1939. I felt that it was right to just write them and turn them loose and not take myself or the stories too seriously. I had hoped to achieve an easier way for a man to write: that is, a more natural way. I believe that this was a worthwhile thing to go after. I believe writing achieved in pain and torture is not necessarily better than writing gladly achieved.

If anxiety, then, is the thing for the writer to get rid of

at his work, it follows that the way to get rid of it is for the writer to have implicit faith in himself, in his character, and in what he is apt to write. He must believe that it is not necesary for him to be careful if being careful makes him anxious and tired. He must believe that it is possible for him to achieve writing as good as he might ever achieve anyway by working easily, swiftly and with gladness. This means that he must have something to say, that he is experienced enough not to need to brood about how to say it, and experienced enough as a human being to know what the sum of what he is to say is to be.

In short, if a writer's character is all right, how can anything he writes not be the best he *ought* to write? How can it not be what his writing ought to be? How can it not be as important, as necessary as writing achieved by any other means?

There is, in short, no exact and final way in which a writer may write, and if one way achieves great art it may not necessarily be great art *solely* because of the way in which it was achieved, it may be great art in *spite* of the way in which it was achieved, it may be great art because the writer had character, and it may finally be that he got tired because he did not get to his character in the simplest or most natural manner.

Now, it may also be that for our world, time and rate of living some of the elements in the great literary achievements of the past are either no longer comfortably achievable or even desirable. This writer believes that even the masterpieces of writing frequently have too much art in them, for instance. Too much art of a kind, that is. *All* is art of course, a matter of degree. The question is, then, Can writing be good art and still be gladly achieved?

I think it can.

The Writer on the Writing

It may be that the flaw in the lives of the great writers who got tired was that they were too much writers and too little human beings. Too little, that is, men like all others, men not living only the literary life but living the whole one.

Anybody *cannot* learn to write, cannot learn to create life or a sense of life through writing. But if a man is a writer, he definitely can learn to write, and this will be learned, as I have said, by creating his character, by working at it all the time.

San Francisco, August 31, 1949.

THE ASSYRIAN

I had traversed Asia Minor and Syria, visiting the ancient seats of civilization, and the spots which religion has made holy. I now felt an irresistible desire to penetrate to the regions beyond the Euphrates, to which history and tradition point as the birthplace of the wisdom of the West. Most travellers, after a journey through the usually frequented parts of the East, have the same longing to cross the great river, and to explore those lands which are separated on the map from the confines of Syria by a vast blank stretching from Aleppo to the banks of the Tigris.

AUSTIN HENRY LAYARD, 1849

CHAPTER ONE

When the taxi stopped the Assyrian looked away from the barefooted woman walking with the basket of twigs balanced on her head and noticed the hotel.

"Is this the Aviz?" he said to the driver in English.

"Yes, Aviz," the driver said in Portuguese.

He had expected it to be in the heart of the city, a modern building, perhaps something like the Torni in Helsingfors which he had visited in 1935. Instead, it was a small castle set inside a triangle-shaped garden surrounded by quiet streets. There was a high black iron fence around the grounds and a palm tree as high as a telephone pole at the entrance.

He wasn't sure he wanted to try to spend a few days here. The concierge boys at the Palace in Madrid had agreed among themselves after discussion that the best hotel in Lisbon was by far the Aviz, and he had sent along a wire asking for a room that morning just before riding out to the airport. They had mentioned two other hotels and he would have asked the driver to go along to one or another of them, but he had forgotten their names.

The twigs in the basket, he decided, must be for fuel, though not for this day, as it was bright and warm. The woman, old and stern, wearing brown rags, had beauty of body and moved proudly. He turned to watch her a moment as she moved past the taxi. She looked straight ahead, and seemed to be blinded by a patience that had long ago become second nature. Her feet were large, strong, thick skinned and almost black. He had never before seen a woman with thirty pounds of junk balanced on her head.

"They use their heads all right," he thought.

The driver had the door open now and was getting the luggage out and a small boy in uniform was coming down the steps of the hotel to the taxi, his young face solemn with the responsibility of an important job at an hotel.

He handed the boy his brief-case.

"You carry this," he said. "I'll carry the suitcases."

"No, no," the boy said, trying to hand back the brief-case.

"What's the tariff?" he said to the taxi-driver.

The man said something in Portuguese that was meaningless, so he brought out some of the currency he had acquired at the airport exchange and lifted three twenties.

"About three dollars I guess this is," he thought. "It was a long ride, but perhaps it's fare and tip."

The driver said something probably numerical and the traveller said, "More?"

The Assyrian

"No, no," the driver said.

The traveller gave him the three twenties.

The driver smiled and said, "Obrigado."

The driver then picked up both suitcases to carry them into the hotel while the small boy struggled with him for one of them so that he would not be left out in the cold completely. The driver refused to give over, however, and the boy trailed along beside him.

"Obrigado," the traveller thought. "What's that mean? In Rome if I had offered a taxi-driver what I offered this man he would have asked for three times as much, I would have given it to him, and then he would have asked for a tip, and in all probability mentioned either that he had two children or that he had been chauffeur to a Captain in the United States Army for two years, a man named, most likely, Jorge Schmith."

The hotel looked pretty good inside. He knew the kind of place it was immediately: small, quiet, dignified, expensive and exclusive.

A young woman who wore a summer dress of yellow and green was sitting in an enormous chair smoking a cigarette, the daughter of an English banker, no doubt, or a minor government man, or an old soldier.

The traveller nodded to her, and she turned to see if someone was seated behind her. No one was of course. She then turned back to examine him, and almost simultaneously looked slightly up and away. It were as if she had said, "If we have met, I don't remember where, and if we are to meet again, it's not to be across a lobby this way."

The clerk at the desk looked as if he might be a medical student at Yale.

"Paul Scott," the traveller said. "Did you get my wire from Madrid?"

"When did you send it?" the clerk said in perfect English.

"About four hours ago," the traveller said, glancing again at the girl. He had not expected to find her looking at him, but since she was, he smiled a little as if to say: "Oh yes, we've met: we met twenty seconds ago."

The girl looked around again to see if someone else was in the room, and of course it was still only herself. He was nodding to her, that's all.

"We have no wire from you," the clerk said.

"Well, I want a room," the traveller said. "Here's my passport."

"Our rooms are all taken."

"Let me speak to the manager please."

While the clerk was fetching the manager, Paul Scott lighted a cigarette and handed the small bellboy his tip, about a dollar. The boy accepted the money gratefully, said the appropriate word, and stood by waiting for developments.

"Worked here long?" the traveller said.

The boy replied in Portuguese that he did not speak English.

"Well, if you want to get ahead, learn English," the traveller said. "It's the coming thing."

The boy listened and tried to make something of the strange sounds, smiling and then becoming shy because the truth was he hadn't understood a word.

The traveller was looking at the girl steadily and she was trying not to notice that he was.

"I know I won't get a room," he thought, "but so much the better. I'm tired of this place already, and this girl bores me at fifteen yards."

Before being turned away by a hotel he liked to take the matter up with the manager. There was no sense getting turned away by anything less than the top man, and there was always the chance that this man might get the impression he had a lot of American green to trade in the black market.

That's how it had been in Madrid. After a chat with the manager, he had gotten a first-class room and then after a bath and a good steak for lunch the manager had noticed him at the desk asking about the town's amusements and had invited him into his office.

"Do you have, perhaps," the manager had said, "undeclared American dollars? I can give you ten pesetas a dollar above the official rate, but of course we must do this privately. My mother is very sick."

He had told the man that he believed he had five or six hundred dollars undeclared and the man had said, "You are very kind."

It turned out, however, that every dollar had been declared and it would be folly for the manager to alter the figures on the declaration. Thus, a commonplace sneak-play in Spanish finance had been frustrated.

"Perhaps you have a friend with undeclared dollars," the manager had said.

"No," the traveller had said. "I don't have a friend in the world."

The clerk and the manager of the Aviz Hotel appeared together. The clerk went behind the counter but the manager remained outside.

"We have no rooms," he said quickly. "We receive reservations weeks and sometimes months in advance."

"I don't plan to stay very long."

"Tonight only?"

"Tonight and part of tomorrow morning."

"I can count on it?"

"Of course. Isn't there a resort a little out of town?"

"Estoril?"

"Yes. I'll go there tomorrow."

"Very well."

The manager went behind the counter to examine the room chart.

"I have a very good room, but only until noon tomorrow."

"Bath, of course."

"All our rooms and apartments have baths and showers."

"Good. I haven't had a *shower* in a month."

The manager and the clerk worked together on writing things down from the passport, and then the clerk took a very large key attached to a very heavy piece of round flat metal and led the way to the elevator, the small bellboy struggling alone with the luggage at last. The traveller did not interfere this time. Still, the boy scarcely made it into the elevator, the inside of which was like the inside of a horse-drawn carriage, all brown velvet and soft brown leather.

"Who's the lady in the lobby?" the traveller said.

"I beg your pardon?" the clerk said.

"That girl sitting alone in the lobby? Who is she?"

"Her name's Borrego."

"You mean she's not English?"

"Oh no. She's Portuguese."

"Well, she *speaks* English of course."

"Oh yes."

"She *looks* English."

"It happens," the clerk said. "Some people have told me I look *French*."

"Yes, but that's understandable. Almost anybody in Portugal is apt to look a little French, I suppose."

"Oh no," the clerk said. "We have the Moorish types. They do not look French at all."

"The women who carry baskets on their heads," the traveller said. "Are they the Moorish types?"

"All the types carry baskets on their heads in Portugal," the clerk said, "except the upper classes."

"I certainly would like to see that girl in the lobby carry a basket on *her* head."

"She cannot carry a basket on her head," the clerk said. "Her mother was not trained in it, and so she was not, also. Her father is Victor Borrego, our greatest critic."

"Of what?"

"I beg your pardon?"

The elevator, which had moved very slowly, now stopped. With a key the elevator boy unlocked the metal grill gate and pushed it forward. The bellboy worked with his burden and the clerk moved to step out, but the traveller remained seated on the leather bench.

"Your greatest critic of what?" he said.

"Of *all* the arts," the clerk said. "Literature, music, painting, sculpture. We are a small country, so he is not known in America."

The traveller got up.

"What's the rest of her name, and what's she like to do?"

"I don't understand," the clerk said.

"I mean, does she write or paint or anything fantastic like that?"

"Oh no. They are very rich."

"What's she doing sitting alone in the lobby?"

"They have lunch here two or three times a week. We have the best food in Lisbon."

"Who do you mean by *they*?"

"Her father and mother and her brother and sister. The Portuguese are all family people, rich or poor."

47

They were standing in the court of the top floor now. The bellboy had gotten the luggage into the room and was proudly on his way back to the elevator. He stopped to hand the key to the traveller.

"Obrigado," he said.

"What is that word I've heard several times?" the traveller said.

"It means *thank you* in Portuguese," the clerk said.

"*Obregardo*, is that it?"

"Again?"

"Obregardo," the traveller said slowly.

The clerk listened carefully this time.

"I think not," he said. "I will write it and then say it."

The traveller handed him the envelope he kept in the inside pocket of his coat for just such an occasion, and on it the clerk carefully printed the word, and then said it.

"Ah," the traveller said. "I get it. Obrigado."

"Yes, that is the way to say it."

They stepped into the room and the traveller was not surprised to find it large and well furnished. There were twin beds and good pieces of the usual furniture, but the bath was enormous, with tile everywhere excepting the ceiling: brown, green, white and black. Very cool and clean.

"Lunch is from one to three," the clerk said. "Dinner eight to ten."

"O.K. If I step into the dining-room at five minutes to three, or five minutes to ten, will that be all right?"

"Oh yes. There is always somebody at the tables until five o'clock from lunchtime, and sometimes at night after dinner they sit there until twelve."

"Good. Now, what is that girl's name?"

"Obrigado."

The clerk was smiling.

48

"I knew you'd be surprised," he said. "Yes, that's her *name*. Obrigado Borrego. They are very proud people."

"That's good," the traveller said.

He was getting a little bored.

"I am speaking this way because I know you are the American writer," the clerk said.

"One of six or seven dozen," the traveller said.

"When her father learns you are in Lisbon, I believe he will ask you to his home," the clerk said.

"He will? How will he learn I am in Lisbon?"

"Such news gets around very quickly."

"I don't get it," the traveller said, "but it's O.K. with me."

"The manager," the clerk said. "He does not read very much and he does not know who you are. I shall tell him this afternoon. Perhaps you may keep this room as many days as you like."

"Hot dog," the American writer said softly.

"Hot dog?" the clerk said.

"That means *very nice* in American."

The telephone bell rang and the writer picked up the receiver.

"Yes," he said.

The clerk moved to go.

"Wait a minute," the traveller said.

"Mr. Scott," he heard the manager say, "I am Mr. Sousa, the manager. I have on the line the newspaper writer Rodrigo Azevedo. He is asking when it will be convenient for you to give him an interview of two hours."

This was something new, perhaps improved, for ordinarily they asked for an interview of five minutes and then stretched it out to two hours.

"Any time at all," the writer said.

"Your convenience, Mr. Scott," the manager said.

"How about five o'clock this afternoon, then?"

"Very good. I shall tell Mr. Azevedo. Thank you."

The writer hung up.

"Who's Rodrigo Azevedo?" he said to the clerk.

"He is the best newspaper writer in Lisbon," the clerk said. "He has interviewed them all. The kings who come to Lisbon when they have no more kingdom, the American moving picture stars on their honeymoons, the statesmen, the rich men from all over the world. He is at the airport for every landing and he examines the list. That is how he knew you were in Lisbon."

"How did he know I came to the Aviz?"

"It is the best hotel."

"I see. Now, which of my books have you read?"

"All of them."

"In English?"

"Yes."

"Which do you like the best?"

"The last one."

"*The Runaway Rock?*"

"Yes."

"Well, that's very kind of you. I happen to have a copy of it in my suitcase and I'd like very much to inscribe it to you."

"Thank you very much," the clerk said. "My name is Eduardo Dos Santos."

The writer opened one of his suitcases, looked around in it, then opened the other, found the book, opened it, wrote in it, and handed it to the boy.

"In a half hour or so," he said, "will you have the boys send up a steak medium rare, a green salad, and some fresh fruit."

"Yes, sir."

The clerk went along and the writer began to unpack.

The Assyrian

He threw laundry out of both suitcases onto a bed, pressed the button for the valet, opened the door, and in a moment saw an old man, asked him in, handed him a Portuguese twenty, and said, "Express, special, as quickly as possible." The man understood and enquired about shoes to be polished. The traveller brought out his black shoes and removed the brown pair he was wearing, and the old man went off quickly with the stuff.

The writer then brought out the notebook he had bought in Marseille and after finding the place wrote, "Fell asleep on the airplane for about two minutes and dreamed Rosey wept. Picked her up and said, 'Listen, little girl, Papa loves you, but he can't do anything for you. Nobody can do anything for anybody.' Began to sob. Woke up and wondered if I had been heard."

Rosey was the man's daughter by his third wife. He had a son by his first, a son and daughter by his second, and Rosey. He loved them all, each of the children and each of his lost wives, but the three-year-old Rosey ravaged his soul. He hated to think he had lost her too, but he knew he had.

The child's nurse had taken her along to his hotel in New York to leave his mail, and he had run into them in the lobby. Rosey had run into his arms and said, "You coming home, Papa?"

That was the last time he'd seen her. He'd chatted with the nurse a moment, asking about the child's health, about her eating, and not asking about his wife, for he knew she was all right. The nurse had gone off with the little girl and he had hurried to the bar. Then he had gone upstairs and telephoned T.W.A. about flight

51

schedules, and that night two months ago had set out for Europe.

He frequently prayed for the girl, saying, "Please don't hurt Rosey."

He put the notebook aside and stepped into the bathroom to draw his bath.

His wife had no idea how tough this final failure was proving to be, but he was thankful for that, even though they had long ago found their loathing of one another greater than their love or whatever the hell it had been.

He had first seen her early one morning as she came into the Cub Room, accompanied by two college boys.

She had seemed irresistible, arrogant and animal, her small bright face, her child's eyes, her enormous mouth, her long and perfectly white neck, and her incredibly abundant black hair making him laugh as one laughs when one beholds anything perfect.

The college boys had been high on rum and Coca-Colas when he had walked over to the table and said, "I've got to know your name. What is it?"

"What's yours?"

"Paul Scott."

"You say that," she said, "as if it meant something, or ought to, but it doesn't. So your name's Paul Scott, so my name's Katey, so what?"

The college boys roared with laughter.

"Ah, don't you know who he is?" one of them said. "He's Paul Scott. Whoever thought we'd ever meet Paul Scott? Ah, sit down, Paul old pal, and have a drink."

"Thanks," he said. "Which of you is engaged to Miss——"

"Muffet," she said.

"Yes," he said. "Which of you?"

"Ah, neither of us is engaged to her."

"So what?" the girl said.

They had a drink together, then another, and he got up and said, "It wouldn't have done not to have spoken with you a moment," and then to the boys he said, "I wonder if you know how lucky you are to know her."

"We sure do," one of them said.

He hadn't learned her name because he had refused to bring the matter up again, and on his way to his hotel in the taxi he had felt ashamed of having forced himself on her.

It was four that morning when he had finished his shower before going to bed. At half past four the telephone bell rang and the hotel operator said, "A Miss Katey Muffet to speak with you, Mr. Scott. Shall I tell her you're not in?"

"Let me speak to her please," he said.

He was put through and heard her say, "It's Apartment 9-C at 939 Fifth Avenue."

She hung up, he wrote the address down, lighted a cigarette, and tried to think what to do. He had only a month ago separated from his second wife. It might be more than a year until they would be divorced. He was still sick of longing for their two kids. He just naturally couldn't get into something like this. And yet he knew he would. He knew he would *insist* on it. He knew the matter was fixed and ended. They would be married. It was absurd, but it would have to be.

He began to walk up and down the length of the living-room, trying with the reasoning part of his nature to make sense, but he knew it was no use. Had she not behaved precisely as she had, he might have had a chance.

He knew he was sunk, for in spite of his efforts to reason, he was delighted. Still, he went to bed, as if to give the girl and himself one last chance. He was almost asleep when the bell rang again and he heard the operator go through the same rigmarole about who it was.

"Let me speak to her please," he said again.

"I'm glad you haven't left yet," she said, "because I'm starved, it's half a mile to the kitchen, I don't like to get food for myself, and there's a delicatessen that's open all night on 6th Avenue next door to the St. Moritz. Will you bring me a ham and swiss cheese on rye?"

Again she hung up.

The shower was refreshing after the bath in Lisbon. He stretched a moment, remembering how incredibly long he had managed to keep himself alive.

He had always been his own best friend, and he had always had compassion and charity and humour for himself, the stranger, the impostor whose integrity was finally unassailable.

When he was dressed except for tie and shoes, he stretched out on the bed, for the tiredness would not go, would not let up, and he must not let himself lose a chance to lie on a bed and rest. Was there a chance still, no matter what?

There would be lunch to eat in a few minutes. There would be the newspaper interview at five. There would be the taxi ride to the Casino at Estoril. There would be the gambling there. There would be bed and sleep tonight, and there would be tomorrow.

He was glad Katey didn't know how it was with him because it might put her to thinking she must try to be sympathetic or helpful and he preferred her the way she was: separate, aloof, detached, proud, just as vulnerable as himself, just as pathetic, and just as clean and ugly and

54

lonely. They were human enough and it wouldn't do for either of them to be even a very little more human.

He had always known the end would catch up with him suddenly. It had caught up suddenly with his father at the age of thirty-seven. It had caught up suddenly with a first-cousin who had been only seventeen, a fellow on his mother's side of the family he had met for the first time in the pathetic deathbed in the wretched hospital in the ridiculous town in the San Joaquin Valley. It had caught up suddenly with his father's younger brother at thirty. It had always caught up suddenly with both sides of the family, the Scotch side and the Assyrian side, and now he knew it was suddenly catching up with him.

The longer he'd lived the more he'd become acquainted with the Assyrian side, the old side, the tired side, the impatient and wise side, the side he had never suspected existed in himself until he was thirteen and had begun to be a man. It was then that he had learned to speak the strange and almost impossible language, staying at the homes of his mother's relatives, listening with them to the phonograph records of the songs of the old country— the songs of all the peoples of that part of the world—singing the songs, speaking the language as if it were a secret shared by only a handful of people miraculously salvaged out of an extinct race. Even his skin began to grow dark when he became a man, and he encouraged his cousins to call him by his Assyrian name, Belus Alahabad, and he began to understand how superior he must be to most other people in that his very race was finished and had no need to clamour for irrelevant rights of any kind.

When he heard the clatter of dishes and the bumping of wheels in the court outside his door, he knew it was lunch, and he got up, but when he sat down, he found that he could not eat, though he was starved. He went to the bathroom, angry and ashamed, for he knew he was ill from bitterness about himself. He knew he didn't care about anybody else in the world, not even Rosey if the truth were told, he cared only about himself, and always had.

He returned to the table, and without reasoning that he must do so, he began to cut into the steak and to eat. In ten minutes the entire lunch was finished.

CHAPTER THREE

It was several minutes after three when he stepped out of his room, having decided to hire a taxi, ride to Estoril, have a couple of brandies, gamble a moment, and come back to the hotel in time for the two-hour interview with Rodrigo Azevedo.

He stood in the court a moment to notice how bright the light of day was, and how spaciously the hotel—if you could call it an hotel—had been designed. The court was three or four times the size of his room which was not small, the ceiling was three-quarters glass, the floor was bright green, yellow and white tile, and there were a half dozen different kinds of plants growing out of pots along the walls; that is, they were growing discreetly, as if not to disturb the refined tone and texture of the place. They were all strong plants which he seemed to feel ordinarily leaped about wildly and had accidents of power, some handsome and some grotesque, but here, at the Aviz, these same plants had calmed down, become restrained, abandoned humour and exhibitionism, and settled into the peaceful ways that promise long life. The stalks of the plants were clean and strong, the leaves uniform, and the yellow and blue blossoms did not appear to have exploded into being : they were just there, and not especially proud of it or very likely to become miserable in a day or two about decaying and dropping. Or so all this seemed to him in the instant in which he paused on his way to the elevator and took in the scene.

"They are convict plants," he thought as he thought other things, too ; as he noticed where the doors of the other rooms on that floor were ; as he wondered how his luck would be at the Casino ; as he tried to put Rosey out of his mind, saying, "She's here and going, and nobody is ever going to be able to help her, not her father, not her mother, and no one she ever meets" ; as he also remarked to himself that when he had gotten up at half past nine that morning he had believed he was on his way to breakfast and a walk to the Prado in Madrid to have a look at what he had heard was the greatest picture museum in the world, full of El Grecos and Goyas ; and then suddenly instead of bothering about breakfast had casually asked when the next plane would be leaving for Lisbon and had learned that if he went straight back upstairs and packed he would make it ; and that is what he had done. Of course there had been the usual stalling with customs at the airport, but all the better, for he was able to get a cup of coffee, buy some more postcards for Rosey, put one in the mail, and look through the latest issue of *Time*.

The flight itself had been high, smooth and swift. In less than two hours he was in Lisbon. In another half hour he was at the Aviz. In another hour he had unpacked, bathed, lunched, and now he was on his way to Estoril.

"The plants are convicts, though," he thought, but he was thinking of a penitentiary that had the shape and meaning of a church.

57

He noticed that the elevator boy, not much larger than the bellboy, was also a convict. The boy was speechless and expressionless because it was the law of the penitentiary.

And he found Eduardo Dos Santos in his own small prison.

"Now, about Estoril," he said. "How do I get out there and how long does it take?"

"I will get you a big car," the clerk said. "You will pay the man one hundred scudos or five dollars. That includes tip. He will get you there in twenty or twenty-five minutes unless you want him to drive very fast."

"No, twenty or twenty-five minutes will be fine. I'll have thirty or forty minutes of it, and then I'll get a taxi and be back here at five. If I happen to be a moment late, please let the newspaperman know I'm on my way, will you?"

"I will tell him," the clerk said.

He came from behind his cage and stepped out onto the small high porch. He motioned to the driver of a large car across the street, and the driver immediately drove around and drew up in front of the place. The clerk stepped down to the car and said a few words in Portuguese to the driver, Paul Scott thanked him, got in, and the car went off.

The town had seemed likeable enough from the beginning, but now as he saw more of it he wished everybody he had ever loved, everybody he had ever known, was in it with him, in the clear light of it: all who had lived and died, all who had quieted down and disappeared, all whose love had turned to hate; all with whom he had ever spent time, with whom he had talked and laughed and joked; but when he tried to bring them around to memory he noticed that not one of the multitude came forward; not a blessed one; and he saw no one he knew excepting Rosey in the place, and he saw her alone there, and he didn't like it.

The car scooted about among throngs moving along narrow streets, the driver honking his horn every other instant, slowing down, picking up, staring with amused amazement or anger at someone who had no longer the power or inclination to leap, cursing softly at someone who *did* have the power but refused to exercise it out of the small animal pride of the man on foot, or the man without money. The car came to a broad street, a street that was *four* streets in fact, with broad coarse tile walks, with ancient and handsome trees, with statues, with benches, with birds, with boys and girls, and with barefooted women carrying baskets and jars balanced on their heads.

Then the car came to open country, to a fine highway with the bay to the left and rolling green hills to the right.

It was a place for all his friends to be with him all right, but he couldn't remember any. He must make a friend. He must find time to make a friend. He owed it to himself to make a friend. He had heard a lot about friendship, he had once or twice read Emerson's essay about it, but he had never quite managed to run into one. It was probably because the Assyrian side of him just naturally didn't believe in it. "How does anybody have a friend?" he asked himself. "And how does he know he's got him?" How far could a man test a friend's friendship and still not be unworthy of it? Why should anybody be anybody else's friend unless it was all very polite and safe, and if it was all very polite and safe, how could it be friendship?

He remembered once knowing for three months in San Francisco a girl he used to visit almost every afternoon for an hour or two, sitting with her in her dingy parlour because she was so beautiful and so able to laugh without making you feel sorry for her. He used to take her little gifts and never hand them to her, but leave them on a table, and one day she handed him as he was going something neatly wrapped that turned out to be a book : *The Rubaiyat of Omar Khayyam* of course. Maybe *they* had been friends, but he couldn't even remember her name or what she looked like. She had always been able to laugh, though, and he had never been able to just let that go. He had gone back again and again to hear the laughter.

"You're from New York, I know," she said the night they met. He was twenty then, so it must have been thirty years ago, and he only wished enough others had heard her to have made it worth her while. She was a small, handsomely proportioned woman of thirty or so whom he had held in his arms a moment when they had first met. A pugilist he had gone to school with had taken him to her place and she had come to the door to greet them with no clothes on. Five years later when he next saw the pugilist, he noticed that he was walking strangely, and after a couple of beers learned that the boy had been fighting syphilis two years, but ought to be out in the clear before long.

Well, nobody could say the Y.M.C.A. hadn't warned them, for he remembered very clearly that he and the pugilist one Saturday afternoon had paid a dime each to get to the basket ball court and the swimming pool, but had first been given the lesson, fully illustrated by monstrosities.

As a matter of fact, he hadn't at that time ever been to New York, but it was his going in August that year that had brought an end to their friendship, for when he got back to San Francisco seven months later and went to her place, she was gone and the situation was something else again. *The Rubaiyat*, but she never asked him if he had liked it or read it, so one afternoon he said, "Have you read that book you gave me?"

"I read it every day," she said. "It's my Bible."

That was the one who had come nearest to being a friend.

The car came to a small port full of small boats, to a light-house, to clusters of brightly painted houses, and then to a small park-like centre that was Estoril, with the Casino up the hill half a mile from the sea. He went into the place and filled out the form which established him as a paying member, then to the bar for two brandies. He saw the four roulette tables working and heard the croupiers making the usual remarks, but this time in Portuguese instead of French or Italian. He had now a little less than five hundred American green, about a hundred and twenty in Travellers' Cheques, 55,000 Italian lire which were worth very little, 12,000 Spanish pesetas worth something or other, 20,000 French francs, worth forty dollars or so. He also had a very big English gold coin that had cost him the equivalent of $80 in Marseille. Every bit of money he had in the world was on him. He exchanged four hundred American green for 10,000 scudos with the understanding that if he won he could buy back the green. The man who made the transaction wore a monocle in his right eye and spoke good English.

"The limit is five thousand scudos' profit on any bet," he said. "That's about two hundred dollars."

"O.K."

He went to the nearest table and put five thousand on the red and the black came up. He put a second five thousand on the red and again the black came up. At a quarter after four he had traded in all of the foreign money, cashed the Travellers' Cheques, and all he had left was six thousand scudos. He would have to leave in fifteen minutes or so to be back at the hotel in time for the interview.

He put five of the six thousand on the red, and it came up. He then stepped across to the next wheel just before the marble was sent rolling and he put five thousand on the black and the black came up. He then moved back to the first table and put five on the red and again the red came up, but the red is always flanked by the black, the black by the red—this must be understood. He then stepped to the second wheel and put five on the red and the black came up. He stayed at this table and played the red again and again the black came up.

He stepped to the bar for another brandy and to do some arithmetic. He was still a lot better off than he had been a minute ago, perhaps no more than two hundred dollars out, which he could make up after dinner that night. The place was open until four in the morning. There was plenty of time. He had another brandy.

He thought he was on his way to the change booth to change the plastic into Portuguese money, but he wasn't. He was on his way back to the red for five thousand and again the black came up. He stayed at the table for another try at the red and again it was black. Now, he had five thousand scudos and a few hundred.

He put five on the red at the same table, and this time as the marble rolled around he was sure he was wrong, so he walked away to the man with the monocle and said, "I've got a very big British gold coin that cost me about eighty dollars in Marseilles. How many scudos can you let me have for it?"

He looked back at the table, and knew it had been black instead of red.

The Assyrian

The man with the monocle examined the coin, referred to a chart, and said, "Two thousand scudos."

"O.K."

He took the two thousand and changed it down to hundred scudo chips and began to play the numbers. He missed on three at one hundred, on six at two hundred, on nine at three hundred, and then he put one hundred and thirty on thirteen because his luck had been so bad, because now he had only one hundred scudos and would have to get back to the hotel by electric train, but the incredible happened, thirteen came up, and of course he got thirty-five for one, or almost five thousand scudos, plus the hundred and thirty left on number thirteen for another roll. It is traditional to leave the amount bet on a winning number on that number, but he moved his play to number two, for absolutely no reason in the world, and number two came up. He crammed his winnings into his trousers' pocket and moved his play from two to twenty-two, but twenty-seven came up. He looked at his watch. It was twenty-seven minutes after four, and he'd better get going. He had almost ten thousand scudos now, or around four hundred dollars. He put five thousand on the red and it came up. He moved to the next wheel and put five on the red again and it came up. He hurried to the third table just in time to get five thousand on the red there too, and again it was red; and it was the same at the fourth table. He went with the plastic to the man with the monocle and they did a little book-keeping. The result was that he got back all of his money, including the countersigned Travellers' Cheques, and about four hundred dollars' worth of scudos which would certainly enable him to stay at the Aviz a few extra days. The man with the monocle was not at all unhappy that he had made a come-back from almost nothing.

On his way to the bar, though, for one more brandy, he thought, "This is disgraceful. Even so, I'm proud of my luck."

He gulped down the brandy, noticed that it was now twenty-seven minutes to five, paid a dollar for his hat, paid the equivalent of seventy-five cents a pack for four packages of Chesterfields, made a deal with the driver of a 1947 Buick and began to ride back to the Aviz. When he stepped out of the car it was two minutes to five.

"Is he here yet?" he asked the clerk.

"Yes," the clerk said. "He's with Mr. Sousa in the private room, next to the bar."

"I'm stinking with gambler's sweat," he said. "Do you suppose it would be rude to get upstairs for ten minutes to shower and change?"

"Oh, no," the clerk said. "They do not expect you until perhaps half past five. You have plenty of time."

He was about to get into the elevator when he saw Obrigado Borrego and the rest of the family appear in the lobby from the dining-room downstairs. They were just leaving after lunch. He watched them move across the lobby.

"Was that them?" he asked the clerk.

"Yes, that was the whole family."

"They're no prouder than anyone else."

He went upstairs and was down again in ten minutes, relaxed and at ease and happy because of the way things had happened—the quick, absurd, meaningless way that somehow came to meaning. No one would ever know how near to disaster he had come so many times in his life, foolishly and deserving the worst, and then at the last minute being forgiven and put in his proper place : which was to have more than enough, to be in a position to throw it around, to use and waste, and then to receive

64

more. Well, in the realm of petty money it certainly had just happened again. It certainly had happened there, and he hadn't been entitled to it at all. He wasn't entitled to it in any other area, either, but who could say it wouldn't happen there, too?

"I want to pay four thousand scudos on account," he said to the clerk.

"Then you will stay a few days?"

"If I may, yes."

"I have spoken with the manager, and he has made arrangements for the other people."

"If they've got their hearts set on that room, they can have it. I'll be glad to move to another room."

"No, they do not know anything about this. They will have a good room too, but overlooking the garden. Some people prefer that. It is a little quieter."

"Well, that's good."

The clerk handed him a receipt for the money, and took him to the private room next to the bar. The newspaper-man and the manager were standing, waiting for him, and a man with a camera was nearby. The manager acted as interpreter and after a drink of brandy for the writer and sherry for the others the manager said, "Well, shall we sit down and begin the interview."

The questions had been numbered and typed out in Portuguese and some of them seemed pretty long and complicated. It turned out also that the manager was not a very good interpreter, so that the first question reached the writer in this form:

"The world today, and you in the world, socially and politically, a man of making, what does it mean?"

"*Making?*" the writer said.

The manager and the reporter asked one another many swift questions and gave many swift answers, so as not to

E   65

keep him waiting too long and then the manager said, "Let me see how to say it. Is it important?"

"What happened to the other question?" the writer said.

"This is the same question," the manager said.

"Well, is *what* important?"

The newspaperman came near blowing up now because he felt the manager was bungling his very carefully worded questions, and they fell to asking and answering again, and then the manager said, "It is difficult to make the Portuguese come out exactly, but Mr. Azevedo says he is asking, Do you believe in the world as a private man and as a man of making—writing, that is."

The writer was about to answer the question with the one logical word, *Yes*, but he knew by now that this newspaperman was no common one with common questions. The man was small, tense, alive, very wise, very angry, and yet extremely gentle, profoundly earnest. His face was dark and covered with pockmarks, his eyes swift but at the same time shy. He smoked one cigarette after another, brushed nervously at the flies, and then looked unhappily at his list of questions, as if perhaps he was putting the writer to too much trouble.

"Oh, no," the writer answered his fretfulness in English. "Please tell Mr. Azevedo," he said to the manager, "that I am extremely glad to meet him and that I am going to answer every one of his questions. Carefully."

The manager paused to make this translation and then said a few words that surely did not mean what the writer had said but probably came near enough to it to be O.K. because Mr. Azevedo smiled and bowed and said something courteous that did not require any answer.

"Now," the writer said, "I think I understand this first question perfectly. I want to think a moment about my answer." He thought a moment, and then went on. "Yes. That is my answer to the first question. I believe the world is a meaningless accident or blessing, depending on a man's health, nearness to ugliness, pain or death ; or his nearness to grace, love or luck. Yes, I believe in the world."

"Ah," the manager said. "Now I will tell him." He spoke in Portuguese a moment and then said, "Meaningless?"

"Yes," the writer said. "Meaningless accident." The manager said these words or something like them to the newspaperman in Portuguese and the newspaperman wrote them down. "Or blessing," the writer went on, "depending on a man's health," and so on and so forth. When the entire answer had been translated and written down the newspaperman leaped to his feet, smiling and showing his tobacco-stained teeth, and then sat down again.

"This is most unusual," the writer thought. "Every critic in America has remarked a dozen times that I have no intelligence, that I can't think or won't, and here is this little guy in Portugal taking me for a visiting intellectual."

Still, he meant to be respectful of the man above all things, and to do his best to answer every question as honestly and as accurately as he knew how.

The questions were all of the same order: that is, perhaps of a high order, and deadly serious, so that the writer could not help now and then making some of his answers with a little of the humour of humility, but not once did he permit a word or a tone of voice to belittle the reporter's respect for the writer, and for himself. The interview was not over until half past seven. The photographer had done a good deal of meandering about the large room, apparently thinking about angles, but he had not taken a picture. Now, when the interview was over and the reporter and the writer were chatting in a language of their own which they had invented during the interview, the photographer took a picture, and then asked them to step out into the sunlight of the balcony, and there he took another one.

During the interview the writer had managed to ask a few questions of his own, and to learn a few things about the newspaperman. To begin with, he was a poet, novelist and dramatist, not a newspaperman at all. He did that for a living, Portugal being a small country, and his children numbering five. He was forty-seven and had had most of his life a little consumption, but not enough to get out of hand and finish him. He had met his wife when he was thirty-seven, very sick, and quite sure he would die soon. He had then been writing for more than twenty years and had had no success of any kind, although he had had a dozen miscellaneous works published. When he had met her his wife had been an illiterate girl of sixteen who probably had Moorish blood in her veins. He was trying to get home at five o'clock in the morning after a night of drinking when he suddenly stopped in the street and began to vomit blood. The girl, just up for the day, carrying something in a basket on her head, put the basket down, ran to him, hugged him, got blood all over herself, scolded him, shook him, and took him to the home of her grandmother where she put him to bed, bathed him out of a basin containing no more than a quart of warm water, fed him, and a few days later slept with him with such a fierceness of love that he was shocked with delight and for almost a whole night believed he would return to the church. He might have done so had it not occurred to him that the girl and her grandmother

68

were Catholics only for the social convenience of it and that actually they believed in something of their own which he wanted to find out about. They were married several days later and for almost five months the girl was not quite sure what his profession was. When she saw the published book he had written after they had met she was unable to believe that he, her husband, had written it, for she had imagined books came into being by themselves, out of some kind of magic.

"Do you love your wife?" the writer asked the man, and the man thought a moment and then said, "We hate each other all the days and nights because it is so much trouble to live, but all the years we love each other."

It was quite a task for the manager of the Aviz to translate these words of the Portuguese writer, but the writer hung onto him until he had got it all straight.

After the interview, the writer went to the desk and asked the clerk to tell him a little about the Portuguese singing he had talked about with the bartender at the Casino.

"Fado?" the clerk said. "You must hear it, I think. Machado's is the best place, and the food is very good, too. Very expensive of course, but very good. I am very eager to know how you like this singing."

"I'll take a taxi to the place," the writer said, "and to-morrow I'll let you know."

"Have you taken a walk in Lisbon yet?" the clerk said.

"No, as a matter of fact I haven't," the writer said.

"It is a nice walk to Machado's," the clerk said. "It is up a hill, through very narrow streets, in the Old City, the part that was dangerous to be in not so very long ago. But now it is not dangerous, it is just nice, and you will see the poor people in the evening when they forget they are poor. You will see them standing in front of their houses talking, or walking through the narrow streets."

"O.K.," the writer said. "I'll walk. Which way do I go, and how long will it take me to get there, and when I get there, what shall I order?"

The clerk told him precisely how to get there; he said if he walked slowly enough it would take a very pleasant three-quarters of an hour; and that the thing to do would be to tell the waiter to bring him one or two of the Portuguese dishes.

The writer decided to see if he could make the walk in an hour instead of three-quarters, for it was a beautiful city, he was enjoying his luck, and he wanted to go slowly for a change, walk slowly, and then come to a place and go in and sit down and eat, and afterwards listen to Portuguese singing.

CHAPTER FOUR

He made the walk from the Aviz to Machado's in even better time than he had hoped. He did not reach the restaurant until a quarter after nine which meant that he had walked well over an hour. He had not followed a straight course, being satisfied to move in the general direction of the place, to have the gambler's sweat bathed out of his hide, to be up and abroad in fresh clothing, to be able to move easily and for a moment at least not to want anything. He was satisfied just to be there, to be in still another country, among still another people, to be walking the streets of still another city in the world; and he knew he had dreamed it all long ago. He knew he had dreamed he would get to Lisbon some day and that it would mean something.

The Assyrian

The truth of the matter was that in remembering what had happened at the Casino in Estoril he had the feeling that he had dreamed it all perhaps not longer than five years ago, and that the dream and the real had precisely coincided, right down to the details, and to the key word involved : *bravo*, for just before his luck began to change, just before he began to win, the word returned to consciousness, and just before the white marble leaped into the red, he said the word aloud, as he had in the dream.

On the way to Machado's he tried to notice everything, stopping frequently to get things straight, but knowing he would never be able to do that, it was not to be so, nothing could be altogether brought out of the sleep and seen real. The people, every one of them, were figures in a dream who somehow had acquired the illusion that they themselves were awake. He noticed that the city had newsboys. This was unique, for in London old men sold papers, in Paris and Rome and Madrid, old men and old women, but in Lisbon small boys without shoes on their feet sold papers, and they ran about the streets crying the headline and the name of the paper. He had done that forty years ago in California.

He stopped one of the boys and bought a paper. The headline said that Forrestal had committed suicide. The former Secretary of War had leaped out of a window at a Naval Hospital. It had happened over the week-end, early Monday morning. The man had been reading around in a book of poetry. It was all in Portuguese on the front page of the paper, but he was able to piece together what had happened. The photograph of the man (which he had seen many times before) now seemed to be filled with the shadow of death, as if the man, when he had been photographed, could not conceal his doom, or as if the camera, through some accident, had found the doom that is in all

71

men. This is almost always so when the photograph of a dead man appears in a newspaper. It is so, most likely, because the end of himself is every instant in every face of every human being—in the eyes and in the mouth.

The suicide was fifty-seven and he had worked hard, he had worked hard all his life. Perhaps he had wanted something and hadn't gotten it, perhaps he had gotten it and it hadn't been worth it, perhaps (as the psychiatrists said) he had been exhausted.

"Every man is an order unto himself," he thought. "That is the place to begin. Man is not standard, statistics do not apply to him, nothing ever happens to any two human beings in precisely the same way—that is the place to begin. The man who destroys himself intends to destroy the world, not himself; the world which he has worked so hard to give meaning to, the world which has resisted meaning; or he has meant to destroy his enemies, but whatever he has tried to do, it has been secret, it cannot be put into statistics, it cannot be explained, the science of statistics is necessary but only as a warning against untruth or a hint as to which way to go more intently after the illusion of truth; and the truth must never be considered anything more, anything better than illusion. That is where to begin," he thought.

He suddenly remembered the idea for a story that had occurred to him when he had first crossed the Atlantic and visited Europe. His character, a boy of twenty-two (he had been twenty-five at the time), is aboard ship, travelling for the first time. He is in the midst of a game of shuffle-board with another boy and two girls when suddenly he uses the board to polevault over the side of the ship, and drowns. Was it suicide?

He had never written the story. He hadn't vaulted, either, but he had laughed about having *almost* done so.

The Assyrian

From time to time he had gone back over the idea and tried to understand it. Finally, he decided the truth of it was inaccessible, but that in all probability had it been himself he would have taken a swim and gotten back aboard ship. And that, he felt, had been pretty much how it had been with him all through his life, in every dimension of it. He had always gone too far, but he had always come back, too. He had always plunged overboard, and then taken a swim, sometimes silently, desperately, knowing that he was struggling for his life, for another chance to find out how far he could go, struggling silently and proudly; sometimes indifferently, scarcely struggling at all, apparently only waiting.

The afternoon of the syphilis lecture at the Y.M.C.A., for instance, he and Packey, the pugilist, had agreed to race the length of the pool three times for a dime. He hadn't had any lunch—he had never bothered very much about eating when something had taken over his mind, such as swimming—and on the last lap of the race there had been nothing left in him by which to keep going. He was at that moment in water twelve feet deep. Small boys were swimming past and around him, and he was drowning, but he refused to lift his voice. Packey got out of the water to establish having won the race, laughing proudly and not noticing that he had gone under once and was going again. Then suddenly he ran around the pool and dived in just in front of where the writer was sinking. When he came up Packey didn't try to take hold of the writer, he began to swim to the side slowly, and the writer found that he could move a little forward in the wake of Packey's swimming. Packey didn't help him climb out of the pool either, and when the writer was out Packey didn't run for help. He flopped down as if that was what he wanted to do, and so did the writer. After a moment the writer got to his feet and wobbled to the can and there had the good luck to heave up most of the water he had swallowed.

Packey didn't bring the matter up, and when they were dressed and out in the hot light of that Saturday afternoon the writer handed his friend the dime he had won.

Three months later they had a fist-fight one morning before school, and the writer refused to strike Packey in the face, directing his blows to the shoulders and arms. It was perhaps at this time that Packey began to imagine he might become a professional.

The writer in turn never told Packey (when they took up again) that he had avoided striking him in the face because Packey had helped him get out of drowning without making a fuss about it. And he wondered if Packey had ever suspected the truth. Most likely he had, but hadn't bothered to give it its proper importance.

It was at this time that Paul Scott decided to try to find out what made men what they were; that is, to be a writer. To watch as carefully as possible the way he himself went, and if possible to notice the way others went. He had been at it ever since, and he had learned enough to know that after all the evidence had been carefully examined the best that could be hoped for was a guess, and a wild one might be just as right as a cautious one.

"Facts," he decided, "which do not set truth free are the biggest lies of all; facts which are not *intended* to help set it free are death penalties meted out by fools upon imbeciles who faithfully accept the verdict of guilt. Beyond the plane of the superficial, beyond the game of social pretending, there is and there can be no guilt; for guilt is cried out in despair because human beings have failed in accuracy. The word signifies nothing. It is a cloak thrown over the eyes of the safe by themselves, so that they need not try to notice any longer that the one called guilty is in fact each of themselves, but in a more terrible trap than their own."

The Ambassador to England during the years of the War had done away with himself, too. A writer of one book, a sensational success, had, and now the former Secretary of War, a grim-faced, tough-looking man. And the barefooted boys of Lisbon were running through the streets, crying the news of it. If each of them made the equivalent of ten cents more than usual that night, a special fondness for the memory of the man was in order.

He walked on under the trees of broad Avenida Libertad, and then came to Gloria Ascension, a short street up a steep hill, climbed by a streetcar built by the man who built the Eiffel Tower, a piece of engineering that had taken the shape of a joke, one end being twice as tall as the other, so that the passengers might be level all the way up or down the hill. The streetcar was jammed and a crowd of fifty or so was waiting for the next load-up, so he climbed the hill slowly and at last came to the first level, to the Old City. It was here that he would soon find Machado's, have supper, and hear the Portuguese singing called Fado.

It was dusk now. The sun was gone, and he was standing in a narrow street, looking back. He saw a shade of green somewhere that had the effect of wrenching his heart suddenly and he wished to God in a kind of sundown panic that he had someone to hold in his arms, someone with whom not to be so alone, someone to whom he could say very softly, "I'm scared to death because the sun's gone and there's that green out there, the tops of trees or a patch of grass or something, and I love you."

He looked about and saw old women and lopsided ones and ones with infants in arms with peaceful dirty faces, staring at the fixed thing—at nothing, that is—and then a fat little waitress came out of a little restaurant to look back, as he was doing, and stood beside him.

"You'll do," he said. "Whoever you are, you'll do."

The girl turned to look up into his face, and smiled, and he said, "Yes, I love you."

"English," the girl said.

"No, just dying."

He turned away from the heart-wrenching green, and began to move further up the street. He came to a lazy fellow with a cigarette dangling in the corner of his mouth who was leaning in a doorway.

"Machado's," he said.

The boy inhaled, exhaled, lifted his head in thought, then went to work on the problem. He took a twig that was lying in the gutter and began to draw a rough map, marking one part of it North. Paul Scott watched and listened and after a full minute it was permissible for him to say thanks and go on.

"Portuguese sailor," the boy said in English.

"Assyrian poet," Paul Scott said.

"English?"

"No, no, I just happened to stumble into the use of that language."

It turned out that Machado's was around the corner. He ran back to the boy and said, "You were right. That was a perfect map you made, and I want to show my appreciation."

He fetched a twenty out of his wallet and handed it to the boy.

"O.K., Pal," the boy said, for by now he knew this was an American.

The Assyrian

Machado's was a good place. The food was bad, but the place itself was good. The waitresses were young, fat, cheerful, a little on the sloppy side, and perfectly able, while waiting table, to go on with their personal lives, to chat and laugh with one another, to be indifferent about the people they were putting food in front of.

Paul Scott's table was served by a waiter, a man of thirty or thirty-five with his shirt sleeves rolled, and to identifiy him as a waiter only a dirty cloth over his left arm with which he wiped table-tops, dishes, his hands and face.

He was drinking coffee when three men with guitars or something like them sat at the table next to his and went to work. After two instrumental numbers a fourth man, the youngest of the group, perhaps twenty-five, stood beside the table and began to sing. The song was what Dos Santos at the hotel had identified as Fado.

It was easy to listen to, and very long. The song started at a quarter to eleven and ended at two minutes to. Somebody bought drinks for the Fadistas and they drank and rested five minutes, and then did another song, equally long, perhaps a little more interesting than the first, which had not by any means been dull. Both songs complained softly and hopelessly and then loudly and bitterly, and one knew the nature of the complaint. It was woman, with all her different names. He listened to one more, got up and began to walk back to the hotel, moving downhill at first, and then going along swiftly but easily, as if he had a schedule. He was back at the hotel a few minutes before twelve.

77

The manager of the hotel was standing near a man smoking a cigar whose face somehow seemed lopsided.

"Oh, Mr. Scott," the manager called out when he saw the writer, "have you met Mr. Paddock?"

The writer walked over to the man with the cigar and shook his hand.

"How are you?" he said.

"When did you get in?" the man said.

"Early this afternoon."

"My wife went to some kind of official shindig, but I settled for the bar and lobby. Have a drink?"

"Sure."

"The boy'll bring them out. I've been fooling with port. At my age it makes you warm but not confident. What'll you have?"

"Well, to save the boy two trips, a double brandy."

"That's all I used to drink myself," the man said. "I'm in the seventies now, so I slow down around nine every night. Another of the same for me," he said to the manager, "and a double brandy for Mr. Scott."

The manager went off, a boy brought the drinks, and the manager did not show up again.

"Well," the man said, "the situation in China doesn't give us a hell of a lot of time for fancy thinking, does it?"

"I haven't studied the situation," the writer said.

"The Commies have just about taken over for sure."

"Well, that's the way it goes, I suppose."

"I'm just back from a little poking around in Spain," the man said. "Hell, if you leave it to the State Department, there's no telling what'll happen. I decided eleven days ago to fly over and see if I could whoop things up a little on my own. I think I've got one ball rolling, anyhow."

"What ball's that?"

"Well, I think we'll soon be getting Spain acceptable as a signatory to the Atlantic Pact," the man said. "That's the way to make the beginning of course. And there's no reason in the world why they shouldn't be. They've been fighting the Commies a damn sight longer than we have, and that's what the Pact's for, so how can we leave them out? They need credits badly, they need our know-how, and anybody who says we don't need every inch of Spain is nuts. You here on an assignment?"

"No, just to look around."

"Have you run into the old boy at the hotel here yet?"

"Who's that?"

"The old Arab," the man said. "He's been living here eleven years now, I believe. The biggest oil man in the world. You've heard about him, haven't you?"

"Do you mean Curti Urumiya?"

"That's him. I tracked him down yesterday for a minute, and we had another conversation today. I told him I've got fifteen million American families reading my papers, and I could promise to do a series of features about him that would clear up some of the lies and nonsense *Time* and *Life* and so many other magazines and papers have been running about him over the past ten years, but, he says he didn't read the lies and he's very busy."

"He's not an Arab. He's an Assyrian."

"Is that so? How do you happen to know his first name?"

"I'm an Assyrian myself."

"I didn't know that, but of course you changed your name, as any sensible American would."

"No, Scott's my father's name. I'm Assyrian on my mother's side."

"Well, what do you know—Scotch and Assyrian. What a combination! You don't speak the language, do you?"

"Yes, I do."

"Well, he speaks perfect English of course," the man said. "Top man of his class at Oxford. Come to think of it the two of you do have something in common. Damned if I know what it is, though. Speaks perfect French too, of course. Don't tell me you didn't know he was here at the hotel? He's got all of the mezzanine, right above us."

"No, I thought he spent his time in Paris."

"His son's there. His son's a man of sixty or so himself, but the old boy likes to pretend *he's* not quite eighty yet. He's not quite ninety would be more like it, but that's beside the point. He's old all right, but not so you can notice it. I like to sit down and take a lot of time talking, but he *stands* and he's got to go before I've had half a chance to win him over to my thinking."

"He doesn't want any publicity, is that it?"

"That's about it, I guess, but he said I could see him again tomorrow for five minutes."

"What's he do?"

"He hangs onto his money and his rights. Only last year he spent close to a million dollars on lawyers and drove off Standard Oil trying to pull a squeeze play on him. He's more like an American than an Arab if you ask me."

"Assyrian," the writer said.

A moment later he went to the taxi across the street and found the driver dozing.

"Estoril," he said. "Casino."

The man said something about the fare.

"Yes, I know," he said. "It's O.K."

He had another double brandy at the bar and then bought three hundred dollars' worth of the plastic from the man with the monocle, and in three minutes needed more.

"I've got all the way to four, haven't I?" he said to the man.

"I don't understand."

"I mean there's action until four o'clock, isn't there?"

"Oh, yes."

"You don't shut down at ten minutes to four or anything like that?"

"No, we stop at four o'clock sharp."

"O.K. Let me have fifteen more of those thousand chips."

He won a couple of times, but lost more frequently than he won, so that at ten after two he was at the bar drinking another double brandy and going over the score again. Everything was gone except the big English gold coin. He couldn't expect to make another come-back from the few scudos that that was worth, and yet it wouldn't do to quit while there was still the barest chance.

The night crowd wasn't much different from the day, except there were now a half dozen American husbands and wives betting ten cents a throw, and fighting each other on the theme of how they were deteriorating.

And of course there were more of the girls working the place at night. During the day there had been no more than seven or eight of them, unofficially encouraged by the house itself, but now there were at least three dozen of them, in nature precisely like the girls at Machado's but done up here, their fat made attractive with plenty of chalk-white powder on their shoulders and arms. They were emotional in their gambling, losing twenty cents with a refined bitterness, explaining loudly to one another what had happened, and how nearly it had come to *not* happening, and how they had thought of playing it another way, and then at the last minute that busy-body Estella had said, "No, play twelve, I have a hunch." Twelve! *Twenty*, not twelve, and there you are, only one chip left.

Well, it was too late now. He'd had his good luck earlier in the day, and now he was as good as broke, and absolutely pooped.

He finished the brandy and went to the man with the monocle.

"Well, it's the red again," he said.

"The red?"

"The gold," he said. "We call it the red in Assyrian. I'm an Assyrian, you know."

He was drunk now on top of everything else.

"Anyhow," he went on, trying to straighten out, "here's the gold again, but of course if I happen to hit, I expect to buy it back, and as much of the rest as I can."

"Of course," the man said.

He took the last plastic and changed it into chips of the lowest value and without confidence began putting them on miscellaneous numbers for thirty-five to one, but out of twenty tries, some of them large enough to make a little difference if he had happened to win, he did not have one winning number. He now had so little left to work with that his discouragement was complete, and as it usually is with losing gamblers he began to loathe the others who were gambling and to be irritated by their manner of doing so, and by their crowding of one another and himself and leaning and stretching to put down a play.

But he knew what was happening and why, and he forced himself to bring a halt to his irritation.

"One more drink," he thought. "This thousand for cabfare home and a cable, and this hundred for a straight-up play on one number." What number? If he picked the right one after his drink he would have thirty-five hundred, enough on which to get even, after all, perhaps. It was fantasy of course, and yet he permitted it. He might just somehow pick the right number when he returned to one or another of the tables after his drink.

He drank and went back and on the way somehow it had been decided for him that he would put the hundred on number nine. When he did so, he was absolutely confident that nine would come up, but it was not so.

Well, the thousand for the taxi and the cable would just have to go too, that's all. He had four thousand paid in advance at the hotel, so the night clerk would pay the taxi, and he would take care of the cable the same way. He put another hundred on the nine, but it came up twenty-two, and he thought, "Hadn't I been thinking of twenty-two all night? Why didn't I play twenty-two?"

So he knew he was in a bad way for sure. He moved to the next table and put a hundred on seventeen because it was nearest and seventeen came up.

At ten minutes to four about two thirds of the players had gone home and he was with the man with the monocle, going over accounts again. It turned out that he had won everything back and about two hundred and thirty-five dollars besides.

But it wasn't worth it. He was safe for a moment again, but what did it prove? The entire amount involved—the whole business—came to a little under or a little over a thousand dollars. In his time he had made more than a million dollars, and where was any of it?

On the way home in the cab he answered his question.

"I've just got to win, that's all. I've got to win against the odds, too."

He was past rest now. When the taxi came to the city he told the driver to take him to a house, and when he got there and saw the girls, he picked the saddest one and went to a room with her and they had two drinks of brandy together and didn't try to talk, and then he went out into the street and saw that it was daylight, and he began to walk, stumbling past a small girl hugging her little sister, asleep on the steps of a school, and he was too tired to feel anything about it, or to try to think of something to do about it, but he knew either one of them might have been his own daughter Rosey.

CHAPTER SIX

He heard a bell ring in his sleep and the part of his mind that had taken instruction from bells asked, "Was that a telephone bell? That is, a real one? Or was it a dream one?"

Another part of him, faintly aware that he was being irritated at an inopportune time, a part that was aware of the questioning that had just been done, prayed that the trouble was unreal and that in a moment all the parts of him could return to the freedom of deep sleep and be unmolested.

There was a long period of waiting, but no bell rang, and just as the man and his parts were about to give over the anxiety of waiting and return to freedom, the bell was heard again. He sat up, located the telephone, remembered everything in an instant, shook his head, and cleared his throat so that he would be able to speak.

A heavy but cordial voice expressed the hope that it had not disturbed him, and then went on about dinner that night at half past nine, if that was not too late. A car would be sent at a quarter after nine to the hotel, the voice went on in slow and easy English, so that it would not be necessary for him to write anything down. He thanked the voice and fell back into deep but active sleep.

An hour later the sleeping man's soul was put through another ordeal, except that this time someone was knocking softly at the door. When he opened the door he saw a little man of fifty or so who immediately said in very quiet English, "I am Mr. Urumiya's secretary. When he heard a few minutes ago that you were at the Aviz he wrote you this note which he asked me to hand to you personally."

"Very kind," he managed to say.

The handwriting was small and swift.

"Will you have lunch with me at a quarter after three? C. Urumiya."

He found his watch on the night-table and noticed that the time was twenty-two minutes after twelve. He got the hotel operator on the line to ask her to give him a ring at a quarter to three, but it turned out that she did not understand him, so he asked for Dos Santos.

"Will you ask the operator to please ring my telephone bell at a quarter to three?" he said.

"Yes, of course, Mr. Scott."

Well, anyway, he could sleep a *little* longer, at least. He was in the bathroom for a drink of water when he heard the telephone bell ring. It was Dos Santos.

"Mr. Scott," he said, "you mean a quarter to three this *afternoon*, don't you?"

"Of course."

"It's twenty minutes to three now."

"Oh. I guess I forgot to wind my watch. Don't bother to ring, then. I'm up."

"Yes, sir," the clerk said.

He went back to the bathroom, brushed his teeth, filled the tub with warm water and got in. At ten past three he was chatting with Dos Santos at the hotel desk about Fado, about the invitation he had accepted for dinner that night with the Borregos, about lunch in a few minutes with Urumiya."

"I think he will expect you in his apartment first," the clerk said.

"He will?"

"Yes, I think so."

"What do I do? Go right up?"

"I'll show you the way," the clerk said.

They took the elevator to the mezzanine and Dos Santos led the way to the door. He knocked softly, waited for the word, and then opened the door for Paul Scott, who stepped into an enormous cluttered room. He saw a man who had probably been quite tall at one time but now seemed small. The man hurried to him with his hand extended.

"I had no idea you were here," he said. "I would have asked you to dinner last night had I known. My grandson who is twenty-two talks about you all the time. He is my daughter's son. What will you have to drink before lunch? I have had to do with a great many of your people. I am fond of the Americans, but of course the ones I happen to meet are my enemies. All human beings are enemies, is that not so? That is why I have this cat. Look at him. How perfect he is, and although a creature which is supposed to be arrogant, my only friend."

The little man who had knocked so softly at the writer's door stepped into the room and even though the old man's back was turned the old man said, "Some Scotch, please." The secretary moved out of sight quickly and quietly, and was back in a moment with a tray on which Paul Scott saw a bottle of Scotch, a silver bucket full of ice cubes, two bottles of water, and a glass pitcher of water.

"Please tell him how you like it, or go to it yourself," the old man said.

"On the rocks, then," Scott said.

"Oh yes," the old man said. "We know what that means. Help yourself, please. I like to be doing something all the time myself. I expected to see an older man, I confess. How old are you?"

"Fifty."

"I looked older at fifty. Well, cheers."

"Cheers," Scott said.

The old man lifted his glass a little, and Scott lifted his and they drank.

"I'm having the same, as you see," the old man said. "I'm no drinker actually—not any more, I mean—but I like to know something about what others are so fond of. Do you like the cat? Of course if you loathe the sight of him, don't think I won't understand. He's almost a monster, I know, but I've gotten so used to him I hardly ever notice."

"I like him all right," the writer said. "What do you call him?"

"Will you believe I have never given him a name?" the old man said. "And he and I have been at this hotel together almost from the beginning. He was a kitten when I found him in the street. Oh, there was absolutely nothing the matter with him, he was just very little and alone and he was mewing with all his might. Well, there he is now on the best chair in my house. He never bores me and nobody can bore him. He's always thinking about something else. Won't you help yourself to another?"

"A little one perhaps," Scott said.

"Please don't stand because I do," the old man said. "I always do. I think it's because I once read somewhere that standing constitutes an excellent form of exercise, and as

I don't like games I suppose I cultivated this form of exercise. But please sit down."

"I'd rather stand," Scott said.

They had instantly recognized one another as members of the same family. That was the reason they were putting off talking in their own language. Each of them knew the other could speak the language, but they had reached a silent agreement that they would begin to speak that language without test or preparation, at the proper moment.

The secretary brought two cablegrams on a silver tray and the old man said, "Will you excuse me a moment while I look into these?"

He tore open one envelope, glanced at the message and placed it back on the tray. He tore open the second one, took in the message at a glance, dismissed the secretary, and then showed the cablegram to Scott.

"Two of my best lawyers lost," he said. "But I'm glad for them. Both young men, about your age, just appointed to the highest positions in law in England. Oh, they'll not earn a tenth as much as I pay them, but men love fame, and this is the crowning of their careers. I've lost them, but I'll cable congratulations."

"They've been knighted?"

"Oh, much better than that," the old man said. "Everybody's knighted these days. There must be a hundred thousand of them. There are only a half dozen of these. It would be something like being appointed a Justice of the Supreme Court in America. Now, that *is* a very big honour in America, is it not?"

"Yes, I suppose it is."

"I see you are not much impressed with such things," the old man said, his eyes smiling. "Well, let me tell you I'm not either. I've been offered a few little odds and ends of that sort by kings and tribal chiefs and dictators and all the others, but I've managed to get along without them. What better title does a man need than his own name if he has made it stand for something? What better honour than a yes that means yes and a no that means no?"

"Surely there is honour in *perhaps* also," Scott said.

The old man burst into laughter.

"I'm delighted you caught me up there," he said, "for it occurred to me as I was speaking that a yes that means yes and a no that means no is so much nonsense. It is *all* perhaps. I am so glad you were not bullied into letting the slip pass, for I myself was unable to let it pass. The other message was from my grandson in Paris. He asks if he may fly here for the week-end. What shall I tell him?"

"What do you want to tell him?"

"To come of course, but one must go to the trouble of trying to think clearly about what is best for the young. I'm afraid of flying. It's the way I travel when I have any distance to go, but I'm an old man. He was scarcely a child when he flew for the R.A.F. during the war. He was spared, as so many others weren't. If I tell him to come along and one of those absurd things happen—they happen all the time—what am I to do?"

"You love this boy very much."

"Ah, indeed, though no one—no one—shall ever guess how much, for I could never know how to measure it. Soon enough the open face of innocence will be gone out of him—he and I shall be enemies—but I live for him. The thought of him comforts every minute I remain alive. And why? Because he is mine, though he does not even bear my name. Because he is mine even more than my own son, even more than my own daughter. Everyone has noticed it. He himself knows it and I know it. He cables

89

me to come here for a week-end—to come here from Paris—a boy of twenty-two. Why? I am an old man. Because he loves me and knows I love him. And we have never spoken as openly as you and I are speaking now. We all want love. It is the only thing we *do* want forever. The cat here. I have pretended for ten years that he loves me because he cannot say that he doesn't. It's safe, but I know it's untrue. He loves cream and his thoughts, whatever they are. Well," the old man said suddenly in another tone of voice, "I didn't have time to order what I would have liked for you, but I hope you will enjoy what it is. Shall we go?"

The secretary stepped into the room again and the old man turned and said, "Tell Van to come. Very special congratulations to the others. Put the copies on top of everything else on my desk."

The hotel dining-room was big and full of light. The tables were set far apart and it was impossible for even a half dozen waiters in tails attending to one table to make too much of themselves. This was evident immediately when a half dozen of them came alive as the old man and the writer appeared. The headwaiter came to escort them to the old man's table in the corner while two others hurried to the table to be ready with the chairs and two others stood by to receive instructions about food and drink.

"A double Scotch on the rocks," the old man said instantly when he sat down. He then mentioned in French two kinds of wine he wanted, and then asked Scott what he'd like to start.

"I always start with something my Greek housekeeper makes for me," the old man said.

"I'll go along with that," Scott said.

"Oh no," the old man said, "it's something like ravioli

90

made with spinach and chicken." He said something in French to the headwaiter and a wagon loaded with hors d'oeuvres was pushed alongside the table. The writer asked the waiter to let him have an assortment, and before the waiter had finished his work another waiter had set before the old man, piping hot, his ravioli, and was pouring melted butter over them. The old man instructed the waiter to put some ravioli on another plate for Scott, so that he might know what they were like. The old man ate with zest. He ate swiftly, like a hungry man.

The headwaiter stood nearby, although his work was finished. This was the proper moment. The old man began to speak loudly in Assyrian.

"This man," he said. "Please do not look at him. He hangs around this way all the time, to hear something he might pass along—for money of course. I have waited for this opportunity for many years. He is trying to understand what I am saying so loudly but of course he can't, for it is not in English or in French or in Portuguese— but you understand what I'm saying, I know."

"Yes, I do," the writer said.

"I'm so glad you do," the old man said in the secret language, "because I get so little opportunity to speak our language. My own son says he has forgotten it, and as for my grandson he speaks it as if it were Oxford English. But he *does* speak it. You will notice that. Now, in a moment, you will notice that this man will step to the table to move a fork half an inch because even though I am speaking so loudly, he cannot make any of it out. There is one telephone operator at the hotel who is also of this order. It is nothing any longer, a little game that amuses me. And I know precisely what to let them hear, and what the results will be. This sort of thing must seem strange to an American. Ah ha. Here he is now. Did you notice—the fork? He is listening and I am eating and talking. He cannot understand. Therefore the knife. Did you notice? I am absolutely bursting with laughter inside. And yet what I give him four times a year is more than he earns here in wages the entire year. Now he is gone. I shall look about at the flies. And at him of course, too."

The old man stopped eating for an instant, lifted his round head serenely and glanced outward into space, taking in the bewildered headwaiter, the flies, and that part of the table not hidden by the screen at which a banquet for perhaps thirty or forty was in progress.

"The English of course," the old man said, and the writer heard someone at the banquet say, "And so it gives me the greatest plezzure to present to you Sir Adkey Baddington." This was followed by applause.

"They do enjoy cheering," the old man said. "I am not speaking of the British. I am speaking of people who are eating. Well, our friend is in distress. Before lunch is over I must say something to you in English for him to hear. It will happen suddenly."

The writer and the old man chatted in the secret language all during lunch, and then suddenly the old man said in English, "You must understand of course that at any moment everything may be lost. I have neither government nor army. I am one man alone, a private citizen of the world. If they choose to take by force that which belongs to me, I cannot stop them."

The headwaiter listened and poured a little more white wine into the two glasses. Then the old man said in the secret language, "He is saved, and so is the game. He will think about what I have said all afternoon and then he will write it out, and present it to his employer."

"Surely you're not serious?" the writer said.

"Of course I am."

"But what you said is meaningless or certainly useless."

"Of course, but he *heard* me say it. That's the important thing. The words must be preserved, kept on file, put with the other words he has gathered, the game must go on."

"Who is his employer?"

"One day one, another day another. Lisbon is full of this sort of nonsense, and those who deal in it. I love my work, and I have my grandson. And of course the cat. The game amuses me, for I know we are all absolutely helpless. I only wish I could be around long enough to know how it is all going to turn out."

"Perhaps you will be."

"Perhaps. My grandfather lived to be a hundred and nine, my father a hundred and one. I'll be satisfied with ninety-nine."

"You may not need that many more years to find out."

"Yes, I know. I'd like to know how several other things turn out as well."

"Well," the writer said, "I have already outlived my father by a good many years, and he outlived his by several, but fortunately I have several sons and several daughters."

"They are the only thing," the old man said. "Until of course they have children of their own that you like even more than you like them, and then of course you have just about all there is for any of us to have."

"Mine are all rather young," the writer said, "for I began getting married when I was thirty-five."

"You *began*, you say?"

"Yes, I've had three wives, and I have just separated from the third. We have a daughter of three. I have a son of fourteen by my first wife, a son of eleven and a daughter of eight by my second."

"Ah. You married what sort of girls?"

"Pretty ones."

"Ours?"

"No."

"From our part of the world?"

"No."

"Well," the old man said, "so much the better, I suppose. We are so nearly finished, we might as well be finished together."

"People are all the same," the writer said.

"Not altogether," the old man said. "I know it is the style these days to believe that there is no such thing as nationality, but I believe there is such a thing."

"It is surely an unimportant thing," the writer said. "Being alive is nationality enough for anybody, I should imagine."

"Yes, it is, no doubt," the old man said, "but the other little bit sometimes, in some cases, seems to make being alive just a little more fun. For instance, I have for many years felt that I have (for being who and what I am) outwitted the foolishness of life, and I must confess it makes me very happy. I mean, I survived, although my race didn't. Now, isn't it so that you have felt the same way?"

"Yes, I believe I have, but I think it would have been so had I been a mixture of French and Italian, for instance, instead of Scotch and Assyrian."

"Ah, I see what you mean. Yes, there is something to that. The pleasure we get from surviving is personal, not collective. Yes, I can see how that could very easily be the case. Still, I couldn't possibly enjoy anything more than to be talking to you this way in our own language."

"It's the same with me," the writer said.

94

The Assyrian

They sat at the table until half-past five, talking in Assyrian, and then the old man went upstairs for his nap and the writer took a taxi to Estoril; but this time he only sat at the bar and drank Scotch on the rocks, chatting in a mixture of English and something like Portuguese with the barboys and with the man with the monocle in his eye.

CHAPTER SEVEN

He was about to get up and go for a walk, down the hill and past the shops of Estoril, when Paddock, the publisher, puffing at a brand-new cigar, and accompanied by a blonde elderly woman, charged up to him at the bar and said, "I didn't come out here to gamble, Scott. I came to have a talk with you about Urumiya. The kid at the desk told me you came out here yesterday and I took a chance that you might be here again today. This is my wife."

"How do you do?" Scott said.

The woman nodded, mumbled something, and glanced over at the gambling tables.

"Give me some money," she said to her husband.

"Ten dollars, that's all," the husband said.

The woman took the money and went off to gamble. Paddock leaned against the bar.

"I hear you had lunch with the old boy."

"Yes."

"Well, I went up to his place and caught him for a minute just before he settled down for his nap. He says nothing doing. Now, what about that cat up there? What's the cat got to do with anything? Why does he keep talking about a great big black fat tomcat, anyway?"

"He likes that cat," Scott said.

"Oh, Christ," the publisher said. "O.K. What can you tell me about him?"

"What do you mean?"

"I think I owe it to the American people to make his importance known, and to make him attractive to them."

"I thought you said he told you nothing doing."

"He did, but that doesn't mean anything. Now, you had lunch with him, and I understand you spoke Syrian together."

"Assyrian."

"Yes. Well, whatever it is. The point is that I'm asking you as a patriotic American to let me know what you know about him."

"Is that what you're asking me?"

"Oh, now, listen here," the publisher said. "I've talked plain American to Mussolini, Franco, the Pope, Mikoyan, Vishinsky, the King of England, and a hell of a lot of others."

"Hitler?"

"I spent twenty minutes with him ten years ago this month, just before the blitzkrieg. Now, as a patriotic American, what about Urumiya?"

"Well," the writer said, "as a patriotic American, I'd like to know what you mean by a patriotic American?"

"Oh, hell," the publisher said. "You writers are all alike. You know damn well what I mean. I mean a patriotic American."

"Well," the writer said, "that's settled. I can't tell you anything about him because I don't know anything. If I happened to know something I wouldn't know how to interpret it or what value to give it because I don't believe there has absolutely got to be another war in the next year or two."

The Assyrian

"Yes, so I gathered from the interview that came out in this afternoon's paper. Have you seen it?"

"No, I haven't."

"Well, whoever the man was who interviewed you, he's got you saying some pretty high-falutin' things about the international situation for a fiction writer."

"I answered the man's questions," the writer said. "I didn't thank you for the drink last night. What'll you have? Port?"

"I'll have some of that Scotch on the rocks, too."

"Two more of these," the writer said to the barboy.

"Now, listen," the publisher said. "I was very close to F.D.R. the last five years of his life. All I can tell you is this: things are moving very fast. We can't afford to get caught with our britches down again. All right, so where does Urumiya come in? Christ, you know exactly who and what he is, don't you?"

"I have a pretty good idea," the writer said. "Why?"

"You also know where his oil is, don't you?"

"Yes."

"All right," the publisher said. "I'll tell you what I'm willing to do. Hang around Lisbon awhile. Get to know him. Get me his story. Call it an assignment—a personal one, off the record, between you and me. How about it?"

"I don't intend to see him again."

"Why not?"

"I'm flying to Paris in the morning."

"I'll pay you not to fly," the publisher said.

"No thanks."

"Why not?"

"I don't like your papers."

"Say, are *you* a Communist, too?"

"I'm an anarchist."

"I *thought* you were something away over on the left,"

the publisher said. "Do you believe in the overthrow of the American government by force?"

"Ah, nuts."

"Well, I don't," the publisher said. "I'm offering you a chance to square yourself."

The writer was hopelessly drunk with boredom and irritation.

"He's just a nice old man," he said. "I don't know anything else about him. What's all the excitement about?"

The publisher turned and walked away.

The writer had one more drink before getting up to take the walk through Estoril he had planned to take.

CHAPTER EIGHT

He walked an hour, though there was very little to the place itself, being a place of holiday—clean, good-looking shops full of the usual crap; three hotels for tourists, each of them bright and neat and quiet-looking; and then the streets and houses of the Portuguese themselves: nice and warm and familiar-looking, the kids playing in front of the houses all gravely taken up with the problem of the game: that is, to get away from the boredom, the unhappiness and the desperation; to get away from the hopelessness, the anxiety, the despair; to find in a simple problem a decent moment of peace, of action, of meaning. He watched each game until he was noticed, and then, knowing his watching would spoil the fun, he moved on quickly, but it was there every time, in every kid's face: "What are we going to do about the poverty? What are we going to do about all the things we need and don't have and can't get? What are we going to do about all

98

the time we've got and nothing to go with it? What are we going to do about poor, sick, foolish, mad Mama, and angry, hollering, ignorant Papa? What are we going to do about *now*? What are we going to do about tonight and tomorrow? What are we going to do about ourselves?" And in each kid's face was the one answer to all of the questions, the answer to the hundreds of thousands of variations of the one question: "Nothing. We ain't going to do anything."

He found the beach and meandered along it for half a mile or so, smelling the water and the faint scent of fish, stopping to notice and pick up pebbles, thinking all the time of Rosey, hearing her soft, almost-whispered speech when he picked her up after a nap and asked her a preposterous question like, "Did Rosey sleep well?" and the little girl said, "Yeah," but said it as if the word had come out of another life and place and reality, as if it were a whole note in a piece of forgotten music.

"Rosey, would you like to hear a story about a boy named Tom?"

"Yeah."

"Rosey, would you like to have a little boy of your own, a brother?"

"Yeah."

One day in January he had stretched out on the sofa in the living-room and fallen asleep. The little girl had gotten up from her nap and found him asleep. He became aware of a sweet presence, and felt on his face the breathing of someone smelling of tender life. He opened his eyes and there was his daughter, crying bitterly; crying because she had seen the death that is in a man's face.

"Where was you, Papa?" the child had sobbed. "I came here. Where was you?"

He rushed light to his eyes, smiling to his lips, love to

the child, and tried to explain to her what had happened : tried to tell her about tiredness.

"Yes," she said softly. "You was far away but you came back."

"That's right, honey," he said. "You want to go for a walk with Papa and get an ice cream soda?"

"Yeah."

He found the nurse half-asleep in the kitchen, reading a book about martyrs, and he asked her to dress the girl so he could take her out. When he got back it was almost six and his wife was still out, from lunch at "21" with three of her pals, all young mothers.

When she came in a half hour later he said, "When are you going to start getting acquainted with Rosey?"

"Why? What's the matter with her?"

"Nothing, but I should think you wouldn't be able to drive yourself away from her."

"Oh, Rosey's fine," his wife said. "I've got to get out once in a while. If we're going to the opening tonight, you'd better shave and get dressed. You look like a bum."

"I'm going to shave every morning from now on," he said. "Rosey saw me asleep on the sofa and burst into tears."

"I don't wonder," she said. "Well, let's have a drink at least."

"I see you've had a couple already."

"Two before lunch, four after."

"For a girl of twenty-two, that's quite a lot for the middle of the day. How miserable are you, anyway?"

"Just so-so," she said. "Nothing special. All my friends keep buying new clothes, though. I thought you were rich."

"Well, I'm not."

"Aren't you going to try?"

100

"Try what?"

"Try to get rich."

"Don't talk nonsense."

"You used to try. You used to make a lot of money."

"I still try, but not to make money," he said. "It was always an accident that I ever made *any*."

"A man who gets married so many times and has so many children ought to try a little harder, I think."

"So you can buy more clothes."

"Yes, of course."

"O.K., I'll try a little harder."

"When?"

"Right now. Would that be soon enough?"

"It's O.K. with me," his wife said. "If you want to spoil our evening, go ahead. I'll give the tickets to my mother."

He tried hard to get rich by writing until a quarter after eight. His wife came into his workroom from the bath and said, "You don't write the way you used to write any more, and everybody I know says that's the way you ought to write again, but I tell them they don't know what they're talking about."

"You always did know how to make small talk," he said. "You always did know how to make what you mean very clear."

"What do *you* think I mean?"

They went to the opening, and then to the Cub Room. When they got home it was after four, and when they got up it was past noon. They were invited to dinner that night, and they had asked a half dozen friends to dinner the next night; and the night after that something else was sure to break for them, something wonderful to keep the old game going. If they stayed home and everything seemed serene and it appeared as if he could begin at last to make plans to get to work, they would have a fight during supper, his wife would get up and leave the house and he would think about it fifteen or twenty minutes and then go to the little bar around the corner where she always went after a fight and sit down with her and they would have two or three drinks and talk about their separation and divorce and then go home and peek at Rosey asleep and fall into one another's arms with something that wasn't exactly tender love but wasn't exactly anything else, either, although they knew neither of them could abide the thought of the other; and knew they didn't understand, didn't know what to make of it, didn't know what was going on or what would be apt to be going on in a day or two; and yet they were forever trying to think up a good name for Rosey's brother if, as luck would have it, he might come to pass.

The man walked along the beach at Estoril and remembered, as he did every day, the way of his life, the meaningless way of it, the accidental way of it; and how, in the end, as in the beginning, a man is alone.

CHAPTER NINE

He was a simple-minded man and knew it and was only now and then envious of those who were intelligent or seemed to be—that is, who had made something of being thinkers, something respectable, that is; something cultured people, as they were called, could take seriously or respect even; something formal; something dignified; something *too* dignified; something so dignified that one knew the pose concealed the basic horror, the basic falsity; something so dignified one felt its desperate and pathetic unreality, its covering-up; but he had no illusion

102

of superiority here : he knew he was nothing, he knew he
had failed, and even though he also knew they (the intelligent posers) had failed even more profoundly, he did
not feel superior ; and he did not feel pity or compassion
for them, he simply felt that it was all right, they were
all right : everybody went along as he was made to go
along : the Jesus-huggers hugging Jesus ("Oh Jesus," he
thought every time a new one made the big grab, every
time an old one gave it a new twist, writing about it so
carefully, so expertly, "Oh Jesus, deliver us from Jesus,
deliver us from the Jesus-huggers.") ; the psychiatry boys
—surely the best of the lot but too hep, too frigging above
it all, too informed about every little detail, too sure
about how to interpret every little particle of the whole,
too smug, too dull, too boring—the psychiatry boys going
about their business with the same expert confidence ; the
sneaky Marxists with their eyes, their ever watchful eyes,
their clever questions, their clever eyes as they wait for
the fool's reply ; not the sneaky Marxists alone, the
sneaky Stalinists, the sneaky Trotzkyites, the sneaky
Socialists, the sneaky Democrats too, the sneaky Republi-
cans ; they all had one thing in common: they sneaked
through the minds and souls of the great imbecile, man,
without love, without hatred, even, without anything—
they just sneaked, that's all. The aesthetic boys did him
no good, either, though he tried again and again to
follow them, to make sense out of their cautious, disciplined, careful building, their making something of
something, something more of it, something less, something else, something different, something astonishing,
something clever ; he tried always to be humble and to go
along with them and perhaps learn something, but it
always ended with his knowing they were hoodwinking
him ; so then he would ask, "What the hell is everybody

looking for? What the hell does everybody want to be, and want others to be?" And the answer was never any good at all. "Dead. Dead and gone. Or alive; or indifferent about being alive; or careless about it; or glad about it; or amused. Or alive but free of one's own self. Still alive but free of one's own tiresome self; liberated from one's own illusion of one's own absolute self, the hopeless hide bathed, the fool's face washed and shaved, the whole jumping strutting struggling freak hidden by clothing. Perhaps they're looking for a better lie to take the place of the broken-down one. No, they're looking for peace, that's all. Wasn't peace of mind supposed to be the theme of a best-seller of six or seven years? And wasn't that followed by peace of soul; and wouldn't peace of soul be followed by peace of body, peace of nervous system, peace of internal organs, peace of bowels, peace of head (for people with sinus, for instance, or migraine), peace of tail? What the hell are they looking for? A way out. A way to the right way out. A way to leave. A way to go. A way to have had it, to have had enough of it, to be done with it. A decent way to give it all over to the giver of it all, with thanks for the bother. A decent way to stop being so important to one's own unworthy self, which was always bored with every bit of it, which was always helpless to refuse any of it, to say enough, leave off, there is nothing to me, nothing you can give me that can make anything of me I want to be, enough. A decent way to say to the giver take back your man, all of him, and do the same with the other living things: they were all unholy, but worst of all was always that phoney, man, that snarling animal that got up off its front legs. That grunting thing which learned to blow its nose. That bathed thing which grew dirtier and dirtier after centuries of soap and water, sicker and sicker after centuries of medicine, whose manners became more and more evil after centuries of politeness, whose thinking became more and more meaningless after centuries of practice and instruction; that charmless charlatan who had to be a hero. That believing thing which believed anything because it could believe nothing. Oh boy, we're Christians. Oh baby, we're Jews, we're just as nice as Christians and even official Christians are beginning to say so. Oh man, we're Mohammedans and it certainly is important and better. We is Baptists, we is this, we is that, and the Lord (Oh boy, the Lord) he is the One, he is behind it all, and we is behind him, and somebody or something is behind us, or else who doing all that pushing? And, oh Comrade, we are the children of the Man-Father, the latest thing, the wise man who went to Yalta and was so superior because he did not go as a personality, like Roosevelt or Churchill, but went as our Father, as a couple of hundred million instead of one little old teeny-weeny one, that's who we are, and we're acoming, man, how we're acoming.

He was the simplest kind of man, knew it, took no pride in it, and was always a little more polite with all of them than they ever were with one another, loving the girls and letting it go at that. As long as the girls were able to remain girls, he loved them.

He said something of all this to the girl after dinner, and she said, "Why? Why is that the way it is with you?"

"I don't know," he said, "but so it is, and so it is *now*. I am thinking of you, but do not be afraid. I do not mean you personally, nor myself, either. I just mean, so it is. Will you excuse me? I'd like to speak with your father."

He got to the hotel at three in the morning, after an hour at the Casino. He had finally lost everything, including the gold coin, but it was no matter, it was just that he'd hoped to win enough to put gambling out of his mind for a week or two because he wanted to see about quieting down and finding a good book to read—a long book to read very slowly for a month or so, a book he could like, out of which he could pick the lies and laughs —but now he would have to cable somebody—who? Katey? Good God, would he have to cable Katey for five hundred dollars?—and fly back to New York, go to a ball game and stir it all up again and around and forget the details, or drop in at a hospital someplace and tell somebody, "I'd like to be made very peaceful for two weeks."

The night clerk handed him his key and a letter.

"A man brought this about an hour ago," he said.

He opened the envelope and read, "No matter what time you get in, will you please telephone."

The number followed but there was no name.

The clerk got him the number. "Do you still feel that way?" she said.

"Yes, I do."

He listened a moment, borrowed the equivalent of ten dollars from the clerk, and then went out to see if he could find a taxi. After a few minutes he stopped one and handed the driver the address. The driver said something in Portuguese that was meaningless and drove off. It was ten minutes before another taxi showed up, but there were people in it. He began to walk toward town, hoping to find a taxi, but after a half hour he turned around and went back to the hotel. The clerk got the number for him again and he said, "I can't find a taxi. Do you have a car?"

"Oh," she said. "Good night. I'm going to sleep."

He went upstairs and without bothering to take a shower fell into his bed and went to sleep. When he woke up at noon he saw an envelope which had been slipped under the door. He recognized the handwriting. He put the unopened envelope on the night table and went back to sleep, waking again in an hour because the telephone bell was ringing.

"How long do you sleep?" she said.

"What's the matter?"

"I'm downstairs. We're all to meet for lunch at three."

She stopped and he couldn't imagine what to say, and then she said, "Well?"

"Can I meet you at Machado's in fifteen minutes?" he said.

"Machado's? That's a restaurant, isn't it?"

"Well, can I meet you anywhere but here in fifteen minutes?"

"Number 51 Aereo," she said. "But don't get out of the taxi. I'll get in."

"O.K."

He showered, dressed and went by taxi to the place, and she stepped in.

"Give the driver this address."

She handed him a card which he handed to the driver and after a half hour he said, "Where is this, anyway?"

"It's a small house we have in the country that we hardly ever open."

"Do you have to be back for lunch?"

"Oh yes."

"You want me to *look* at the house, is that it?"

"Why are you being ugly?"

"It's ten minutes to two. If we get to the house in five minutes, that will give us five minutes to look at the house."

"Five minutes is something."

"O.K. After lunch get some sleep and then let me take you to the theatre, only we won't go to the theatre."

"No, after lunch we are driving to Cascaes where we are spending a month with my father's brother's family."

"Nuts."

"What did you say?"

"I said O.K., I'll come to Cascaes."

"You can't. I couldn't see you a moment if you did."

"Why not?"

"Here's the house. Do you like it?"

The taxi turned up a drive on a slope and he saw a small stucco house painted light green, surrounded by a small grove of olive trees.

"I'm crazy about it," he said when they were inside, but he was holding her in his arms then.

On the way back to the hotel she said, "They will be in the lobby waiting. I've never been late before."

"You're only about a half hour late."

"My father will be suspicious."

"You're not a child."

"Yes, I know."

"I'll come to Cascaes tonight and if I don't see you by noon tomorrow, I'll fly to Paris."

"Do you want to marry me?"

"No. Why? Why should I make you unhappy?"

"If you said you wanted to marry me, we might be able to meet in Cascaes."

"Your father knows all about me. I told him last night. We can't pretend I want to marry you. I'll be wandering around Cascaes from nine until ten tonight, and tomorrow from ten until noon."

"Ask the taxi to stop. We're almost back and I have to get out of the taxi alone."

He stopped the taxi and got out.

"Will I see you in Cascaes?" he said.

"No."

"Will you come back to Lisbon?"

"No."

"Will you come to Paris? I stay at the George Sank."

"No."

"Are you all right?"

"Yes. Goodbye."

"O.K."

He paid for the taxi and walked away from the hotel which he saw up the street. After an hour he went back, and up to his room. He wrote a cablegram to his wife asking for money and a boy picked it up. He then ordered some food and when it came sat down and ate. Then he stretched out on his bed to think because here it was again : he wanted more.

He didn't know what he wanted, but he knew he wanted more of it, whatever it was, whatever was available, whatever had ever been available, whatever it actually came to : more time? more fun? more trouble? more meaninglessness? more children?

He got Dos Santos on the phone and said, "Could you come up here a minute?"

When the clerk saw him he said, "Is something the matter, Mr. Scott?"

"Why?"

"Are you ill?"

"Well, maybe I am. Did you send the cablegram?"

"A boy is coming to pick it up."

"Tear it up. I'm flat broke. That means I haven't any money and I'll tell you what I want to do."

The clerk telephoned the desk about the cablegram.

"I have a little money," the clerk said.

"Yes, that's what I mean. I want to borrow whatever you can lend me. I want to go out to the Casino and win enough money to pay for an aeroplane ticket. When does the next plane fly East?"

"East, Mr. Scott?"

"Yes."

"There's a plane for Beirut, Basra and Bagdad at nine in the morning."

"Reserve a place for me."

"Yes, sir."

"Do you know a good doctor in town?"

"Oh yes."

"I don't know when I'll be finished at the Casino, but as soon as I get back I'd like him to come here and give me some pills."

"I'll get him. He is my cousin. But if you do not win?"

"It won't be the first time."

"I have only a little money."

"It'll do."

He reached the Casino at six and was back at the hotel at one in the morning of his birthday, fifty years old now. Eduardo Dos Santos was sitting in the lobby with a man of fifty-five or sixty. The clerk got up and went to Scott.

"We have been waiting since eight o'clock, but it's all right. Did you win?"

"Yes, I have everything. Did you reserve a place on the airplane?"

"Yes."

"Well, I'm sick. Will the doctor go to work now?"

"Oh yes."

They went upstairs and the doctor examined him in silence for ten minutes. The doctor then sat in a chair and fell to thinking and the man did not disturb him. Then the doctor said in English, "You want the truth of course."

"Yes."

The doctor turned to his cousin, and said something in Portuguese.

The clerk said, "He asks that I tell you."

"O.K."

"You must not take the airplane."

"Why not?"

"Your heart won't stand it."

"My heart's always been good."

"It's not good now. Do you want to hear it?"

"I wouldn't know the difference. This is something temporary."

"I don't think so," the doctor said. "Besides, something temporary can kill a man."

"I've got five hours of sleep ahead. I'll be O.K. in the morning."

"I would like you to stay in bed for two or three days," the doctor said. "I will look in every two or three hours."

"I've got to take the plane in the morning."

"Why?"

"Because in case you're right I want to be where I'm going."

"I cannot stop you," the doctor said. "How many hours is the flight?"

"Ten or twelve or fourteen, I suppose."

"Perhaps you will get there all right."

"Yes."

"Well," the doctor said. "Will you stretch out and relax for a little while and no one talk, and after a half hour or so I'll listen again."

When the doctor listened again he said, "I do not think you will get there. You must stay here until I am sure you will get there. Tomorrow I will call in two or three others. There is an American doctor that I will call, too."

"Listen, I'm awfully grateful, but I've got to take the plane."

"Do you want to kill yourself?"

"I want to take the plane."

"I believe that you are the kind of man who will live a long time with a bad heart if you will slow down and never speed up again," the doctor said.

"I believe that, too."

"You must become a vegetable for a long time, and then an old man."

"Most likely."

"You must not have appetites."

"I can understand that."

"I must ask you to stay. You are a reasonable man."

"I'm deeply grateful."

"Well, good luck, then," the doctor said. He was smiling and he extended his hand.

"Thank you," the man said, taking the hand. He turned to the clerk.

"You've been a good friend, Eduardo. Let me pay for my ticket now, and my hotel bill, so that in the morning I can just get up and go."

"Yes, sir," the clerk said.

The three men went downstairs and the man paid for everything. The doctor and the clerk said good night and went home, and the man, instead of going upstairs to bed, sat down in the lobby. It was three o'clock, and he wished the plane was leaving now instead of in six hours. He didn't feel like sleeping at all. He didn't feel like stopping, slowing down, catching up. He had never caught up, and it was no use trying to do so now. He had been thinking of Rosey when something secret began to happen that frightened him very deeply.

"Christ," he thought.

He tried to stand but couldn't, then almost did, then fell, tried to see but couldn't, and then heard shouting, although he had seen the nightclerk fall asleep, so it wasn't the nightclerk, and all he himself was doing was trying to breathe, as if he were a fish out of water, and he believed he must also be flapping or trying to flap in the damned darkness like such a fish, and then it seemed that he was going to be finished.

"Well, I made fifty anyhow," he thought, and then forgot everything.

When he felt his face it was sticky and when he opened his eyes he found that he could see. He could see the large red and green flowers in the rug. He'd had it, but he wasn't quite finished yet, he was just sprawled on the floor in the lobby, and the place was very quiet. If the night-clerk hadn't come to help him he hadn't been out very long, so now he would begin to find out what it came to. He was able to get to his feet, but something was out of commission somewhere now because the whole left side of him, from head to foot, wanted something, something it had once had but didn't have any more. He tried the left side and it was out of commission all right, but the other wasn't, and he got out a handkerchief with which to wipe his mouth clean of spit and sweat and noticed that it was the handkerchief he had bought in Paris, a first-class handkerchief that was proving to be useful. It was thirteen minutes after three now. He got to the counter and said to the nightclerk, "I want to go upstairs now," but the man didn't stir.

"Wake up," he tried to say very loudly, but the words came out quietly. While he was waiting he thought, "Well, I won again, and I've paid for everything, so I'm all set."

"Wake up," he said again, and this time the nightclerk

opened his eyes, sat up with a start, got to his feet, and then went to the elevator.

"Listen," the man said. "Everything's paid for, but I'm not packed. Will you help me pack and then get me a taxi?"

"You wish to leave *now*?"

"Yes. I want a taxi to take me to the airport as soon as possible. There isn't much to pack but I'd like you to help me."

"Yes, sir."

He sat and watched the nightclerk pack.

Getting a taxi wasn't easy, though, so he didn't leave the hotel until half past four. It was daylight then and a nice day. It was going to be a fine day. He sat on a bench in the waiting room at the airport and began to wait for nine o'clock.

He had gotten all that he deserved, all that he was entitled to, all that he had bargained for, all that he had insisted upon. He'd had it and he was satisfied. "I never gave a shit for any of it anyway," he thought. "There was always a little rhythm anyway, and there still is. I got out here all right, and I'll get on the plane all right, too, the same as the other travellers going East, and I'll get there, too."

He was certainly glad it hadn't been on the floor of the Aviz Hotel anyway. That would have been silly.

At nine when the airplane began to lift up and push out into space, he thought, "Well, I made it again. I kept the rhythm. I met the schedule. I'm going. I'm on my way."

THE PARSLEY GARDEN

One day in August Al Condraj was wandering through Woolworth's without a penny to spend when he saw a small hammer that was not a toy but a real hammer and he was possessed with a longing to have it. He believed it was just what he needed by which to break the monotony and with which to make something. He had gathered some first-class nails from Foley's Packing House where the boxmakers worked and where they had carelessly dropped at least fifteen cents' worth. He had gladly gone to the trouble of gathering them together because it had seemed to him that a nail, as such, was not something to be wasted. He had the nails, perhaps a half pound of them, at least two hundred of them, in a paper bag in the apple box in which he kept his junk at home.

Now, with the ten-cent hammer he believed he could make something out of box wood and the nails, although he had no idea what. Some sort of a table perhaps, or a small bench.

At any rate he took the hammer and slipped it into the pocket of his overalls, but just as he did so a man took him firmly by the arm without a word and pushed him to the back of the store into a small office. Another man, an older one, was seated behind a desk in the office, working with papers. The younger man, the one who had captured him, was excited and his forehead was covered with sweat.

"Well," he said, "here's one more of them."

The man behind the desk got to his feet and looked Al Condraj up and down.

"What's *he* swiped?"

"A hammer." The young man looked at Al with hatred. "Hand it over," he said.

The boy brought the hammer out of his pocket and handed it to the young man, who said, "I ought to hit you over the head with it, that's what I ought to do."

He turned to the older man, the boss, the manager of the store, and he said, "What do you want me to do with him?"

"Leave him with me," the older man said.

The younger man stepped out of the office, and the older man sat down and went back to work. Al Condraj stood in the office fifteen minutes before the older man looked at him again.

"Well," he said.

Al didn't know what to say. The man wasn't looking at him, he was looking at the door.

Finally Al said, "I didn't mean to steal it. I just need it and I haven't got any money."

"Just because you haven't got any money doesn't mean you've got a right to steal things," the man said. "Now, does it?"

"No, sir."

"Well, what am I going to do with you? Turn you over to the police?"

Al didn't say anything, but he certainly didn't want to be turned over to the police. He hated the man, but at the same time he realized somebody else could be a lot tougher than he was being.

"If I let you go, will you promise never to steal from this store again?"

"Yes, sir."

The Parsley Garden

"All right," the man said. "Go out this way and don't come back to this store until you've got some money to spend."

He opened a door to the hall that led to the alley, and Al Condraj hurried down the hall and out into the alley.

The first thing he did when he was free was laugh, but he knew he had been humiliated and he was deeply ashamed. It was not in his nature to take things that did not belong to him. He hated the young man who had caught him and he hated the manager of the store who had made him stand in silence in the office so long. He hadn't liked it at all when the young man had said he ought to hit him over the head with the hammer.

He should have had the courage to look him straight in the eye and say, "You and who else?"

Of course he *had* stolen the hammer and he had been caught, but it seemed to him he oughtn't to have been so humiliated.

After he had walked three blocks he decided he didn't want to go home just yet, so he turned around and started walking back to town. He almost believed he meant to go back and say something to the young man who had caught him. And then he wasn't sure he didn't mean to go back and steal the hammer again, and this time *not* get caught. As long as he had been made to feel like a thief anyway, the least he ought to get out of it was the hammer.

Outside the store he lost his nerve, though. He stood in the street, looking in, for at least ten minutes.

Then, crushed and confused and now bitterly ashamed of himself, first for having stolen something, then for having been caught, then for having been humiliated, then for not having guts enough to go back and do the job right, he began walking home again, his mind so troubled

117

that he didn't greet his pal Pete Wawchek when they came face to face outside Graf's Hardware.

When he got home he was too ashamed to go inside and examine his junk, so he had a long drink of water from the faucet in the back yard. The faucet was used by his mother to water the stuff she planted every year: okra, bell peppers, tomatoes, cucumbers, onions, garlic, mint, eggplants and parsley.

His mother called the whole business the parsley garden, and every night in the summer she would bring chairs out of the house and put them around the table she had had Ondro, the neighbourhood handyman, make for her for fifteen cents, and she would sit at the table and enjoy the cool of the garden and the smell of the things she had planted and tended.

Sometimes she would even make a salad and moisten the flat old-country bread and slice some white cheese, and she and he would have supper in the parsley garden. After supper she would attach the water hose to the faucet and water her plants and the place would be cooler than ever and it would smell real good, real fresh and cool and green, all the different growing things making a green-garden smell out of themselves and the air and the water.

After the long drink of water he sat down where the parsley itself was growing and he pulled a handful of it out and slowly ate it. Then he went inside and told his mother what had happened. He even told her what he had *thought* of doing after he had been turned loose : to go back and steal the hammer again.

"I don't want you to steal," his mother said in broken English. "Here is ten cents. You go back to that man and you give him this money and you bring it home, that hammer."

"No," Al Condraj said. "I won't take your money for

something I don't really need. I just thought I ought to have a hammer, so I could make something if I felt like it. I've got a lot of nails and some box wood, but I haven't got a hammer."

"Go buy it, that hammer," his mother said.

"No," Al said.

"All right," his mother said. "Shut up."

That's what she always said when she didn't know what else to say.

Al went out and sat on the steps. His humiliation was beginning to really hurt now. He decided to wander off along the railroad tracks to Foley's because he needed to think about it some more. At Foley's he watched Johnny Gale nailing boxes for ten minutes, but Johnny was too busy to notice him or talk to him, although one day at Sunday school, two or three years ago, Johnny had greeted him and said, "How's the boy?" Johnny worked with a boxmaker's hatchet and everybody in Fresno said he was the fastest boxmaker in town. He was the closest thing to a machine any packing house ever saw. Foley himself was proud of Johnny Gale.

Al Condraj finally set out for home because he didn't want to get in the way. He didn't want somebody working hard to notice that he was being watched and maybe say to him, "Go on, beat it." He didn't want Johnny Gale to do something like that. He didn't want to invite another humiliation.

On the way home he looked for money but all he found was the usual pieces of broken glass and rusty nails, the things that were always cutting his bare feet every summer.

When he got home his mother had made a salad and set the table, so he sat down to eat, but when he put the food in his mouth he just didn't care for it. He got up and went into the three-room house and got his apple box out of the

119

corner of his room and went through his junk. It was all there, the same as yesterday.

He wandered off back to town and stood in front of the closed store, hating the young man who had caught him, and then he went along to the Hippodrome and looked at the display photographs from the two movies that were being shown that day.

Then he went along to the public library to have a look at all the books again, but he didn't like any of them, so he wandered around town some more, and then around half-past eight he went home and went to bed.

His mother had already gone to bed because she had to be up at five to go to work at Inderrieden's packing figs. Some days there would be work all day, some days there would be only half a day of it, but whatever his mother earned during the summer had to keep them the whole year.

He didn't sleep much that night because he couldn't get over what had happened, and he went over six or seven ways by which to adjust the matter. He went so far as to believe it would be necessary to kill the young man who had caught him. He also believed it would be necessary for him to steal systematically and successfully the rest of his life. It was a hot night and he couldn't sleep.

Finally, his mother got up and walked barefooted to the kitchen for a drink of water and on the way back she said to him softly, "Shut up."

When she got up at five in the morning he was out of the house, but that had happened many times before. He was a restless boy, and he kept moving all the time every summer. He was making mistakes and paying for them, and he had just tried stealing and had been caught at it and he was troubled. She fixed her breakfast, packed her lunch and hurried off to work, hoping it would be a full day.

The Parsley Garden

It was a full day, and then there was overtime, and although she had no more lunch she decided to work on for the extra money, anyway. Almost all the other packers were staying on, too, and her neighbour across the alley, Leeza Ahboot, who worked beside her, said, "Let us work until the work stops, then we'll go home and fix a supper between us and eat it in your parsley garden where it's so cool. It's a hot day and there's no sense not making an extra fifty or sixty cents."

When the two women reached the garden it was almost nine o'clock, but still daylight, and she saw her son nailing pieces of box wood together, making something with a hammer. It looked like a bench. He had already watered the garden and tidied up the rest of the yard, and the place seemed very nice, and her son seemed very serious and busy. She and Leeza went straight to work for their supper, picking bell peppers and tomatoes and cucumbers and a great deal of parsley for the salad.

Then Leeza went to her house for some bread which she had baked the night before, and some white cheese, and in a few minutes they were having supper together and talking pleasantly about the successful day they had had. After supper, they made Turkish coffee over an open fire in the yard. They drank the coffee and smoked a cigarette apiece, and told one another stories about their experiences in the old country and here in Fresno, and then they looked into their cups at the grounds to see if any good fortune was indicated, and there was : health and work and supper out of doors in the summer and enough money for the rest of the year.

Al Condraj worked and overheard some of the things they said, and then Leeza went home to go to bed, and his mother said, "Where you get it, that hammer, Al?"

"I got it at the store."

"How you get it? You steal it?"

Al Condraj finished the bench and sat on it. "No," he said. "I didn't steal it."

"How you get it?"

"I worked at the store for it," Al said.

"The store where you steal it yesterday?"

"Yes."

"Who give you the job?"

"The boss."

"What you do?"

"I carried different stuff to the different counters."

"Well, that's good," the woman said. "How long you work for that little hammer?"

"I worked all day," Al said. "Mr. Clemmer gave me the hammer after I'd worked one hour, but I went right on working. The fellow who caught me yesterday showed me what to do, and we worked together. We didn't talk, but at the end of the day he took me to Mr. Clemmer's office and he told Mr. Clemmer that I'd worked hard all day and ought to be paid at least a dollar."

"That's good," the woman said.

"So Mr. Clemmer put a silver dollar on his desk for me, and then the fellow who caught me yesterday told him the store needed a boy like me every day, for a dollar a day, and Mr. Clemmer said I could have the job."

"That's good," the woman said. "You can make it a little money for yourself."

"I left the dollar on Mr. Clemmer's desk," Al Condraj said, "and I told them both I didn't want the job."

"Why you say that?" the woman said. "Dollar a day for eleven-year-old boy good money. Why you not take job?"

"Because I hate the both of them," the boy said. "I would never work for people like that. I just looked at

122

them and picked up my hammer and walked out. I came home and I made this bench."

"All right," his mother said. "Shut up."

His mother went inside and went to bed, but Al Condraj sat on the bench he had made and smelled the parsley garden and didn't feel humiliated any more.

But nothing could stop him from hating the two men, even though he knew they hadn't done anything they shouldn't have done.

THE THEOLOGICAL STUDENT

I began to meet the theological student about a quarter of a century ago in the plays of certain Russian writers. Tolstoy, Dostoyevsky, Chekhov, Andreyev and Gorki seldom wrote a play in which the theological student did not appear. The theological student seemed to be the playwright himself looking back at his youth with an amused but admiring eye. He was certainly a good man to have around—young; nervous; pale; often pimply; not the least bit handsome; ridiculous and pathetic; ill-clothed; ill-fed; eager for tea; full of the lore of heaven, hell and earth; and yet for all that a man who could be counted on to liven matters up considerably, for he was a devil at heart.

He was certainly always in the midst of a desperate struggle with sin, which appeared to be an overwhelming longing to kiss the girls, a longing that never failed to startle him and bewilder them. Some of the girls were women with children older than himself. These rather liked him, for he was clumsy, inexperienced, inept, and therefore amusing to them. More in charity than in passion they permitted him to breathe heavily in their arms, only to discover later in the afternoon that he was thinking of killing himself. His habit of coughing nervously in their faces made them cry out, "Oh, Alexander Alexandrovich!" —which he took for an expression of love. He disgraced himself in company by his ill-timed remarks and by his uncontrollable desire to escape being good.

He was useful to each playwright, however, in that it

seemed perfectly natural for him to explain why humanity was unhappy.

In the plays of Tolstoy the theological student blamed man's unhappiness on women, and sometimes went so far as to mention certain physical parts of them to which men were so powerfully attracted that they could not give their undivided attention to God or farming ; and then, in another play, Tolstoy would have the theological student blaming something else.

Once, I believe it was the railroads, tempting men to run away. (From women of course, although the playwright mentioned only crying children and members of the local government who were forever greeting people in a most insincere manner.)

Another time the theological student, having had no stronger stimulant than a cup of tea, shouted that man is a beast because of his stomach ; and went on to ask if anyone had recently noticed how frequently men sit down to eat, how much precious time is wasted in eating or in planning to do so, and what mischief attends the circumstance of a stomach full of meat, wheat, greens, cheese, wine and water.

Dostoyevsky's theological student claimed that man was unhappy because his very birth had been a nervous disorder.

Gorki's theological student was the best of the lot, though, for he hated everything which made life miserable, and everything made life miserable. The theological student proceeded quite logically to find fault with God, whereupon another side of Gorki, embodied in another character in the play—a notorious waster of sixty who had recently read a book from cover to cover—came forward with an attack on the government, blaming it for his present age and ill-health, and remarking profoundly that

126

he had once been thirty—no, even less than that—twenty !
But now what? A ridiculous thing in a ridiculous black
cloak ! (Looking meaningfully across the room at Tatania
Lvovna, age 18, and detecting in her the faintest trace of
admiration.)

Having met the theological student and having found
him an odd sort of fish—in no particular greatly different
from anyone else I had met in the Russian plays—I began
to wonder what it was that he was supposed to be study-
ing. Whatever it was, did he study full-time or part-time?
Did he study at school or at home? Or was he called a
theological student simply because he was young? None of
the playwrights was very clear about any of this, other
than to hint that what the theological student *wanted* was
perfection.

At length I decided for myself that he studied theology
books, and I decided to do so also.

A whole small mezzanine balcony with a floor of thick
glass was devoted to books of theology at the Public
Library in Fresno. Climbing the steep narrow stairway to
this section of the library was like climbing upward on a
small cramped ship. Once there, the feeling of sailing was
very great, and the faces of the other readers seemed
flushed by a mild fever, as if they were all a little seasick
and were trying their best not to throw up. They were
certainly dizzy from the height, the hot air, and the
narrowness of the aisles between the shelves of books. I
joined them and began to examine every book on the theology shelves.

Every book seemed depressing, but I was fearful of
putting one of them back in its place until I was reasonably sure it was absurd and did not have hidden away in it
somewhere what I was looking for.

The Theological Student

What *was* I looking for? It did not occur to me at the time—nothing much occurs to anybody at the time and we might as well come right out and admit it—but whether I knew it in so many words or not I was very definitely looking for a theology which I myself might have written, or might one day write. That is to say, I was looking for what I believed was the only true theology. Robert Burns had already summed it up with Scotch economy, but one frequently forgets the remarks of poets. "A man's a man for all that" was right enough, and the implication of laughing about it was in the remark, but I imagined there would be a fuller recitation on the theme.

There wasn't, however.

The millions of words in the hundreds of books were little more than nonsense. Even so, I took home with me after each visit two or three of the theology books which I felt might not prove to be altogether senseless, and read around in them until I was convinced that the author was as ridiculous as any theological student in any Russian play.

No writer is more pathetic than the one whose passion is to complicate, and theology appeared to be a matter of complicating. If it was a matter of believing, why not believe and be done with it? Swedenborg sweated like a horse and wrote a couple of million words that must have had the effect of making it impossible for any reader ever again to smile, itself a kind of theological act, although uncomplicated and surely no more meaningless than Swedenborg's two million words.

All of which brings me to the plot of this story.

One evening on my way home from the Public Library I was met in the Santa Fé freight yards by a man who was profoundly complicated and desperately theological.

128

The Theological Student

"Do you know," he called out from a distance of twenty yards, "that the world is going to end tonight?"

"What time?" I called back.

"Don't know the exact hour," the man said, "but it will be sometime tonight."

From his shoulders the man brushed dirt which had gotten there when he had leaped from a freight train and fallen.

"Did you just get to town?" I said.

"Yes, but I was born here twenty-seven years ago," the man said.

"Are you ready for the end of the world?" he went on, as he took to brushing dust from his pants.

"As ready as I am for anything else," I said. "Are *you* ready?"

"That's the trouble," the man said. "I'm not. I'm not at all."

Suddenly the man fell down.

"Do you know where the Emergency Hospital is?" I said. "It's at the back of the Police Station on Broadway, across from the Public Library, but if you don't want to go there, you can go to the County Hospital. It's across Ventura Boulevard at the Fair Grounds, but I suppose you know where these places are. I live on the way to the County Hospital and I'll go with you as far as my house. Maybe you can pick up a ride."

The man leaned on me and we stumbled in silence past Inderrieden's Dried Fruit Packing House. Crossing Ventura he fell again, and an automobile stopped. The driver of the automobile got out and came to the man and said, "What's the matter?"

"He ought to get to a doctor," I said. "He's hurt."

The driver of the automobile helped me get the man into the car. On the way to the County Hospital the injured man took one of the three books I had borrowed from the Public Library and opened it.

"*Either-Or*," he read. "By Sören Kierkegaard. Who's he?"

"I don't know," I said.

"A man ought to know who these people are," the man said.

He began to read the book. When we reached the hospital his grip was so tight on the book that I felt sure it would be damaged and the girl at the desk in the Public Library would examine the damage, and then me, and wonder how it had happened, but not say anything.

The driver of the car—a man who had remarked on the way to the hospital that his name was August Bockbell, a name I have never forgotten, perhaps because the driver—sensing that the other man was dying—gave an account of his *own* life, which included almost killing his elder brother over the ownership of a pocketknife—helped the injured man into the reception room, and then went off, apologizing that it was necessary for him to do so.

I did not go with him because the injured man was still reading the book I had borrowed from the Public Library, and it seemed to me that it would have been rude under the circumstances to ask him to return it. He was reading the book with incredible swiftness. When it was necessary for the injured man to go off with the nurse and a young man in a white coat who did not seem to be much of a doctor, I followed them down a hall to swinging doors, partly from anxiety about the man himself and partly from anxiety about the library book. At the swinging doors the nurse told me to return to the reception room. I wanted to ask her to please get my book for me, but instead I said, "He's going to be all right, isn't he?" The nurse gestured severely, as if to say, "No difficult questions at this difficult time, please."

I returned to the reception room and sat down.

When I examined the two remaining library books, I discovered that my library card with my name and address on it was in the book by Kierkegaard which the injured man had taken. My library card was as important to me as a passport is to a traveller. I had thought of waiting only ten or fifteen minutes for the book, but when I discovered that my library card was in it, I decided to wait two hours if necessary.

It was necessary to wait longer than that, however, during which time I grew very hungry—half-sick from it, in fact—and very angry, too. At first I was angry at the nurse who entered the reception room every ten or fifteen minutes in a state of confusion and excitement and refused to listen to what I had to tell her or to tell me about the condition of the injured man. After awhile I became angry about the man himself, whether he was to live or die—for he had most rudely taken off with a book I was charged on my honour to return to the Public Library in the same condition in which I had found it. Finally, I became angry about Kierkegaard, a man concerning whom I knew absolutely nothing except that he had written a book with the strange title of *Either-Or*.

After having waited more than three hours for the return of my book, the nurse came up to me in the reception room in a manner which revealed unmistakably that she meant to speak, and began by announcing a hopelessly garbled version of *my* name.

"Yes?" I said.

"He's dead," she went on. "Dr. Humpkit (at least that's what I *thought* she said) did everything possible for him, but it was just no use."

"I'm sorry. The thing I wanted to tell you was to please let me have my book."

"What book?"

"The book by Kierkegaard."

"He said it was *his* book. *His* library card with his *name* and *address* on it is in the book, at any rate."

"The card in the book is *my* card," I said. "Why do you get everything wrong? I was walking home from the Public Library with three books when I met the man in the Santa Fé freight yards. He had just jumped off a train and had hurt himself, so I helped him to Ventura Avenue where he fell down and a motorist stopped and brought him here. In the automobile he took one of the three books I had borrowed from the Public Library and kept it. Now he's dead, and just because my library card happened to be in the book, you've given *him* my name. Well, I'm sorry he's dead whoever he is, but I'd like to have my book back just the same."

"He himself told us his name," the nurse said. "I am entering it in the hospital records. We shall return the book to the Public Library for him."

"You've been to school," I said, because I was so angry and hungry, and then left the hospital and began walking home.

When I got there I found the street full of automobiles. The house was full of uncles and aunts and cousins from all over the city.

My uncle Khosrove was the first to see me, for he was sitting alone on the steps of the back porch smoking a cigarette.

He got up and shouted at the top of his voice into the house, "I told you it was a mistake. Here he is now, the same as ever, but very much in need of food."

The Theological Student

Everybody inside the house came tumbling out, and then, after having seen me, they all hurried back in to set the table.

After I had had all the food I could get into my belly, my mother asked very sweetly, "Why did they come in an ambulance and say that you had died?"

"If I had known they were going to come in an ambulance," I said, "I would have come with them instead of walking three miles on an empty stomach at ten o'clock at night. They didn't tell me they were going to come in an ambulance."

"We've been terribly worried about you," my uncle Zorab said.

This was too much for my uncle Khosrove.

"We've been terribly worried about you!" he mocked. "When the man from the County Hospital told us you were dead, we were afraid you would not recover."

He turned to my uncle Zorab.

"Why do you talk nonsense?" he said. "Is it possible to worry about someone who is dead?"

My uncle Zorab cleared his throat nervously as he said, "Well, all I can say is, we worried, and here he is alive!"

"Man," my uncle Khosrove shouted, "will you never understand the very simplest sort of thing? There has been a mistake, as I said. Your worrying did not bring a dead man back to life. The boy's been involved in some sort of typical American complication. Unless you understand this now, there is no telling what terrible distortions will come into the telling of this family episode in years to come. Now that the boy has had his supper, let him tell us the whole story, and then one by one let us return to our own homes and our own lives. Whoever it was that died, we shall all join him soon enough, and it is quite all right." He turned to me. "Now tell us what it was that happened which the people of the hospital reported to us as having been your death at the age of twenty-seven. I tried to tell these people that it was not you who had died, for you are not twenty-seven years old, but they replied that perhaps you had given twenty-seven as your age in a last attempt to be impressive. How old are you, and then tell us the story."

"I'm fourteen," I said.

And then I told the whole story, accurately, point by point.

My aunt Khatoon took to weeping softly for the young man who had died, claiming that he had died for *me*, so that I might go on living, a theory that made my mother angry; but my grandfather twisted his moustaches and said, "All very well and good, but who the devil is this man Kierkegaard to make such an ungodly fuss in this desolate and far-away village which is trying to pass for a city?"

"He is the man who wrote one of the three books I borrowed from the Public Library this afternoon," I said, "but that's all I know about him."

"Well," my grandfather said, "that's fine. Now, all of you—get out of here. Go home where you belong. If it's for him you've been crying, there he is trying to get meat from between his teeth, so go home."

Everybody embraced lightly by way of celebrating my survival; there was kindly whispering among the women; the small boys took to wrestling in the living-room; and then at last everybody was gone excepting the Old Man and my uncle Khosrove. These two exchanged quarrelsome glances and then my uncle Khosrove said, "I know what you are going to ask him. Well, I'll give you the answer, to save him the trouble. You are going to ask him

134

what he means by getting into complications of all sorts every other Friday, and I will answer for him that he doesn't mean anything at all by it. Some people come into this world asleep and go out of it asleep, and that is very thoughtful of them. A few others—like myself and this boy, my nephew Aram Garoghlanian—come into this world asleep, and then one fair Friday wake up and look around and notice what we are."

"What are we?" the Old Man asked politely.

"Armenians," my uncle Khosrove said quickly. "Could anything be more ridiculous? The Englishman has an empire to govern. The Frenchman has art to guide and measure. The German has an army to train and test. The Russian has a revolution to start. The Swiss have hotels to manage, the Mexicans mandolins to play, the Spaniards bulls to fight, the Austrians waltzes to dance to, and so on and so forth, but what have *we*?"

"Loud mouths to shut up?" the Old Man suggested.

"And the Irish," my uncle Khosrove went on. "The Irish have a whole island in which to be poverty-stricken; the Arabs a thousand tribes to bring together in the desert; the Jews child prodigies to send on concert tours; the Gypsies wagons and fortune-telling cards; the Americans chronic nervousness which they call freedom, but what have the Armenians?"

"Since you insist, tell me," said the Old Man. "What have the Armenians?"

"Manners," my uncle Khosrove said.

"Are you mad?" the Old Man said. "Nothing is so unnatural as a polite Armenian."

"I did not say *good* manners," my uncle Khosrove said. "I said manners. The good or bad of it I leave to others. Manners is what we have, and very little of anything else. You are going to ask this boy what he means by getting into complications of all sorts every other Friday. Your asking is manners. Well, go ahead and ask him. I'm going to the Arax Coffee House for a couple of hours of tavli. My going is more manners."

"Before you go," the Old Man said, "I think you ought to know I wished to ask the boy to report to me about the book by Kierkegaard, if he ever reads it. Now, I will go to the Coffee House *with* you."

The Old Man got up and yawned enormously. He yawned in three movements, after the fashion of symphonies, very slowly, wildly, and finally slowly and wildly by turns.

He went out of the house by the front door while my uncle Khosrove took the back. The screen doors slammed one-two, and I went looking for half a watermelon to eat, as I was very thirsty.

The following day I went out to the County Hospital and after a great deal of effort identified myself, retrieved my book, and took it home to read. The injured man had reached page 99, for he had folded the edge of that page over, so that he might easily find his place when next he took it up. After reading an hour and three-quarters I too reached page 99, and decided that I did not wish to read any farther. I took the book back to the Public Library and as I had expected the girl at the desk noticed the damage, examined it, examined me as I whistled softly, but did not say anything. I climbed the steep stairway to the mezzanine and continued my search for the book of theology that I hoped to find.

That evening I reported to my grandfather that Kierkegaard appeared to have been a Dane who had been born in 1813 and had died in 1855 after having spent the greater part of his time struggling with the devil, the church, and the complications of theology.

The Theological Student

"Died at the age of forty-two," the Old Man said. "Struggling with the devil is most destructive, I see, but perhaps had he *not* struggled he would have lived only twenty-two years and left behind him not even the book he wrote. Have you read the book?"

"He wrote more than one book," I said. "I read the first 99 pages of one of them, and then I got tired of it."

"What did he say in the first 99 pages?"

"I'm not sure, but he *seemed* to say that everything is not enough."

"That is how it is with these fellows who are forever struggling with the devil," the Old Man said. "And the unfortunate man you met yesterday in the Santa Fé freight yards, what about him?"

"He died. Yesterday was the end of the world for him all right, just as he said."

"His real name?"

"Well," I said, "I have a name written down here from the book at the County Hospital which is *supposed* to be his name, but I am sure it is only another mistake. It's no mistake that he's dead, though. I suppose he might have lived had he not fallen into the hands of people so sure of themselves, and so quick to get things accurately wrong. I'm sure he didn't expect to die, for he turned down a page of the book, so that he might go on reading it. Here's the name I got from the Hospital book. Abo Mogabgab."

"How can that be?" the Old Man said. "Abo Mogabgab is the man from whom I buy my clothing, the Syrian with the shop on Mariposa Street, a man older than myself. Here, look into the lining of this coat at the label and read to me what is said there."

I looked at the label inside the coat and read aloud, "Abo Mogabgab."

137

"A magnificent example of American efficiency and theological accuracy," the Old Man said. "A man has been killed and a coat label has been given a funeral. And yet, here we are, all of us who are still alive, none the worse for the terrible efficiency or the fierce accuracy. Thank you for reporting to me on the gospel of Kierkegaard. I am still eager to learn, but I find that the farmer's gospel is still the best we have. Now, the vine is planted thus; and thus is it tended; and thus protected from rabbits; and thus are the grapes harvested; and thus are they made into wine; and thus dried by the sun into raisins; and in the winter thus it is that the branches of the vines are pruned; and in the spring thus it is that the vines are watered. What other gospel is half so pleasant, since it is all out in the weather? To hell with these stifling chambers in which poor men sit and confuse themselves. When they are all through for the day, don't they get up and go home and eat a bowl of stewed raisins with a piece of black bread, or drink a glass of wine with a lamb-chop, or eat a bunch of grapes with cheese and crackers?"

"I guess so," I said and went home.

When I got there I spent three hours in the backyard, working. My uncle Khosrove sat on the steps of the back porch and watched.

At last he got up and said, "For the love of God, what is it now? Why are you pestering the life out of that poor old Malaga vine? You have cleaned and repaired it until it looks like the ghost of a wretched old man, and only a moment ago it resembled a handsome, dreaming youth. Matter is beautiful only in its imperfections. Only blockheads seek perfection, which is death. Let perfection seek you. You needn't seek it. Now, go inside the house and sit down and eat half a cold watermelon. You are not perfect, the vine is not perfect, but you can eat watermelon and pass water, so do so."

"What nonsense," I thought, but as I ate the watermelon I wondered if my uncle Khosrove was not just about the best theological student of them all.

THE PLOT

The plot was as follows :

The L Street Boys would dig the three-feet deep, six-feet long, three-feet wide hole in the middle of the short-cut across Kazakian's empty lot that ran from M Street to the alley between L and M. They would dig the hole at midnight, after everybody in the neighbourhood had gone to bed, so that Apkar Popcorn, as he was called, who was the first to use the path in the morning, would not suspect anything. They would cover the hole with plaster-laths, newspaper and dirt.

At half-past five in the morning they would hide behind Kazakian's house and watch Apkar Popcorn fall into the hole.

The L Street Boys were the Shimshamian brothers, Husik and Jaziyire, called Fussy and Jazz ; the Melkonian brothers, Arsen and Ardash ; Fat Kishmish ; Shag Bareko-mian ; Haig or Ike Ardzrooni ; and George Vrej. But it was Fussy and Jazz Shimshamian who were the creators of the plot. The backyard of their house on L Street faced the backyard of Apkar Popcorn's house on M Street. Two of their chickens had wandered across the alley into Apkar Popcorn's garden and Apkar Popcorn had captured them, but he had denied it, and now the boys wanted to get even.

The other L Street Boys didn't know about the chickens, they just liked the idea of making a hole for Apkar Popcorn to fall into, so they dug the hole and covered it precisely as planned, and at half-past five in the

141

morning they gathered together behind Kazakian's house. Apkar Popcorn left his house on M Street every morning at exactly a quarter to six, and he always used Kazakian's short-cut on his way to town, so the boys knew they would see something unusual in a few minutes.

At twenty minutes to six a tiny woman entered the short-cut on M Street and began to move upon the hidden hole. This was not what the L Street Boys had had in mind, but the woman had appeared so suddenly and was moving with such speed upon the trap that everyone became speechless.

At last Fat Kishmish said to Fussy Shimshamian, "That looks like your mother, Fussy."

"No," Fussy said, "my mother's home baking bread."

"Isn't that your mother, Jazz?" Fat Kishmish said to Fussy's brother.

"Yes, it is," Jazz Shimshamian said. "What's she doing on M Street?"

"That's Jazz and Fussy's mother," the L Street Boys said to one another.

"Well, aren't you going to stop her?" Ike Ardzrooni said.

"How can I stop her?" Fussy said. "She'd kill me."

"You've *got* to stop her," George Vrej said. "One of you has got to stop her. You just can't let your mother fall into a hole. We dug the hole for Apkar Popcorn, not for your mother."

"Jazz," Shag Barekomian said, "you've got to stop your mother from falling into the hole."

"It's too late now," Fussy Shimshamian said.

The L Street Boys stopped breathing to watch Mrs. Shockey Shimshamian fall into the hole they had dug for Apkar Popcorn. The woman had only two or three more steps to take. They saw her left foot go through the false surface, and then every bit of her plunged forward onto the surface, and then into the hole. They heard a scream.

The trap had been perfectly set and concealed, and it had worked perfectly.

After the woman had disappeared into it, the L Street Boys turned and ran. They ran straight down San Benito Avenue across the Southern Pacific tracks to the outskirts of China Town, and there, outside Chong Jan's Wholesale Produce House, they stopped to think and talk things over.

It was agreed that no member of the organization would confess knowing anything about how the hole had come into being, and there the matter ended.

Mrs. Shimshamian was not seriously injured, but she did go to bed for a week.

The open hole remained in Kazakian's empty lot for several years and was finally filled with garbage from Mr. Kazakian's home.

Every morning at a quarter to six, on his way to town, Apkar Popcorn glanced at the hole. It broke up the monotony of his walk very nicely.

THE FOREIGNER

Hawk Harrap, whose father came from somewhere in Asia Minor and used to sell vegetables and fruit from a wagon drawn by a horse, was of my time in Fresno, so I remember the days when he was a kid in overalls hustling *The Evening Herald* or sneaking in to the fights at the Civic Auditorium or playing hookey from Emerson School to sell soda pop at the County Fair and make a lot of money.

His father was Syrian but seldom spoke the language, as he had married a woman who was Scotch-Irish. Harrap was his name on all the school records, although his father's name was something that only *sounded a little* like Harrap. He was given the name Hawk by myself for being as swift as that bird or as swift as I imagined that bird was. By the time we were at Longfellow Junior High School together, the nickname was on the school records, too. Actually, his mother had named him Hugh after a dead brother.

The day I first met Hawk at Emerson School, in 1916, he took me to a boy named Roy Coulpa and insulted him by saying, "Roy, you're an *Italian*!" It did not seem to matter at all that Roy Coulpa *was* Italian. It was Hawk's tone of voice that was insulting. After making this painful and preposterous remark, Hawk shoved me into Roy with such force that we fell and began to wrestle. Roy was surprised and angry, and strong enough to make me exert myself. The school playground was Fresno dirt, so a lot of dust got kicked up as each of us broke free of all kinds of

holds. The match stopped when the recess bell rang, and
Roy and I got up and had a look at one another. We
looked around for Hawk, too. We were not permitted to
move until we heard the second bell, at which time we fell
in at the entrance of the school. When a third bell rang
we marched to our classrooms. Hawk was standing among
the two dozen spectators. When I caught his eye he
winked, and I wondered what the hell he meant.

After school he and Roy and I walked to California
Playground, and there the three of us wrestled for the fun
of it.

The point is, it was impossible to dislike him.

Hawk lived on O Street, so he and I walked home together when Roy set out for his house across the S.P.
tracks on G Street, beyond Rosenberg's Packing House.

"What are you, anyway?" Hawk said as we walked
home. "Even the teacher can't pronounce your name."

"I'm American," I said.

"The hell you are," Hawk said. "Roy's Italian, I'm
Syrian, and I guess you're Armenian."

"Sure," I said. "I'm Armenian all right, but I'm American, too. I speak better English than I do Armenian."

"I can't talk Syrian at all," Hawk bragged, "but that's
what I am. If anybody asks you what you are, for God's
sake don't tell them you're American. Tell them you're
Armenian."

"What's the difference?"

"What do you mean what's the difference? If you're
Armenian and you say you're American everybody'll
laugh at you. The teacher knows what you are. Everybody knows what you are."

"Aren't *you* American?"

"Don't make me laugh," Hawk said. "I'm a foreigner.
My father sells vegetables from a wagon."

The Foreigner

"Weren't you born in America?"

"I was born in Fresno. I was born in the house on O Street. What's that got to do with it?"

"Well, I'm American," I said. "And so are you."

"You must be looney," Hawk said. "But don't worry, you'll find out what you are soon enough."

One day months later, after lunch, Miss Clapping, our teacher, suddenly stopped teaching and said, "You Armenian boys who go home for lunch have got to stop eating things full of garlic. The smell is more than I can stand and I'm not going to put up with it any longer."

Hawk turned to see how I was taking the insult.

As a matter of fact lunch for me that day had been dried eggplant, okra and stringbeans made into a stew with chunks of shoulder of lamb, in which garlic was absolutely necessary.

The day wasn't so cold, however, that the windows of the room could not be opened or the radiator turned off. The classroom was air-tight and over-hot.

"Open the window," I said to Miss Clapping.

Hawk gave a hoot of amazement and Miss Clapping looked at me as if she had no intention not to finish my life immediately. The rest of the class stirred in their seats and waited for developments. I decided to kill Miss Clapping and be done with it, but when I got to thinking how I might do it, the scheme seemed impractical. Miss Clapping went to her desk and studied her class book.

"Yes," she said at last. "Here is your name. I'm sure you know how to pronounce it. The Lord knows I don't."

Another insult!

She closed the book and looked at me again.

"Now," she said, "what did you say when I said you Armenian boys will have to stop eating garlic?"

"I said open the window."

"Perhaps I don't understand," Miss Clapping said, her lips beginning to tremble a little.

She put down the book she was holding and picked up a twelve-inch ruler. She stepped away from her desk and stood at the foot of the row in which my desk was the last one.

"Now, tell me," she said, "just *what* do you mean?"

"I mean," I said, "it would be stuffy in this room no matter what anybody ate for lunch. This room needs fresh air. It's easier to open the window than to ask people to cook stuff without garlic."

Hawk hooted again, and without any further discussion Miss Clapping moved down the row to my desk.

"Put out your right hand," she said.

"What for?"

"For being impertinent."

It happened that I had recently learned the meaning of that word.

"I haven't been impertinent," I said.

"You're being impertinent now," the teacher said. "Put out your right hand or I shall send you to the Principal, who will give you a thrashing."

"No, he won't," I said.

"Oh, he won't, won't he?" the teacher said. "We'll see about that. You're not going to make a fool out of me in *this* class. Put out your right hand."

Miss Clapping waited a full minute for me to put out my hand. So many things happened to her face, to her eyes and mouth, that I almost felt sorry for her. I certainly felt disgusted with myself, although I knew she was being ridiculous.

Finally she returned to her desk and with a shaking hand scribbled a note which she folded and handed to a little girl named Elvira Koot who took the note and left the room. The class sat in silence, the teacher tried to occupy herself looking into her book, and I wished I lived in a more civilized part of the country. At last the little girl returned to the room and handed the teacher a note which the teacher read. I was sure the Principal had considered the situation and had urged her to open the window; I was ready to apologize for having made so much trouble; but when I saw the evil smile on the teacher's face I went back to planning to kill her, for I knew I was headed for hard times.

"Report to the Principal in his office at once," Miss Clapping said.

I got up and left the room. In the hall I decided to kill the Principal too. I had seen him from a distance, the usual tall man around public schools; and I had heard about him; but I hadn't believed what I had heard. The report was that he was quite a rooster among the old hens who taught school and that he wouldn't think of giving you a chance to tell your side of a story. If one of the old hens said you deserved to be punished the rooster punished you. Instead of reporting to his office immediately, I left the school building and walked home.

My mother was in the kitchen cutting up half a dozen cabbages for sour cabbage soup.

"What are you doing here?" she said.

"I don't want to go to that school any more," I said.

I tried to explain as accurately as possible what had happened. My mother listened to my side of the story and cut up the cabbages and put them into a five-gallon crock and poured salt over them and put a piece of apple-box wood on top of the cabbage, and on top of the wood she put rocks the size of eggplants. She said nothing until I was finished, and then she said, "Go back to the school and mind the teacher. Hereafter when there is garlic in your lunch, eat a sprig of parsley. Do not be so eager to defend the honour of Armenian cooking."

This attitude infuriated me.

I went to my room and put some things together—a pair of socks, a sling shot, three pebbles, a key I had found, a magnifying glass, and a copy of The New Testament I had won at Sunday School—and tied them into a bundle, to run away. I walked two blocks and then went back to the house and threw the bundle on the front porch and went back to the school and reported to the Principal.

He gave me a strapping with a heavy leather belt. After this greatest insult of all, I dried my eyes and went back to my class and sat at my desk.

After school Hawk said, "See what I mean? You're a foreigner and don't ever forget it. A smart foreigner keeps his feelings to himself and his mouth shut. You can't change teachers. You can't change Principals. You can't change people. You can laugh at them, that's all. Americans make me laugh. I wouldn't fool with them if I were you. I just laugh at them."

What happens to a man like Hawk Harrap as the years go by?

Well, I had been out of the Army about a month when I decided to drive from San Francisco to my home town before summer ended, and try to find out. It was mid-October, and I wanted to eat some grapes and figs and melons and pomegranates and new raisins, anyway.

I reached Fresno early Saturday evening and telephoned Roy Coulpa and my second cousin Mug Muggerditchian and took them to dinner at El Rancho on Highway 99, just past Roeding Park.

It was 1945, and it was good to be breathing the air of the San Joaquin Valley again, and to be talking to fellows

I had known most of my life, who had just come home from the war, too.

Mug mentioned two of his cousins who had been killed, and how it had affected their mothers and fathers; and Roy mentioned some Italian boys I had known long ago who had been killed, and a boy who was a mess from injuries to his head and spine, who probably wouldn't ever escape from the Army hospitals.

One thing led to another and then Roy Coulpa remembered Hawk Harrap.

"Hawk beat the draft," Roy said, "and as far as I'm concerned I'm glad he did. It would have been silly for a guy like Hawk to go through all that chicken, or get himself messed up by a lot of complicated injuries. He's got a half-interest in The Wink, a little bar on Broadway, but he's not there very much. He drives to Hollywood or Frisco or Reno or Las Vegas and has fun the same as ever. I ran into him in the bar about a month ago. Well, you know Hawk. He winks and takes care of himself. He was behind the bar but not in a white coat. He came out and sat down and we threw the bull a couple of hours. When I asked him how he had managed to beat the draft, a professional fighter three years, six feet one, two hundred pounds—well, maybe you remember the way he always was, even if you haven't seen him in ten or fifteen years. Swift and serious, but you always know he's laughing inside.

"'Roy,' Hawk said, 'you know the time to make money is when there's a war going on. That's no time to be saying yes sir and no sir.'

"Well, *somebody* made a lot of money out of the war," Roy went on. "I know Hawk didn't make it *all*, but I'm glad he made *some* of it."

Roy Coulpa told a half dozen stories about Hawk

Harrap, and then he told this one which he got from Hawk himself :

Immediately after the war, Hawk took to walking around Hollywood with a cane, a discharge button in his lapel, and a gentle, thankful look in his eyes. He limped into the best places and reluctantly told stories to beautiful girls about his fighting in the Solomon Islands, in Casablanca, in Anzio, in Normandy—in the infantry, in the engineers, in the Navy, in the Marines.

Sometimes he would limp with his right leg, sometimes with his left. Sometimes he would shake all over and apologize and ask somebody for atabrine and accept another Scotch-over-ice instead and calm down and apologize some more and say he would be all right soon—sixty or seventy more attacks and he would be finished with malaria.

Sometimes he would have twitches in his face and ask a beautiful girl who had just mentioned her brother, named Jim, to please never, never mention that name in his presence again, and twitch some more and shake his head and shut up like a clam, trying to be mysterious ; and then he would try to control himself enough to hint to her why he could not bear to hear that name, what had happened to his best pal, Jim Sooney, in the break-through at Bastogne.

Well, Jim Sooney and Hawk were old friends from O Street. Jim was Assyrian, not Syrian, but they were good friends just the same.

Jim and Hawk bought a hundred acres of good land in Reedley during the war and made a lot of money growing and shipping fruit and vegetables.

There was a pretty good farmhouse on the land to which Hawk sometimes invited friends for an all-night game of stud, and one Saturday night after the war he was there at sundown, waiting for the boys to arrive. All over the land watermelons were ripening, and he enjoyed seeing them. When it was night, around eight, Hawk was sitting in the rocking chair on the front porch of the farmhouse breathing the good air when three cars stopped on the road beside his watermelon patch, and out of the automobiles eleven boys and men fell on Hawk's watermelons. Hawk watched them a few minutes and then went into the shack and got the rifle off the wall. He strolled down the dirt road of his land and took everybody by surprise.

He said he was just back from Germany where he had almost lost his respect for mankind, and now that he'd come home and was trying to earn an honest dollar, here they were, showing their appreciation for all the private sacrifices he had made in helping to win the war and save civilization. Here they were, stealing his watermelons, taking bread out of the mouths of his children. He warned everybody to follow his instructions and not try to run, or he would shoot to kill. He had gone through a lot in Germany. He had been taught to kill, and he could easily kill every one of them. He counted the watermelon stealers over and over again, saying in a kind of madness, "One, two, three, four, five, six, seven, eight, nine, ten, eleven—almost a dozen. I killed twenty-seven Germans with a machine-gun once, and they hadn't done anything to me at all. Now, every one of you, lie down according to size, on this road."

A number of the watermelon stealers had recently been discharged from the Army and told Hawk so. He asked them not to provoke him. He hadn't made up his mind what he was going to do with them just yet, and he didn't want to be provoked into making an unfair decision.

Everybody stretched out in the road, and Hawk asked them to count off, which they did, or tried to do. The younger boys, twelve years old or so, were crying now.

The Foreigner

Hawk said, "I wish I knew what to do. I must ask God for guidance. I don't want blood on my hands if it's not His will."

Somebody said, "It's not His will."

"We're not sure about that yet," Hawk said. "We're only poor ignorant misguided human beings. God brought me home from Germany. He will answer my prayer."

So then Hawk prayed.

"O God," he said, "these boys and men have come to steal my watermelons and I've caught them with their pants down. As you know, I served faithfully at Anzio, Normandy and Bastogne, suffering terrible embarrassment and being underpaid. Now that I have come home at last to my wife and five children, these men have come to take the bread out of their mouths. I have caught them, and I must do my duty. O God, please tell me what my duty is. Amen."

After a minute of silence Hawk said, "I thank you, O God."

A man lying on his belly in the dirt turned his head and said, "What did God say?"

"He said my duty is to kill every one of you, and I'm sorry, I must do my duty. I expect you to die like men and boys. Let the first volunteer stand at attention. I promise him a painless death."

Nobody moved to volunteer and the smaller boys wept harder than ever and begged for mercy. Finally, the boldest man got to his knees so that Hawk wouldn't take him for a volunteer and said, "For God's sake, man, I was at Bastogne myself. We'll pay for the watermelons, but don't do this crazy thing."

"Don't provoke me," Hawk said, "or I'll shoot you on your knees."

Now, Jim Sooney and four others stopped their car in

the road and got out to see what foolishness Hawk was up to this time.

The man on his knees appealed to Jimmy Sooney and the others, but Hawk ordered the man to fall on his belly, which he did.

Hawk badgered the watermelon stealers a half hour, asking each of them to recite his name, his age, his address, his birthplace, his nearest of kin, his religion, blood type, race, amount of insurance carried, favourite movie actress, combat decorations, secret ambitions, and whether he liked apple pie for dessert better than jello. If a man said apple pie, Hawk said he was sorry for the man : if a man said jello, Hawk said he was afraid the man had made a poor choice. He asked the men to change their religions, and they were all glad to do it.

Finally, because he wanted to go in and start the poker game, Hawk struck a bargain with the watermelon stealers. He said he wanted to hear some good choral singing of hymns. If the group sang well enough to bring tears to his eyes, he would turn them free. He ordered everybody to kneel and sing, but the men couldn't think of one single hymn to sing. At last one of the small boys began to sing, *Nearer, my God, to Thee*, and the others tried to join in.

"It's not that the hymn isn't heartbreaking," Hawk said. "It's your lousy singing. Try another hymn."

The boy who seemed to know a hymn or two began to sing *I Love Life*, but Hawk cut him short, saying that that was not a hymn at all but a dirty semi-classical number. The boy thought a moment and tried again. *When the Roll is Called Up Yonder*, he sang, and the others tried to join in, but when the choral singing broke to pieces and the little boy tried to save them all by sobbing through the whole song alone and looked eagerly into Hawk's face, Hawk was still unmoved.

"One last chance," Hawk said. "I can give you only one last chance. I shall name a song and you must shout it out with all your might. If you hear me singing with you, then you shall know that I want you all to live. I want you all to go home and live decent, Christian lives. I want you all to sing *Onward, Christian Soldiers.*"

The watermelon stealers began to sing, but Hawk remained silent through three choruses.

At last Hawk began to sing, too, and the men and boys jumped up and ran off to their cars, slipping and falling and slamming doors and driving off.

Then Hawk Harrap and Jim Sooney and their friends went into the farmhouse and started the all-night poker game.

Nobody laughed while Roy Coulpa told the story, and there were tears in his eyes when he stopped talking.

"What's the matter?" Mug Muggerditchian said.

"Nothing," Roy said. "I just feel sorry for those guys."

"Hawk was only having a little fun," Mug said.

"I don't mean the watermelon stealers," Roy said. "I mean the guys in the war."

THE POET AT HOME

The Ralph Gallops were four people.

Ralph himself was a man of thirty-seven who, according to his wife Elizabeth, was never the same from one day to another, which she felt was a good way for him to stay.

Elizabeth Gallop was, according to their five-year-old son Philip, the most beautiful girl on 53rd Street between 6th and 5th Avenues, New York, New York, 1949.

Philip, according to his three-year-old sister Molly, was a very bad boy.

As for Molly, she was, in her own words, da best.

The Gallops lived in a five-room apartment on the third floor of an old but solid nine-storey building on the north side of 53rd Street. There was a small kitchen with refrigerator, gas stove, sink, cabinets, and yellow linoleum on the floor. In short, it was the usual small place in which to start stuff cooking and get out, for it was too small for anything like a table, and although it had a chair with a green leather seat which also served as a stepladder, it was not the sort of kitchen anybody could settle down in and loaf.

Ralph Gallop often remarked that the kitchen might have been three times as big, for he felt that a home without a big kitchen was at best temporary. The kitchen had a door onto the hall which was very useful in that grocery deliveries arrived there.

The front door opened onto a good-sized hall in which

stood an old-fashioned iron coat hanger painted white and a spinet piano named George Steck New York Paris London which was also a player-piano.

Ralph Gallop had picked this item up at a second-hand piano store on 56th Street for $500, including two dozen old rolls.

The piano was not yet paid for.

Over the piano was a more or less oval mirror with a white plaster frame carved into a floral design with a girl cherub on one side near the top and a boy cherub on the other. The boy was complete. Although the cherubs had no wings they gave the impression of flying, and Philip and Molly Gallop frequently looked up and watched the cherubs as if they were actually flying. The girl's face was mature and fat and sweet, and the boy's face was thoughtful and angry. The faces of the cherubs, that is.

The mirror was not paid for, either.

To the left of the hall was the medium-sized dining-room which contained the oak table, painted white with black pickling, as Mrs. Gallop pointed out when speaking of her furniture. The chairs were of the same oak, with leather seats and backs, two red, two green, two yellow. One green and yellow chair stayed in the living-room as a rule.

To the right of the hall was the living-room with the two grey corduroy sofas that were also beds. These stood against the wall across from the fireplace. Between them was an end table on which stood a very big lamp with a black sack shade. The lamp had once been a metal roll for the printing of wall paper with a floral design.

It had cost $150, and was not paid for.

The fireplace had a white wood frame around tan marble, and a roll screen from Jackson's that had cost $75.

This item was paid for because that was the way Jackson's did business.

There were no fireplace implements around the fireplace because, besides being expensive, the kids would only take them and wreck the joint, Ralph said. There was a large wooden bucket from Sherry's Wine Store at one end of the fireplace and in it were generally three logs. On the bucket was pasted a small square picture of a snow landscape. In front of the fireplace were two three-legged low stools, with clover-shaped holes at the centre of each seat, and curved legs. These items were from Jackson's, too, and were paid for, but Mrs. Gallop had had them painted white and pickled black, to match the rest of the furniture.

The piano was the colour of all pianos, of course, but it was Mrs. Gallop's plan to have it painted some day. She might paint it herself, as she had painted the bench, but Mr. Gallop was opposed to the plan.

"A piano ought to look miserable," he argued. "It is absolutely not necessary for *everything* in this house to be white with black pickling."

The liquor from Sherry's that had come in the wooden bucket was also paid for, Sherry's also being a cash house, so to say.

Across from each sofa or couch in the living-room was a chest of drawers in which Mrs. Gallop kept some of her stuff. Two book shelves full of books and magazines stood at the open end of each sofa.

The hall, the living-room and the dining-room practically constituted one unit, almost one room, the living-room windows overlooking 53rd Street, the dining-room windows overlooking the court or yard or garden, in which two sycamore trees and several bushes were spending their time.

The rest of the house was another unit : two bedrooms, two baths, halls, doors, closets, chests, sofa-beds, and so on.

The children occupied the rear bedroom because they would not be so apt to breathe gasoline fumes from that room. They had a good bath, but it had no shower, which Mr. and Mrs. Gallop's bath had.

All walls were grey, all ceilings white, the floors uncovered hardwood.

Immediately to the left of the living-room as you entered from the hall was the radio-phonograph-television in bright tan, an Admiral, with a small but adequate television screen, and storage space for record albums and pianola rolls.

Now, on the final Sunday evening of the cold month of January, the Gallops gathered together around their television set, for Mrs. Gallop had promised that they could look at the television after dinner for a half hour. This promise was not made to the children, it was made to Mr. Gallop, for it was he who had longed all afternoon to stop work and make himself comfortable on the sofa and see what was going on in the television world.

Elizabeth Gallop, fooling around all day in the kitchen and all over the house, had informed Mr. Gallop that he could not waste his time at the television until after supper, and then for only a half hour, and *with* the children.

"You just stay right at your work," she told her husband immediately after Sunday breakfast at half past ten in the morning.

"But today's Sunday," Ralph Gallop said, "and besides, I haven't got a thing to do."

Ralph Gallop had a desk he had picked up at Bloomingdale's during a sale for $39.50, a swivel Bank of England chair he had found in a second-hand store on Third

Avenue, for which he had paid $15, and a tall chest with an open front upon whose shelves he had placed books he had found irresistible on the bargain counters of book-shops. These objects occupied a small area at the end of their bedroom, and they constituted his office or studio. Every morning Elizabeth Gallop quickly made up the two couches that were also their beds, removed the soot from the window sill just beyond Ralph's desk, swept the floor, and told her husband to step into his office and go to work.

Ralph Gallop was a playwright among other things, very much among them, too. That is to say, he wrote plays because ten years ago, long before he had met Elizabeth, he had written a play that had been produced on Broadway. The play had been given one performance, and Ralph had never quite forgotten that he had had a play on Broadway. He had never forgotten that the first-night audience had been composed of the same people who go to the openings of plays by Eugene O'Neill and George Bernard Shaw. He had never forgotten that all of the critics had seen the first two and a half acts of the play, and that George Jean Nathan himself had stayed to the very end. And he had never forgotten the play itself. It was about some people who spent thirty hours in the depot of a small town in Montana because the train they had wanted to take was wrecked, there was a snow-storm outside, and there was nowhere else for the people to go.

The play was called *A Good Way to Go*.

One smart-aleck critic reviewed the entire play with one sentence. He wrote, "*A Good Way to Go* is gone, thank God."

This review achieved a small amount of fame as the shortest review of a play ever written, and Ralph Gallop now and then permitted himself to enjoy the review's fame

L   161

by pointing out that *he* was the playwright who had written the play.

Ralph Gallop and Elizabeth Archer met at a beer party in Greenwich Village given by a painter named Galetzky who had seen Ralph's play and had maintained that it was a great play. This man lived in one room on the second floor of a rickety building on Bleecker Street into which through some miracle more than thirty men and women had fitted themselves and were able to drink beer, smoke cigarettes, talk about art and culture, sing, dance, fall in love, or out.

Ralph Gallop fell in, but not exactly at first sight. As a matter of fact, Ralph had gone to the party with a woman who wrote poetry in words she herself made up that were not in the English or any other language. She said her poems were *pure* poems. She wrote them under one name only, Stella, in order to be different from the poets who wrote poems under two or three names, such as Edwin Arlington Robinson, Robert Frost, Stephen Vincent Benét and Pauline Novak. This last writer of poems was someone Stella knew very well and disliked very much, and that was how it happened that her name had come to be connected with the names of the other poets. Stella recited five of her poems to Ralph Gallop and then she began to recite one more, but by that time Ralph was thinking of a good way to get away from her forever and forget that she had ever lived.

In those days Ralph had enjoyed being careless about who he took walks with or who he had a cup of coffee and a doughnut in the Automat with or who he went to a museum or a movie with, and that was how it happened that he had taken Stella to the beer party at Galetzky's.

He hadn't known that she liked to recite her poems.

Ralph Gallop managed to get away from Stella on the

pretext that he would bring her another can of beer, but he kept going until he got to Elizabeth Archer, at that time a total stranger.

"You don't happen to write poems, do you?" Ralph said to Elizabeth, not even stopping to notice her.

"No, I don't," Elizabeth said.

"Good," Ralph said. "Suppose we get out of here and go for a walk?"

Elizabeth Archer looked Ralph Gallop straight in the eye and then moved away. She just didn't like him. This made Ralph mad, in a way, for he wanted to know who she was to act that way with *him*, a man who had had a play on Broadway only three years ago. He watched her for half an hour or so, and at the same time kept his eye on Stella, but fortunately she was busy reciting her poems to a man with a black beard who wore a dirty white corduroy coat. At last Ralph came face to face with Elizabeth again, little suspecting at the time that this girl who did not write poems was soon to be Mrs. Ralph Gallop and that they were going to have a son right away, and two years later a daughter.

"Don't you know who I am?" Ralph said.

"No, I don't," Elizabeth said. "Who are you?"

"Ralph Gallop," Ralph said happily.

"Who's he?"

"Well, I happen to be the only man at this party who's had a play on Broadway, that's all."

"Oh," Elizabeth Archer said, for she hadn't taken him for a man who had written a play at all and she was just as impressed as Ralph Gallop had expected her to be.

He began to fall in love with her at that instant, and since he hadn't had a good look at her close up yet, he felt that he had better have one right away and get it over with. He hoped she would live up to the nice, respectful

163

manner in which she had said "Oh" and changed her attitude from one of scorn to one of admiration. He had his close-up look at her and made the following remarks to himself in a loud clear voice: "About twenty. Healthy. Intelligent. Brunette. One hundred and fifteen pounds. Five feet five. Ambition, marriage. Not in love. Interested in Ralph Gallop. About to fall in love."

Again Elizabeth Archer moved away from Ralph Gallop. He drank another glass of beer and then left the party. He stood in the street, behind a parked car, and watched the people at the party come out of the rickety building and disappear. At last Elizabeth Archer stepped into the street, but with her was Stella and the bearded man in the corduroy coat. He watched the three of them walk up the street, and then followed them. Stella and the bearded man went off together at the corner, and Elizabeth Archer stood at the bus stop. There were half a dozen others waiting for a bus, so Ralph joined them and when the bus came he got aboard and took a seat across the aisle from Elizabeth who immediately remembered him but did not smile or speak.

Elizabeth Archer got off the bus at Times Square, so Ralph Gallop got off, too. He had expected her to hurry along and disappear among the people of Times Square, but he found her waiting for him.

"In case we never meet again," Ralph Gallop said, "I want you to know I love you the way no man has ever loved any woman."

"Why?" Elizabeth Archer said.

"Oh, I don't know," Ralph said. "I haven't been myself lately."

Ralph didn't laugh, but Elizabeth knew he was kidding. She also knew he meant what he was saying, and even though she wasn't in love with him—after all, he was a

rather goofy-looking fellow until you got used to him—
she was beginning to enjoy the surprises in him.

"Have you been sick?" she said.

"No, not at all," he said. "I've been bored with my
health, that's all. Feel my shoulders. Go ahead, don't be
afraid. I'm as strong as a bull, but sick and tired of it.
Feel my shoulders."

Elizabeth Archer reached out and gently touched
the muscles of his right arm. They were as soft as
rubber.

"See?" Ralph said. "And I haven't struck a man in
anger in my life. I nearly struck a woman tonight who
writes poetry, but I decided against it. No, I haven't been
sick, but I can tell you I'm sick *now*. I've been sick for
two hours. Notice how pale I am? It's because I love you,
and if I knew your name, I'd say it."

"Elizabeth."

"Yes," Ralph said quickly. "I knew it wasn't Constance."

"Constance?"

"Oh yes," Ralph said. "The minute I saw you I knew
your name wasn't Constance, Elizabeth. Now, I've said
your name, just as I said I would, and to tell you the
truth, I wish we could step into Rudley's or Riker's or
Nedick's for a cup of coffee."

"Who's Constance?" Elizabeth said.

"How should I know who she is?" Ralph said. "I never
met anybody named Constance in my life."

He paused a moment and then his whole face, his whole
body, grew sorrowful and lonely and he said very softly,
"Elizabeth."

He looked at her out of sad eyes that still somehow had
a great deal of mischief lurking in them and he said, "The
minute I saw you I knew your first name wasn't Constance
and I knew your last name wasn't Petrazzola."

"Why should my last name be Petrazzola?" Elizabeth said.

"It *shouldn't*," Ralph said. "And it isn't."

"Who *is* Constance Petrazzola?" Elizabeth said.

"Well, *Petrazzola* is a grocer I used to know," Ralph said, "but *Constance* Petrazzola is a total stranger to me."

"I suppose you want to know my last name, then?" Elizabeth said.

"Not at all," Ralph said. "Not at all. I don't go around asking young women I hope are going to become married to me to tell me their last names. I don't believe in that sort of thing. Petrazzola's first name was Pietro, which makes a rather rollicking group of sounds : *Pietro Petrazzola*. Just think of it. A man with a name like that selling salami and cheese. Why, he ought to be singing in grand opera, just as *you* ought to be in a house with me, cooking my supper and washing my clothes and having our children.

"Having our children," he said again, this time very softly. "Will you take my arm at all?"

"At all?" Elizabeth said.

"I mean," Ralph said, holding his arm out to her, "will you take it, so that we can walk together to Rudley's or Riker's or Nedick's for a cup of coffee and a doughnut?"

Elizabeth Archer took Ralph Gallop's arm at Times Square and they walked past Rudley's, past Riker's, past Nedick's and all the other little coffee shops on Broadway and came at last to Columbus Circle, and there Ralph Gallop held Elizabeth Archer in his arms and said, "Now, what was it we had in mind, Elizabeth? I seem to feel we've forgotten something."

"Coffee at——" Elizabeth began to say, but Ralph interrupted her. The interruption began slowly and lightly, as if it weren't sure it meant to be an interruption at all. Elizabeth expected it to be a very short interruption at best, but it turned out to be a very long one. At last the interruption ended.

"Rudnick's," Elizabeth said.

"You mean Nedley's, don't you?" Ralph said.

Elizabeth Archer was beginning to be overwhelmed by something or other, for immediately after the interruption she was surprised to discover that he was no longer goofy-looking. She didn't like being overwhelmed and she didn't like his not being even a *little* goofy-looking any more and she didn't believe a man like him could ever be clearly understood—he'd made a mess of the simple names of the places where they had meant to have some coffee. She couldn't believe a man who could never be clearly understood could possibly be a husband and a father, and yet she was beginning to be overwhelmed by a feeling that it was she herself who was making it impossible for him to be clearly understood. It was she herself who was making him carry on the way he had been carrying on, and therefore she was an important part of that way, an important part of him, and how could she ever think of marrying anybody else? How could she ever think of marrying somebody who wasn't instantaneously transformed by her as *he* had been transformed? And yet what could she possibly look forward to with him, excepting excitement and trouble and fun and children and hard work being his wife and their mother the rest of her life? The whole business was so overwhelming that tears appeared in her eyes even as laughter twinkled in them, and of course he noticed both the tears and the laughter immediately.

"No man," he said, "has the right to make a girl whose last *name* he doesn't even know so sad and glad. Why, a thing like that can make a man forget his real fame. A man can get so conceited about a thing like that that he doesn't even want to remember that he wrote *A Good*

Way to Go which had one performance on Broadway and was unanimously voted the worst play of the year. What *is* your last name, Elizabeth?"

"Archer."

"What?" Ralph Gallop almost shouted. "Are you the grand-daughter of the drama critic, William Archer?"

"My grandfather's name was John," Elizabeth said.

"Thank God for that," Ralph said. "I could never have a cup of coffee with a grand-daughter of a drama critic."

Suddenly he noticed that she was still in his arms.

"How does it happen, Elizabeth Archer," he said, "that you are in my arms in Columbus Circle instead of far away somewhere, someone I never dreamed lived, someone I might never *see*, even? How did this happen? Who am I to be worthy of such a miracle? Why, I can already see our children gathered around us on a Sunday evening, listening to the beautiful lies we have agreed to tell them about ourselves and the rest of the people in the world. And all because you're in my arms in Columbus Circle instead of far away somewhere. Now, you and I know we weren't made for each other any more than any other two people in the world were made for each other, but doesn't it seem for a moment as if we were? Doesn't it, though? Who are you, Elizabeth Archer, to make me ask myself all sorts of unanswerable questions? Who are you to do that?"

"I am——" Elizabeth began to say, but again Ralph Gallop interrupted her. This interruption began precisely as the first one had, and it continued precisely as that one had, but then it continued some more, and then some more, and then at last it stopped.

"Nobody," Elizabeth said.

"My God," Ralph Gallop said, "that's who I am, too. You wouldn't think that a man-nobody and woman-nobody could seem to amount to so much in Columbus Circle, would you?"

Elizabeth Archer stepped away from Ralph Gallop.

"What's the matter?" he said.

"People are watching," Elizabeth said.

"Oh," Ralph said. "People. Oh yes."

Ralph glanced at the people, which turned out to be an old lady in black and white rags, including lace, who was selling red roses.

"Buy a red rose for your wife?" the old lady said. "Buy a pretty red rose for your pretty wife?"

"Yes," Ralph said. "Yes, a pretty red rose for my pretty wife. How much?"

"Twenty-five cents," the old lady said.

"I can't afford twenty-five cents," Ralph Gallop said.

Elizabeth Archer was stunned and confused now, for she couldn't believe he had said such a thing. Surely he didn't mean to bargain with a poor old lady. Elizabeth was almost relieved that he was swiftly turning out to be like everybody else—stingy and a little pathetic somewhere in his nature—because if he *was* these things, then good, for she need not be overwhelmed and she could go quietly back to her furnished room and her job as stenographer for a lawyer and forget all about the long life of hardship and fun and excitement and children and trouble and all the rest of it with him. Just let him be somewhere in his nature pretty much the same as the others and she would be free again.

She watched Ralph Gallop dig into his pocket and she heard him say to the old lady—but the old lady was smiling now, she was delighted, something was going on between the two of them that she didn't understand— "Here in this hand is all the money I have."

He opened his hand onto the old lady's. The old lady glanced at her hand, closed it quickly, smiled at Elizabeth, nodded as if to say something especially important, and then walked away.

"A pretty rose for my pretty wife," Ralph Gallop said.

Elizabeth took the rose and looked at it.

"Why did you tell her you couldn't afford to pay twenty-five cents for a rose?" Elizabeth said.

Ralph Gallop laughed.

"Oh," he said, "if you think for a moment that I'm any different from anybody else in the world when it comes to money, I'm afraid you're mistaken. I'm not. I'm not different from anybody else in the world when it comes to anything at all. I said I couldn't afford it because I can't. If this is the end of our life together, there it is. I love money. Is it the end?"

"I don't know," Elizabeth said. "Something happened between you and the old lady. What was it?"

"Something happened between you and me," Ralph said. "What was *that*?"

Now, he was still another person, and even though who he was this time was not any clearer than who he had been at the party, on the bus, in Times Square, walking up Broadway, and standing in Columbus Circle, she wanted to try to get better acquainted with this person, too.

"Well," he said. "I can't offer to take you to Rudley's or Riker's or Nedick's any more, but I *can* offer to walk with you to your door."

"I don't want to go home," Elizabeth said. "It's just a room and it's Saturday night and I haven't got anything to do. Why can't you tell me what happened between you and the old lady?"

"Perhaps I can tell you," he said. "I *flirted* with her."

"You can't be serious."

"I *am* serious, and I *did* flirt with her."

"But why?" Elizabeth said.

"Can't you guess?"

"Do you mean she flirted with you?"

"Listen," Ralph Gallop said suddenly. "I love people when I see them. I can't help it."

"Is that the way you love me?" Elizabeth said. "If you *do* love me?"

"Yes, it is."

"You mean you love me because you see me?"

"Yes, I do," Ralph said. "Love isn't blind, the way they say. Love is the most open-eyed thing there is.

"The old lady wasn't always an old lady," he went on. "She was young and pretty once, and I flirted with her because I saw her young and pretty again."

"How do you see *me*?" Elizabeth Archer said.

"I see you exactly the way you are now," Ralph said. "That's why I believed a moment ago that it was a miracle that you were in my arms and that in all probability you would go along with me the rest of my life and be the mother of our kids."

"Don't you believe that *now*?" Elizabeth said.

"I have *your* doubts," Ralph said.

"Oh," Elizabeth said.

She thought about this remark a moment, and then she handed him the rose and said, "Well, I'd like you to pin the rose on me, anyhow."

She was far away now, and the miracle was no longer a miracle. It was an ordinary accident, like two or three million others like it every day, and there they were in Columbus Circle, a man of thirty-one and a woman of twenty-one. There he was holding a rose he had bought for his wife, and there was his wife, no longer his wife at all, far away, and a stranger.

171

"I haven't got a pin," he said.

"I didn't *expect* you to have one," Elizabeth said.

She opened her handbag, fished around in it a moment, and brought out a pin which she handed to him. Ralph Gallop pinned the rose on the lapel of Elizabeth Archer's grey flannel suit, and then Elizabeth Archer stood on her toes and kissed him on the cheek the way wives sometimes do when they want to appreciate or patronize their husbands.

"What's that for?" Ralph said.

"I wish I knew," Elizabeth said.

Her handbag was still open. She fished around in it again, brought out three one-dollar bills, and put them in his hand.

"I'd like you to take me to Rudley's or Riker's or Nedick's for some coffee," she said.

They were together until two o'clock that morning, moving from one Rudley's or Riker's or Nedick's to another, talking and falling in and out of love again and again as Ralph became different people and Elizabeth, going along with him, became different people, too.

He didn't interrupt her in speech again that night, and they had a fight at her door about nothing, but they went walking up Fifth Avenue the following afternoon and stepped into St. Patrick's because it was the handsomest church around; and even though he had been baptised in the Presbyterian Church and she had been christened in the Methodist Church, they enjoyed being in St. Patrick's together, and they became a little more acquainted with one another there, praying together, or just breathing.

They tried very hard almost every day to get completely acquainted with one another, but Ralph Gallop was never the same from one day to another, or for that matter from one hour to another, and neither was Elizabeth Archer, and so after six months of trying, they decided they'd need a lifetime in which to get acquainted, so they got married, and a month later Ralph got drafted into the Army, and a year later Philip was born and Ralph was sent overseas, and when he got back there was a great deal more of him for Elizabeth to get acquainted with, and a great deal more of her for him, and pretty soon Molly was born, making everything more complicated than ever.

Now, three years after the birth of Molly they were gathered together around the television and Ralph Gallop was trying one channel after another, trying to find something appealing to him which he was sure would also appeal to Philip and Molly and Elizabeth. At last he found some acrobats jumping around and watched them, and then he watched a clown, and then jugglers, a man and a woman, and then the half-hour was up, and Mrs. Gallop turned off the television and took the children into their room and put them to bed.

"Come and say good night to Philip and Molly," she said, so Mr. Gallop went into the dark room and hugged first the little girl and then the boy, and then he stepped out of the room, and Mrs. Gallop closed the door.

They went into the living-room together and Mrs. Gallop said, "What did you write this week?"

"Well," Ralph Gallop said, "I wrote part of a new play, but it's very bad."

"You'd better write a good play," Mrs. Gallop said, "if we're ever going to get out of debt."

"Yes, I know," Ralph Gallop said.

Mrs. Gallop made some coffee and they drank three cups each and ate some doughnuts and remembered again some of the excitement and fun and trouble they had already had together, and guessed about some of it that they would be likely to have in the future.

173

"Know what I think I'll do?" Mr. Gallop said just before they went to bed at midnight. "I think I'll get up tomorrow morning and go out and get myself a job, the way I did last November for a week."

"You'll get up and sit down at your desk and go to work," Mrs. Gallop said, "that's what you'll get up and do."

"O.K., if you say so," Mr. Gallop said, "but you know I can't write."

"Oh, you can write all right," Mrs. Gallop said.

"I always get bored," Mr. Gallop said.

"Well, cut it out," Mrs. Gallop said. "Don't get bored any more."

"O.K. but I wish I wasn't a playwright," Mr. Gallop said.

"You're *not* a playwright," Mrs. Gallop said. "How can you pretend to be a playwright when all you've had is one performance of one play on Broadway?"

"Oh, I can pretend all right," Mr. Gallop said.

Finally, after talking an hour or so in the dark room which was also Mr. Gallop's office, they fell asleep and Mrs. Gallop dreamed that Mr. Gallop wrote a very good play and it was produced and was a success and Mr. Gallop was as famous to everybody in New York as he was to her, almost, and they paid all their debts and had a lot of money left over, and then sat down one night and ate half a pound of caviare.

Mr. Gallop dreamed that they had a whole bucketful of caviare. He went straight to the caviare with Mrs. Gallop and the kids and they ate all they liked. Mr Gallop left out all the details about writing a good play first.

The Gallop home contained a big, fat, long cabinet that was very handsome. This item stood along the wall of the dining-room, and in it Mrs. Gallop kept the family silver, the tablecloths and napkins, the bottles of liquor bought at Sherry's for cash, and other things of that order.

On top of the cabinet was Mr. Gallop's sixth marriage anniversary gift to his family, as he put it. This was a solid silver tray, punch-bowl with ladle, and twelve cups, from Cartier's.

Mr. and Mrs. Gallop had been walking down Fifth Avenue one evening in October when they saw the silver set in the window of Cartier's and Mr. Gallop said, "That set probably costs three thousand dollars."

"Yes," Mrs. Gallop said. "It's the most beautiful set of its kind I've ever seen."

The following day Mr. Gallop stepped into Cartier's and asked to see the set, and a very dignified man who was nice enough not to take Mr. Gallop's interest lightly showed it to him. This man might have taken Mr. Gallop's interest lightly because Mr. Gallop was poorly dressed that day, hadn't shaved, and was ordinarily treated patronizingly by department store clerks because he so often looked broke, but the man in Cartier's was not like the salespeople at Gimbel's and Macy's and Woolworths. He acted as if Mr. Gallop had a perfect right to examine the punch-bowl set, and he treated Mr. Gallop as if Mr. Gallop had a great deal of money in spite of the fact that his black-and-white tweed coat was old and worn and tattered all over. The man brought out the whole set and Mr. Gallop examined it carefully, even lifting one of the cups and pretending to drink something out of it.

"How much is it?" Mr. Gallop said.

The man did some figuring on a scratch pad.

"One thousand and fifty dollars, including Federal and City tax," he said at last.

"Is that all?" Mr. Gallop said. "Yesterday afternoon my wife and I saw it in the window and I said the set probably costs three thousand dollars. Are you sure that's all it is, one thousand and fifty?"

"Yes, sir," the man said.

"I'll take it," Ralph Gallop said.

He went with the man into an office and sat down and filled out a form and asked the man to have the set delivered the following Monday.

When the set arrived the following Monday, Mrs. Gallop unpacked everything and set it on the cabinet in the dining-room. She looked at it a long time and then she said, "Now, what in the world ever made you do a thing like this?"

"It's my sixth marriage anniversary gift to you and the children," Mr. Gallop said. "Do you like it?"

"*Like* it?" Mrs. Gallop said. "It's the most beautiful silver I've ever seen, but you know we can't afford anything so expensive, and besides our sixth marriage anniversary isn't until March next year."

"I thought we'd enjoy it a few extra months before our sixth anniversary," Ralph said.

"Well," Elizabeth said, "I suppose we can at least *look* at it a few days, and then let them come and take it back."

"Nobody's going to come and take it back," Mr. Gallop said.

"Oh, you know you're talking nonsense," Mrs. Gallop said. "We're head over heels in debt already and we can barely scrape up enough every month to pay the rent and the grocery bill. You know very well we can't afford it."

"I'll let you in on a little secret," Mr. Gallop said.

"What is it?"

"It's not three thousand dollars," Mr. Gallop said. "It's one thousand and fifty dollars complete, including all the different kinds of taxes. That's a saving of almost two thousand dollars right there."

"It's no saving at all," Mrs. Gallop said. "How did you ever manage to get them to deliver it without paying them for it?"

"Well," Mr. Gallop said, "they're not a cash and carry house. They're a credit and deliver house, and I agreed to accept their offer of credit and they agreed to deliver it."

"But of course you've got to pay them *something* right away," Mrs. Gallop said. "How much is it?"

"The first payment is one hundred and fifty dollars," Mr. Gallop said.

"Have we got that much to spare?" Mrs. Gallop said.

"Will you please stop worrying about it?" Mr. Gallop said. "A Company like that is never in a hurry. I'll take care of it."

"Well, what about the down payment?" Mrs. Gallop said.

"I'm going to take care of it, I said."

"When?"

"Who knows?" Ralph Gallop said. "In my profession, anything can happen. One day a man's poor, the next he's rich."

"You're acting as if this was one of your rich days," Mrs. Gallop said.

"Not at all," Mr. Gallop said. "You wouldn't want me to pass up a bargain like this, would you? It makes the whole house look different. More as if the people here planned to leave fine things to their heirs. In my profession, a man *ought* to leave fine things to his heirs."

"In your profession," Mrs. Gallop said, "a man ought to have a little common sense."

"No," Mr. Gallop said, "my profession calls for a man

with *uncommon* sense. A man with common sense doesn't write plays for a living, he works in a bank."

"But *you* don't write plays for a living, either," Mrs. Gallop said. "You just write them. When are you going to write one that men with common sense like producers and directors are going to feel will make them a lot of money instead of the kind you keep writing?"

"You never know," Mr. Gallop said. "You never know."

"Well," Mrs. Gallop said, "let's look at all the fine silver on the cabinet in the dining-room and let's have the children look at it a couple of times, and then they can come and take it back."

"I didn't buy it for them to take back," Mr. Gallop said. "I bought it for us to have and enjoy and leave to our heirs."

"Our heirs," Mrs. Gallop said. "We've already left them just about all we're *ever* going to leave them. Philip's exactly like you, with a little of me thrown in, and Molly's exactly like me, with a little of you thrown in. They've already got everything we're ever going to leave them. I'm sorry we're not going to be able to keep the set because I do like it so much."

"Well, what are you waiting for?" Ralph Gallop said. "Fill the bowl with something and let's drink out of it."

"Lemonade?" Mrs. Gallop said.

"I don't like lemonade," Mr. Gallop said. "Fill it with cold water out of the kitchen tap, but be sure the water runs until it's nice and cold. Don't put any ice in it. Just a silver punch bowl full of plain cold water. We'll drink out of it, enjoy it, and when Molly wakes up after her nap she can have a drink out of it, and when Philip gets home from school, he can have one, too."

Mr. and Mrs. Gallop drank cold water out of the silver punch bowl, and later that day so did the children. They loved cold water out of a silver bowl in a silver cup, and Mr. Gallop explained to them that when he and Mrs. Gallop died or got divorced the children could have the set between them, but if there happened to be other brothers or sisters they would have to divide it among them.

"When are you going to die, Papa?" Philip Gallop said.

"Not for a long time yet," Mr. Gallop said.

"When are you going to get divorced, then?"

"Not until I die, most likely," Mr. Gallop said.

"Oh, is divorce the same as dying?" Philip said.

"Yes, it is," Mr. Gallop said. "Notice how cool the silver is when you lift the cup to your lips?"

"Oh yes," Philip said.

"Do *you*, Molly?" Mr. Gallop said.

"Oh yes," Molly said.

The family drank a lot of cold water out of the silver bowl that day, and the following day they tried it with milk, and it wasn't half bad with milk, either, although Philip and Molly preferred water.

A week later they tried the bowl with root beer, and that was the best of all as far as the kids were concerned, especially when Mr. Gallop dumped a pint of vanilla ice cream into the root beer.

Every Saturday night Mr. and Mrs. Gallop emptied a half dozen cans of beer into the bowl and ladled it out into the silver cups and drank beer, sitting at the dining-room table and talking. The pianola would generally be going when they drank beer and every now and then they'd get up and waltz out of the dining-room into the hall and then into the living-room and back again for more beer. The pianola could keep going as long as they wanted it to because it had an automatic lever. Mr. Gallop liked to hear the pianola Saturday nights. His favourite roll was *The Song of Songs*. Mrs. Gallop liked that roll, too, but she liked *Hand Me Down My Walking Cane* and a lot of other rolls, too.

"Anything at all," Mr. Gallop liked to say, "just so it's two players instead of one."

When two players made a pianola roll the music was always lively and rich, so that you could never get tired of it while you were drinking beer.

One night early in November the Gallops invited all of their friends to a chili and beer party, and all of them came, excepting Mrs. Gallop's big sister Madge who had been ill with the flu. Two dozen cans of beer were emptied into the silver bowl and the five couples who had come to the party drank out of it and listened to the pianola and danced.

One bill had been rendered, as they say, by Cartier's at that time, but Mr. Gallop had filed it with the rest of the bills on hand, and the company hadn't brought the matter up again. After the party Mrs. Gallop was upset to find the bottom of the bowl scratched by the ladle because she didn't think Cartier's would like that, but Mr. Gallop told her silver, the same as everything else, was meant to be used and enjoyed, and the scratches made the bowl even more handsome.

"But what will Cartier's think when they come to take it back?" Mrs. Gallop said.

"They're not going to take it back," Mr. Gallop said. "I'm going to pay for it. Everybody admires it."

Now, all this sort of thing, this buying of silver they couldn't afford, and having furniture made to order, and all the rest of it, worried Mrs. Gallop, and she always said that when Cartier's came to take back the set she expected Ralph Gallop to be on hand, as she was going to hide from shame. Mr. Gallop told Mrs. Gallop to stop worrying because it was beginning to do things to her that shouldn't happen to his wife.

"If you want me to stop worrying," Mrs. Gallop said, "send them at least the first payment."

"I only got the bill two weeks ago," Mr. Gallop said.

"We've had the set in the house a month, though," Mrs. Gallop said. "Please send them the first payment. I'll die of shame if they come to take it back."

"All right," Mr. Gallop said. "I'll send them a cheque right now."

He went to his desk and brought out his cheque-book. He studied it a moment, then returned to the living-room.

"We've only got eighty-seven dollars and forty-two cents in the bank," he said. "They'll have to wait."

"Everybody's waiting," Mrs. Gallop said. "Sometimes it scares me."

"Well," Mr. Gallop said, "we've always got the War Bonds. Thank God you bought them. We can turn them in if it will make you feel any better."

"They'll be worth three thousand dollars in only five more years," Mrs. Gallop said, "but if we turn them in now all we can get is two thousand two hundred and fifty."

"Boy!" Mr. Gallop said. "That much? I'll take them to the bank right now and turn them in. Five years from now I won't *need* three thousand dollars."

"The bonds were *supposed* to be for the kids," Mrs. Gallop said.

"We've got three bonds and only two kids," Mr. Gallop said.

"This whole house was furnished on the principle that we would have a good many more," Mrs. Gallop said. "Six sofa-beds, four people. There's room right now for two more, and we could bring in two more sofa-beds any time we felt like it."

"That suits me," Mr. Gallop said. "I'm not the one who has them."

" You're the one who's got to provide for them," Mrs. Gallop said, "so what are we going to do?"

Mrs. Gallop meant what were they going to do about the money, but Mr. Gallop misunderstood her.

"Oh," Mr. Gallop said. "I'm sorry. Do you think for a minute I've forgotten you?"

He held Mrs. Gallop in his arms as if they had just met and had walked from Times Square to Columbus Circle, but Mrs. Gallop shoved him away and said, "I mean, what are we going to do about paying for all the things we have that we can't afford?"

"Well, I'll tell you what," Mr. Gallop said. "I think the first thing we ought to do is stop worrying. We're good for it. We're good for every penny of it, and Cartier's and all the rest of them know it or else they'd be on the telephone two or three times a day."

At that moment the telephone buzzer which Mr. Gallop had had the telephone company attach to the telephone instead of a bell so that the house wouldn't suddenly be filled with a lot of unnecessary noise every time somebody tried to phone them, scaring the kids and scaring Mr. Gallop himself who hated telephones, buzzed, and Mr. Gallop felt a little sick in his stomach. He waited for Mrs. Gallop to answer the phone, but she didn't budge.

"You get it, will you, honey?" he said casually.

The buzzer buzzed again.

"*Me?*" Mrs. Gallop said. "What would I say to them? I'm scared to death."

The buzzer buzzed twice more.

"Ah, to hell with it," Mr. Gallop said. "Let it ring."

The Poet at Home

He knew it wasn't a ring, it was a buzz, but that's what he said anyway.

"No," Mrs. Gallop said. "Please answer it. We can't pretend we don't owe everybody. Be a man. Answer it."

The buzzer buzzed twice again.

"You know I hate telephones," Mr. Gallop said.

"Oh, answer it," Mrs. Gallop said, so Mr. Gallop answered it.

He chatted a moment in a voice that had been deep and frightened at first but had gradually grown lively and joyous, even though all he said was things like, "Yes, of course. Sure. Be delighted."

He hung up and walked the length of the living-room with a great deal of pleasure.

"Charley Athey," he said. "Just about the nicest guy in the world. I was sure it was Cartier's, but so what? Suppose it had been? I would have told them the truth, that's all. Love the set, want it very much, going to pay for it, that's all."

"What did Charley Athey want?" Mrs. Gallop said.

"Asked us over Thursday night for buffet supper," Mr. Gallop said.

"I thought you had no use for him," Mrs. Gallop said.

"Not at all," Mr. Gallop said. "Charley's just about the nicest guy in the world."

Mr. Gallop sat on the sofa beside his wife.

"Tired?" Mrs. Gallop said.

"Exhausted," Mr. Gallop said. "I was sure it was Cartier's. I'm not the kind of man who doesn't pay his bills, you know."

"What kind are you?"

"The kind who does."

"Oh."

Mrs. Gallop put her arms around her husband and held him a moment. Suddenly, Mr. Gallop got to his feet.

"All right," he said. "You don't have to feel sorry for me. I've been working a little hard lately and I *do* get tired this way, but you don't have to treat me the way you treat Philip when somebody at school has beaten him in a fight. I'm as strong as a bull. Resilient, too. Bounce right back. Few men came through the War as well as I did, you know."

"You sat at a desk all through the War," Mrs. Gallop said.

"Is that easy?" Mr. Gallop said. "Besides, I could have told you a lot of lies, couldn't I? I didn't because I *am* resilient. I told the truth. I even told you how scared I was I might get killed in a taxi accident in London or Paris during the War. It takes courage to tell the truth, too, you know. I even told you how I fell over a seat at the Palladium in London the day of the Invasion and hurt my right leg." He stopped a moment, and then said, "I wish I knew what we could do about the money, though."

"How bad did you hurt your leg?" Mrs. Gallop said.

"Oh, it wasn't anything serious," Mr. Gallop said. He lifted his right trouser leg and pointed to his shin. "It was right here," he said. "No scars or anything, though."

"Well," Mrs. Gallop said, "nobody can say you didn't do your part."

"You can say that again," Mr. Gallop said.

"Nobody can say you didn't bleed for America, can they?" Mrs. Gallop said.

"Oh, I didn't bleed," Mr. Gallop said. "It was just a bruise. I cut my hand in basic training, though, and bled a little then, but I can't honestly pretend that it was for America, though. It might have happened right here in our kitchen. I was doing K.P., opening some big cans of

184

tomatoes, and slashed the whole palm of my right hand on the sharp edge of the lid."

"I can just see you," Mrs. Gallop said, "standing there, looking at your bloody hand, and crying."

"That's all right," Mr. Gallop said. "You can laugh all you like. As a matter of fact I did *almost* cry, but not because I'd cut my hand. Some kind of cuts don't hurt, and that was one of them. It was just that I'd been thinking about a play I wanted to write and I'd gotten to a sad part in it when I cut my hand. I didn't cut my hand on a tomato can for America, though."

Molly Gallop came out of the bedroom into the living-room, still half-asleep, smiling and yawning at the same time.

Mr. Gallop picked her up and said, "Now, I suppose if I *hadn't* sat at a desk all during the War and *had* gotten killed, things would now be better in the world; but on the other hand it would be a world without this little girl, and that's not a world I like to think about."

Mrs. Gallop took the little girl out of his arms and went back to the bedroom to dress her. Mr. Gallop got his hat and coat off the iron coat-hanger in the hall and went for a walk down Sixth Avenue.

In the window of the delicatessen store around the corner on Sixth Avenue he saw the displays of jars of imported Russian caviare. He counted his money and found that he had twelve dollars and forty odd cents. The half pound jar of the fine grain Beluga was eleven dollars and fifty cents.

He couldn't afford it, that's all. Veteran or not, he couldn't afford to pay eleven dollars and fifty cents for half a pound of caviare.

Ralph Gallop went into the delicatessen and bought the half pound jar of caviare, a loaf of Russian rye, four hard-boiled eggs, and some dry onions.

After paying for these items, his cash on hand amounted to eleven cents. He had planned to walk down Sixth Avenue to the shop near 44th Street that sold books for nineteen cents, but he turned and went back home.

He was in the kitchen chopping onions when Philip Gallop got home from school.

"What you doing, Papa?" Philip said.

"Oh, I'm making a dream come true, the way I always do," Mr. Gallop said.

"What dream?" Philip said.

"Well, you don't remember when I was in the Army," Mr. Gallop said, "because you were an infant, but all the time I was in the Army I dreamed of getting the hell home to your mother and you, and I dreamed we'd enjoy ourselves all the time. I dreamed we'd eat the most wonderful things there are to eat, and of course the most wonderful of all is caviare. Well, you see, caviare costs a lot of money. Half a pound of it costs more than three or four sacks of flour cost, and flour is what you make bread out of. But bread isn't enough, *all the time*. Everybody is entitled to caviare once in a while, too. So while I was in the Army I dreamed that we'd have caviare any time we wanted it, but when I got out of the Army and we were together again and your sister came to live with us I didn't buy any caviare because it costs so much. I think you know we don't have very much money. Anyhow, this afternoon I paid a lot of money for half a pound of caviare."

"How much did you pay?" Philip said. "A million dollars?"

"Just about," Mr. Gallop said. "Now, caviare goes best on very thin slices of lightly buttered rye bread, with onions chopped fine, and sliced hard-boiled eggs. Well, I'm getting all this stuff fixed up, so we can have half a pound of caviare."

The Poet at Home

"Oh," Philip said. "What about the dream?"

"That's it," Ralph Gallop said. "Caviare. Go along now and let your mother make you comfortable, but don't mention the dream. I want to surprise her."

"O.K.," Philip said, going.

When Mrs. Gallop and the kids came into the dining-room, the table was all set. The family sat down and ate all the caviare. The children didn't like it at all, but Philip, who knew about the dream, forced himself to eat a little of it because he knew the dream was important and he wanted to be in on it. Molly ate peanut butter spread on rye bread.

That was the first time the Gallops had caviare.

"Some day," Mr. Gallop said to Mrs. Gallop when all the caviare was gone, "I'm going to buy a big bucketful of caviare."

Ralph Gallop was not a good cook, but he was an imaginative one. If it is true that a good many of his kitchen creations turned out the way his plays did, it is also true that he frequently achieved dishes that, although they were the first and last of their kind, deeply satisfied hunger.

Having no fierce enemies, the Gallops were never too excited to eat or never too preoccupied not to think about what they would have for supper.

Ralph Gallop liked to read about the last meal of a man condemned to die:

"The prisoner ordered ham and eggs with home-fried potatoes, coffee with thick cream, rye bread toast, and store cheese. He requested four eggs instead of two, ham sliced half an inch thick, and a whole pot of strong coffee. When the meal was served he said the home-fried potatoes should have been fried in butter and sent them back. He

did not get the potatoes the way he wanted them until he
had finished his meal, and just before he left his cell he
remarked to Father McGinnis, 'I certainly would like to
take them along with me, Father.' He walked to the end
firmly and with confidence, nodding and smiling to several
of the newspaper reporters he knew."

Whenever Ralph Gallop read such an account of a
man's last meal, he invariably got up and cooked the same
meal for himself.

Once, however, a man asked for haggis, and it took
Ralph Gallop three days to find out what the dish was and
how to make it. He sat down at midnight one night and
ate almost half of what he had taken so long to cook and
told Mrs. Gallop that it was very good.

"Have some," he said.

"What is it?" Mrs. Gallop said.

"Haggis, the national dish of Scotland," Mr. Gallop
said.

Mrs. Gallop tried a little of the dish and then said,
"What's this stuff?"

"Tripe," Mr. Gallop said.

"Tripe?" Mrs. Gallop said. "Isn't that one of the
words the critics used in describing *A Good Way to
Go*?"

"Yes," Mr. Gallop said, "that was Brooks Atkinson.
But as you see, even tripe, if properly prepared, is very
good."

"Well," Mrs. Gallop said, "I guess you didn't prepare
the tripe in your play effectively, then."

"How could I?" Mr. Gallop said. "I didn't even *know*
it was tripe. I was under the impression it was beef. If
you'll ever go to the trouble of reading the play sometime,
I think you'll find that Brooks Atkinson was mistaken. I
don't expect you to read my unproduced plays, but I

188

think you might take time out from your knitting to read my produced play."

"When did you ever see me knitting?" Mrs. Gallop said.

"Well, anyway," Mr. Gallop said, "you know what I mean. I never expected my own wife not to read my produced play."

"I taste the junk you cook once in a while," Mrs. Gallop said.

"I am not famous as a chef," Mr. Gallop said, "but as a playwright, and I certainly would appreciate your reading *A Good Way to Go* sometime."

"You're not famous at all," Mrs. Gallop said. "How many people know you're a playwright?"

"I know I am," Mr. Gallop said, filling his mouth with the inside or cereal part of haggis, "and that ought to be enough for my own wife, I should think. You've got to learn to read. I'm not asking you to read the writing of men you're not married to, I'm asking you to read the writing of your husband, the father of your children. Now, as soon as Philip learns to read, you can be sure he is going to read *A Good Way to Go*, and what's more, I think he's going to like it, too."

"Where is the play?" Mrs. Gallop said.

"In my desk of course," Mr. Gallop said. "In the top right hand drawer, in the folder marked *Achievements*."

"Oh," Mrs. Gallop said.

"Are you going to read it?" Mr. Gallop said.

"Well, not just this minute," Mrs. Gallop said.

"Then, why did you ask where it is?" Mr. Gallop said.

"I just like to know where the important things are in this house," Mrs. Gallop said. "Where is Philip's Indian hat, with the feathers?"

"It's in my closet," Mr. Gallop said.

"What's it doing there?" Mrs. Gallop said. "Philip turned the house upside down this afternoon looking for it."

"I borrowed it," Mr. Gallop said.

"Did you put it on?"

"Of course I put it on."

Mrs. Gallop tried a little more of the tripe, chewed it slowly, then created a smile that was so much a mixture of scorn and sweetness as to make Mona Lisa's smile seem the dubious achievement of an amateur.

"What's that smile for?" Mr. Gallop said.

"I think it's rude to laugh uproariously under some circumstances," Mrs. Gallop said.

"Such as, when?" Mr. Gallop said.

"Such as when your husband, thirty-seven years of age, steals his son's Indian hat and puts it on," Mrs. Gallop said.

"What's so funny about *that*?" Mr. Gallop said.

"Don't you think it's funny?"

"Not at all," Mr. Gallop said. "You just don't understand writing."

"Now, what's writing got to do with it?" Mrs. Gallop said.

"I just happened to want to try to understand how the President of the United States feels," Mr. Gallop said.

"And putting on your son's Indian hat helped you understand how the President feels?" Mrs. Gallop said.

"It certainly did," Mr. Gallop said.

"I should think you'd examine his *speeches* in order to understand a little more about him," Mrs. Gallop said.

"That's because you don't understand writing," Mr. Gallop said.

"Well, what's an Indian hat got to do with understanding the President of the United States?" Mrs. Gallop said.

"Every President of the United States that I can remember," Mr. Gallop said, "has put on an Indian hat in public, that's what it's got to do with it. I put on Philip's Indian hat this afternoon to see if I could imagine how the President feels."

"How *does* he feel?"

"Fine," Mr. Gallop said.

"Is that all?"

"Well, fine and dandy, then," Mr. Gallop said.

"Doesn't he feel a little silly when he puts on an Indian hat?" Mrs. Gallop said.

"Why should the President of the United States feel silly when he puts on an Indian hat?" Mr. Gallop said.

"Well, the feathers are so big and bright," Mrs. Gallop said.

"He feels fine," Mr. Gallop said, "and I wish you'd stop smiling that way."

Mrs. Gallop stopped smiling.

"I was only thinking of how you must have looked," she said. "How *like* the President, I mean."

"Yes," Mr. Gallop said, "I *did* look like Harry, but more, I think, like Atom."

"Adam?" Mrs. Gallop said. "Who's he?"

"Not Adam," Mr. Gallop said. "A-tom, like the bomb. He's the fellow who put the hat on Harry in Kansas City just before Harry didn't get defeated. His name used to be something else but he brought it up to date a couple of years ago. He looks a little like me, even without the hat and Indian suit. He calls himself Atom Power for All People Irregardless."

"I always thought they had a Chief somewhere or other in their names," Mrs. Gallop said.

"Atom doesn't believe in titles," Mr. Gallop said. "The American Indian is a good deal more evolved than most people know."

"Well, I certainly would like to see you in Philip's Indian hat," Mrs. Gallop said. "Atom Power for All People Irregardless," she added.

"Do you happen to remember the way he looks?" Mr. Gallop said. "We saw him in the newsreel on the television a couple of weeks before the election."

"The President?" Mrs. Gallop said. "Of course I remember the way he looks."

"Not the President," Mr. Gallop said. "Atom Power for All People Irregardless, the American Indian."

"No, I don't remember *him*," Mrs. Gallop said.

"Well, anyway," Mr. Gallop said, "he's about my build. Broad shoulders, long arms, thick black hair, dark intense face with piercing eyes, large Indian nose, and stern lips. About my height. Five feet nine or so."

"You're five feet eight, aren't you?" Mrs. Gallop said.

"Eight and a half, almost nine," Mr. Gallop said. "And I daresay Atom Power for all People Irregardless is undoubtedly a man with my kind of temperament, too."

"What temperament is that?" Mrs. Gallop said.

"Dynamic," Mr. Gallop said. "Rather atomic, rather powerful, and pretty much for all people irregardless."

"Oh," Mrs. Gallop said. "You're not actually part-Indian, are you?"

"No," Mr. Gallop said, "but all people are alike when you get right down to it, and I *do* have a profound respect for Indians."

"Yes, you do," Mrs. Gallop said, "and so does Philip. As you know, he's very good at whooping the way the Indians do."

"Oh yes," Mr. Gallop said. "I taught him. The American Indians are Asiatic racially, you know."

"Is that so?" Mrs. Gallop said.

"Oh yes," Mr. Gallop said. "The theory of anthropologists is that they got onto the North American continent by migrating from Siberia to Alaska across the frozen waters. There's a first-class example of walking on water, if you know what I mean. I feel a profound kinship with the peoples of Asia generally."

"Don't you have any love at all for Europeans?" Mrs. Gallop said.

"Not especially," Mr. Gallop said, "excepting of course the Basques who are still a mystery to the anthropologists. They still haven't discovered where the Basques came from or how their language was evolved."

"It's pretty much the same with you and your language, I suppose," Mrs. Gallop said.

"Well, as a matter of fact, it is," Mr. Gallop said. "I was thinking about my head only last night."

"Is that so?"

"Oh yes."

Mr. Gallop covered his forehead with his right hand and the back of his head with his left.

"You see," he said, "my head is actually not traceable back to the three basic head types of mankind."

"Oh, that's too bad," Mrs. Gallop said. "Come to think of it, it is an odd-shaped head."

"It's a *combination* of all three head types," Mr. Gallop said, "with a slight predominance of the Asiatic or Indian type."

"Not really," Mrs. Gallop said.

"Oh yes," Mr. Gallop said. "An authentic example of a combination of the three head types."

"I should think a man with a head like that,"

Mrs. Gallop said, "should be able to write better plays than Molière, who probably only had a one-type head."

"Molière?" Mr. Gallop said. "I didn't know you knew about him."

"I read *The Misanthrope* at high school, in French," Mrs. Gallop said.

"I never did read that play," Mr. Gallop said. "Is it any good at all?"

"It's about a man who hates the entire human race," Mrs. Gallop said.

"Oh," Mr. Gallop said.

"Even so," Mrs. Gallop went on, "it makes you feel good when you read it, but the point is a playwright with a three-type head like yours ought to be able to write better plays than playwrights with one-type heads."

"Yes, and in all probability, I do," Mr. Gallop said. "In the fourteenth year of my life the hair was shaved off my head and so, unlike a great many playwrights, I've actually *seen* my head."

"What's it look like without the hair?" Mrs. Gallop said.

"Well," Mr. Gallop said, "if it weren't for the face it would look something like a lopsided egg standing on the narrow end, with the top almost flat."

Mr. Gallop lifted a teacup and saucer off the table and rested them on top of his head.

"You could drink tea right off my head," Mr. Gallop said.

"I don't suppose you could do that with very many other playwrights," Mrs. Gallop said.

"Just try and drink tea off Eugene O'Neill's head," Mr. Gallop said.

He smiled proudly and brought the cup and saucer

down from the top of his head with the greatest confidence and ease and put them back on the table.

"Anyhow," Mrs. Gallop said, "I certainly would like to see you with Philip's Indian hat on your three-type head."

"All right," Mr. Gallop said, getting up. "Don't get up. I'll only be a minute. I believe you'll see a remarkable example of the influence of costume on identity. I mean, I believe you'll notice immediately that merely by putting on the Indian hat I actually become an Indian."

"Not really," Mrs. Gallop said.

"Actually," Mr. Gallop said, going. "You'll see."

He returned to the dining-room in a moment. His posture was stiff, the expression of his face was stern and dignified, and he walked as if he meant it. He stood in front of Mrs. Gallop a full minute in absolute silence, apparently thinking.

"It's true," Mrs. Gallop said. "You are actually an Indian. You are actually Atom Power for All People Irregardless."

"Ugh," Mr. Gallop said.

"Well," Mrs. Gallop said, getting up, "I'm going to do the dishes. I think you'd better sit down at your type-writer at the round table in the living-room and go to work because you've stalled long enough. After doing the dishes, I'm going to bed, but I expect you to put in at least two hours of hard work. Be quiet when you come to bed."

"Ugh," Mr. Gallop said.

He took Mrs. Gallop in his strong Indian arms and looked at her out of eyes of steel, then he rubbed his nose all over Mrs. Gallop's nose. She knew that that was the way Indian men kissed Indian women and she rather liked it, for her nose was the most neglected part of her body and was never exercised or stimulated by massage. Mr.

Gallop enjoyed it, too—or rather his nose enjoyed it—and he continued rubbing his nose against his wife's nose for a rather long time. At last he let her be, as an Indian man would—that is, with tender severity, so to say—and he walked Indian-fashion to his desk and carried his portable typewriter to the round table in the living-room and sat down to go to work.

Mrs. Gallop put away the haggis that had not been eaten because she knew he might ask for some of it after six or seven days and be outraged if she had thrown it out. She did the dishes and put them away. It was a few minutes after one in the morning when she turned off the lights in the kitchen and dining-room and went to bed. She saw her husband sitting at the round table in the living-room, wearing Philip's Indian hat, being Atom Power for All People Irregardless.

"Good night, Irregardless," she said, employing the diminutive.

"Ugh," Mr. Gallop said.

Mrs. Gallop went straight to bed and fell asleep, and then suddenly she awoke with a start, got out of bed and ran into the living-room to find out what the matter was, for she had been awakened by a terrible noise that had probably come from a human being. She saw Mr. Gallop standing over his typewriter, making a strange exultant noise with his vocal cords as he clapped his open hand over his mouth gently.

"What in the world is the matter?" Mrs. Gallop said.

"I just finished another play," Mr. Gallop said in plain ordinary English, even though he was still Irregardless, "and I believe it's good."

"Oh," Mrs. Gallop said with relief.

The door of the bedroom opened and Philip and Molly Gallop came out.

The Poet at Home

"Papa just finished another play," Mrs. Gallop said. "Now, both of you get right back to bed. Just because Papa lets out a war-whoop at three o'clock in the morning because he has finished another play doesn't mean you've got a right to get out of bed."

"There's my Indian hat," Philip Gallop said. "Give it back."

Mr. Gallop removed the hat and handed it to his son, who looked at it sleepily but soberly, and then at his father.

"Don't ever do that again," Philip said. "This is *my* Indian hat. I'm an Indian, not you."

Philip put the hat on carefully while Molly watched with envy, even though she yawned at the same time.

Mrs. Gallop took the children to the bathroom as long as they were up anyway, gave them each a drink of water, and then put them back to bed. When she returned to the living-room, Mr. Gallop was holding a rather substantial amount of manuscript.

"Yes," he said to his wife, "I believe this one's a good one."

"What's it about?" Mrs. Gallop said.

"Chickens," Mr. Gallop said.

"Oh," Mrs. Gallop moaned. "Now, why did you go to so much trouble to write a play about chickens?"

"Why shouldn't I write a play about chickens?" Mr. Gallop said. "They're just as interesting as people."

"Well, all right," Mrs. Gallop said. "You'd better get to bed, though."

"The chickens talk of course," Mr. Gallop said, "and except that they're all covered with feathers they're the same as people. Can't you just see the fine set on the stage? A real chicken roost and a real chicken run, and all the rest of it?"

197

"Yes, I can," Mrs. Gallop said, going barefooted back to bed.

When Mr. Gallop got into his own bed he said, "Most people think chickens are all alike, but that's not so. *Chicks* look and act alike, but every chicken is different."

"Shut up," Mrs. Gallop said sweetly.

One day Mr. and Mrs. Gallop were walking through Central Park when the topic of sex came up for a moment. Sex is a fine thing and too long neglected by polite or non-pornographic literature, which appears to have been under the impression for two or three centuries that unless sex figured in a novel in a hot and breathless manner the novel would not be regarded as a major work by a major writer ; or that unless it was treated in a sneaky manner the novel would seem trivial ; or that sex was a spasmodic thing, happening suddenly, generally during dizzy spells, and being something for all concerned to forget as quickly as possible.

It was half past three in the afternoon of a sharp cold day in January. Mrs. Gallop's sister Madge had paid them a visit and had offered to sit and wait for Molly to wake up from her nap and for Philip to come home from school while Mr. and Mrs. Gallop went for a walk in Central Park.

"If you feel like it," Mr. Gallop said, "you can read my play about the chickens. It's on top of the television set."

Madge Archer was almost fifteen years older than her sister Elizabeth, and she behaved as if she were fifteen years younger. She had a large well-proportioned body, a clear speaking voice, a hearty way of laughing, and a love of comfort that would have been sinful were it not that she was not true to this love, was constantly doing something or other or making plans to, scarcely ever slept more than four or five hours a night, and even on Sundays got up at seven in the morning to take a brisk walk.

She was almost always laughing. She laughed so much, she said, because she couldn't get over the fuss her three husbands had made over her.

"Why," she said, "you'd think I'd been the Queen of Sheba, the way they talked and acted whenever I was around. I made them all so nervous."

Madge's husbands had been an archaeologist of fifty who had taught at Johns Hopkins in Baltimore until he married Madge, whereupon he quit his job and went travelling to Mexico and South America with her; a bartender who weighed almost two hundred and fifty pounds and spoke English with a private accent, as if he had invented the language and everybody else used it incorrectly; and an opera singer who soon lost his voice.

That is to say, Madge Archer was an exciting woman.

The only man she'd ever met who treated her as if she were a person, too, in spite of her size and the way she laughed all the time, was Ralph Gallop.

She loved Ralph because he was her little sister's husband and she admired him because he seemed to have mislaid somewhere the answer to two times two.

Madge owned and operated *Madge's*, which was a beauty parlour.

It was Madge who, upon learning how the Gallops had come into possession of the silver punchbowl from Cartier's, had taken Mrs. Gallop to the store and paid the entire bill in cash, both of them agreeing not to tell Mr. Gallop about this, on the theory that he would be offended. They did not know, however, that he knew all about it, having one day telephoned the store to explain what his plans were, only to be informed that the bill had been paid in full by Mrs. Gallop herself. Ralph understood perfectly, but decided not to bring the matter up, for he knew it was important for women to feel they are keeping a secret or that they are doing a very kind thing in a very kind way.

Madge Archer loved the kids, and they loved her because she stuck up for them, arguing with their father and mother about the rights of children.

Now, as Ralph and Elizabeth Gallop came to the zoo in Central Park, Ralph said, "Your sister impresses most of her friends as being a passionate woman, but actually she is a spiritual woman who just happens to have a large body."

"Every man who sees her," Mrs. Gallop said, "tells her within five minutes that she's gorgeous. That's the exact word they use. Gorgeous."

"People don't understand sex," Mr. Gallop said, apparently thinking ahead of the conversation. "I don't mean people *exactly*. *People* understand sex the way they understand the weather. They're O.K. It's the specialists who don't understand it. They've made the relationship of sex to general experience just about what the sneeze is to breathing, and of course that's not accurate at all."

Mrs. Gallop was sure her husband, having brought up the topic of sex in this manner, would talk about it pretty much as he talked about everything else—how to cook Arabian pizzas, for instance, or how to tell the difference between an angry tiger and a lonely one by listening carefully to the quality of the tiger's roar—and so she said, "So what? Who cares?"

She hoped this would discourage him.

"I'm glad you asked me that," Mr. Gallop said, however.

Then he explained all about sex to Mrs. Gallop, and

200

before they knew it they were at the Harlem end of the park and it was time to get home.

They found Madge Archer and the kids very quiet in the living-room, the kids looking at the television, and Madge reading the play about the chickens.

"What do you think of it?" Mr. Gallop said.

"I don't know," Madge said. "I suppose it's very good, though. Why do you call it *Unsuccessful*?"

"That's its name," Mr. Gallop said.

"I know," Madge said, "but what has *Unsuccessful* got to do with it?"

"It's an epic," Mr. Gallop said. "All epics have names like that. The title refers to the fact that the chickens are always getting cheated out of the eggs they lay, and finally instead of being the handsome things they are, all covered with feathers, they are turned into poultry."

"My first husband," Madge Archer said, "told me on our honeymoon that some ancient people worshipped chickens. Did you know that?"

"No," Mr. Gallop said.

"He said they looked upon the form of the egg as the most beautiful form of all," Madge said.

"I don't wonder," Mr. Gallop said.

He went to the kitchen and returned holding an egg.

"It *is* a very beautiful thing," he said.

Madge Archer burst into laughter.

"He said that I was the essence of the egg," she said. "The *essence*, mind you. I'll never forget that word. I think you ought to change the name of your play, though."

"What should I change it to?" Mr. Gallop said.

"Why, to *Successful*, of course," Madge said.

"Oh, no," Mr. Gallop said. "I couldn't do that. It's a play about failure."

"Well," Madge said, "I've got to go now. I'd like to take this along and read it again if you don't mind."

"Do you mean to say you want to read my play *twice*?" Mr. Gallop said.

"I certainly do," Madge said.

"Well, O.K.," Mr. Gallop said. "I certainly feel complimented. My own wife—your own sister—hasn't even read my *produced* play once. Not once."

"Not once," Molly Gallop said to Madge Archer. "Mama hasn't read Papa's play once."

Madge Archer hugged and kissed the kids, her sister, and Ralph Gallop, and then she went off.

"Sex is a very tender thing," Mr. Gallop concluded his lecture.

"Sex?" Philip Gallop said. "What's that?"

"Sex," Mr. Gallop said, "is staying alive and enjoying it."

He went to the kitchen to see about fixing some Arabian pizzas.

One day Ralph Gallop fell asleep in the enormous New York movie house called Radio City and dreamed that while an orchestra played a concerto, apparently by Mozart, a foreign government's secret agents tried desperately to convince him that he ought to write his plays in a manner that would make their political ideology popular with the masses. This was quite exciting because of Mr. Gallop's stubbornness. He insisted that he would not write his plays in any such manner. The agents of the foreign power then threatened to kidnap Mr. Gallop and drown him under the Statue of Liberty. Still Mr. Gallop refused to betray himself. The agents fell on Mr. Gallop and began to tie him up when he awoke to discover that a man and his wife had stumbled over him and only wanted to get to the two seats beyond him. Mr. Gallop almost immediately forgot the dream and watched the Rockettes on the stage.

One evening while the Gallops were taking a stroll down Fifth Avenue, Philip Gallop found an American penny dated 1943, the year of his birth, and felt quite elated about it. And of course it wasn't the money, either: it was the excitement of finding something.

And one day Molly Gallop, while spanking her doll for not eating her supper, discovered that the doll could speak and was thrilled to know such a wonderful thing. Molly Gallop distinctly heard her doll say, "I will eat my supper tomorrow. Don't spank me any more, please."

As for Elizabeth Gallop, she ate the Arabian pizzas and was surprised to find that although she had never before tasted the dish, it was apparently something she had longed to eat all her life, and she was quite excited about this.

Elizabeth's sister, Madge Archer, read Ralph Gallop's play about the chickens a second time, changed the title of the play from *Unsuccessful* to *A Good Way to Stay*, and then she changed the name of the author from Ralph Gallop to Alfred St. Paul and sent the play to a producer, and one day Ralph Gallop remarked to his wife:

"I see in Sam Zolotow's theatrical column in the *New York Times* where the producer Ashley Dust is rehearsing a play by a new playwright by the name of Alfred St. Paul, and the name of the play is *A Good Way to Stay*, which is a lot like the name of my play, *A Good Way to Go*, so you can see how I'm influencing the American theatre. I wonder what the play's about?"

The play opened early in March and Ralph Gallop read the reviews and discovered that it was a success.

He felt a little jealous and never guessed for a moment that it was his own play *Unsuccessful* under another name.

The Poet at Home

Of course Madge Archer had changed the chickens into people—which they were in the first place anyway—so there was no reason for Ralph Gallop to even suspect that the new success on Broadway, *A Good Way to Stay*, was in fact his own play.

This was exciting and wonderful for Madge Archer who received the royalty cheques for Ralph Gallop and put them into a special account which she planned to tell the Gallops about at the proper moment.

Ralph Gallop went right on being an amiable failure, a fine father, a fair cook, a conscientious student of mankind, an amateur playwright, and a devoted husband. That is, he went right on wearing out his old clothes, not having the slightest idea that by March, 1949, he was already a man of considerable means and might one day soon be almost rich.

Madge Archer arranged for Ralph and Elizabeth Gallop to see the 101st performance of *A Good Way to Stay*.

Mr. Gallop began to be suspicious of the play the minute the curtain went up, even though the setting was a back-porch and yard instead of a chicken roost and run.

During the first intermission he remarked to his wife that it seemed to him Alfred St. Paul had by some strange coincidence written a play with a first act very much like the first act of his play *Unsuccessful*, but Mrs. Gallop asked him to be careful, people were listening. It would be preposterous if her husband turned out to be a man who felt that successful playwrights were stealing his work.

During the second intermission Mr. Gallop therefore did not say anything more about the matter, although he felt bewildered by the odd coincidence of the similarity of the two plays.

On the way home on foot Mr. Gallop found it difficult to speak at all, for he seemed to be quite sure that the

204

play *A Good Way to Stay* was very much like the play *Unsuccessful*.

When the Gallops got home Madge Archer tried to get Mr. Gallop to tell her all about the play, feeling sure that he must have recognized it as his own play, but all Mr. Gallop was able to say was, "Well, I thought it was rather entertaining, but certainly not as good as *Unsuccessful*."

Mrs. Gallop said, "Get a load of him, will you? After the first act, he tried to tell me it was a lot like *Unsuccessful*."

"Well, was it?" Madge Archer said.

"Not really," Ralph Gallop said.

Madge Archer went home without telling the Gallops the truth. Finally, she told the truth to Elizabeth Gallop.

"So far," Madge Archer said to her sister, "your husband's play has earned more than eleven thousand dollars, but before it's finished it ought to earn ten times more."

Mrs. Gallop got up and went to the kitchen and drank a glass of cool water out of the kitchen faucet.

"Aren't you excited?" Madge Archer asked her sister.

"I certainly am," Mrs. Gallop said.

"Well, I'll get out of here, so you two can be alone when you tell him," Madge said.

"Who's going to tell him?" Mrs. Gallop said.

"Do you mean to say you're *not* going to tell him?" Madge said.

"Of course I'm not going to tell him," Mrs. Gallop said. "You can transfer the money to our bank account of course, but you and I will tell him our Uncle Thomas Archer died and left me an annuity or something."

"But you've *got* to tell him the truth," Madge Archer said. "For the sake of his career if for no other reason."

"No," Mrs. Gallop said. "It would *wreck* his career."

"How could having a success wreck a playwright's career?" Madge Archer said.

"I'm not thinking of his career as a playwright," Mrs. Gallop said. "I'm thinking of his career as a husband and father. I'm in love with him the way he is, and I want him to stay that way. It's a good way to stay, I think."

And so Madge and Elizabeth agreed to invent Uncle Thomas Archer and have him leave Mrs. Gallop an annuity or something, so that the money in the bank might be accounted for.

Ralph Gallop accepted this story with delight and gratitude, and cultivated a great deal of respect for Thomas Archer, who, it turned out, had been in his youth a playwright himself who had failed and had had to make a fortune in the beer business. Ralph Gallop therefore felt a new respect for beer, too.

THE THIRD DAY AFTER CHRISTMAS

Donald Efaw, who was six years old plus three months, was standing on the corner of 3rd Avenue and 37th Street where his angry father Harry had asked him an hour ago to wait a minute while he stepped into the store for some stuff for Alice who was sick in bed, coughing and crying. Alice was three and she had kept everybody awake all night. Donald's angry father Harry hadn't liked the noise at all and he'd blamed it on Mama. Mama's name was Mabelle "Mabelle Louisa Atkins Fernandez before I married Harry Efaw," the boy had once heard his mother say to a man who had come to fix the broken window in the kitchen. "My husband is part-Indian on his mother's side, and I'm part-Indian on my father's. Fernandez sounds more Spanish or Mexican than Indian, but my father was part-Indian just the same. We never lived among them, though, the way some part-Indians do. We always lived in cities."

The boy wore overalls and an old checkered coat his father had outgrown that might have been an overcoat for him if it hadn't been so ill-fitting. The sleeves had been cut to fit the boy, but that was all. The pockets were out of reach, so the boy rubbed his hands to keep them warm. It was eleven o'clock in the morning now.

Donald's father had gone into the place, and pretty soon he would come out and they'd walk home and Mama would give Alice some of the stuff—milk and medicine—

and she'd stop crying and coughing and Mama and Papa would stop fighting.

The place was Haggerty's. It had an entrance on the corner and another on the side street. Harry Efaw had used the 37th Street exit five minutes after he had gone in. He hadn't *forgotten* the boy in the street, he had just wanted to get away from him for awhile, and from the rest of them, too. He had had one little shot of rye that had cost too much and that was all. It had cost a quarter and that was too much for one little shot of rye. He had gulped the drink down and hurried out of the place and walked away, planning to come back after a few minutes to pick the boy up and then buy the food and medicine and go back home to see if something could be done about the little girl's sickness, but somehow or other he had gone right on walking.

At last Donald stepped into the place and saw that it was not like any other store he had ever seen. The man in the white coat looked at him and said, "You can't come in here. Go on home."

"Where's my father?"

"Is this boy's father in the house?" the man called out, and everybody in the place, seven men, turned and looked at Donald. They looked only a moment and then went back to their drinking and talking.

"Your father's not here," the man said, "whoever he is."

"Harry," Donald said. "Harry Efaw."

"I don't know anybody named Harry Efaw. Now, go on home."

"He told me to wait outside a minute."

"Yes, I know. Well, a lot of fellows come in here for a drink and then go. I guess that's what he did. If he told you to wait outside, you'd better do it. You can't stay in here."

"It's cold outside."

"I know it's cold outside," the bartender said. "But you can't stay in here. Wait outside like your father told you to, or go home."

"I don't know how," the boy said.

"Do you know the address?"

The boy obviously didn't know the meaning of the question, so the bartender tried to put it another way.

"Do you know the number of the house and the name of the street?"

"No. We walked. We came for medicine for Alice."

"Yes, I know," the bartender said patiently. "And I know it's cold outside, too, but you'd better get out of here just the same. I can't have small boys coming into this place."

A sickly man of sixty or so who was more than half-drunk and half-dead got up from his table and went to the bartender.

"I'll be glad to get the boy home if he can show me the way."

"Sit down," the bartender said. "The boy doesn't know the way."

"Maybe he does," the man said. "I've had children of my own and the street's no place for a small boy. I'll be glad to get him home to his mother."

"I know," the bartender said. "But just go sit down."

"I'll take you home, sonny," the old man said.

"Sit down," the bartender almost shouted, and the old man turned in astonishment.

"What do you take me for, anyway?" he said softly. "The boy's scared and cold and needs his mother."

"Will you please sit down?" the bartender said. "I know all about the boy. And you're not the man to get him home to his mother, either."

"*Somebody's* got to get him home to his mother," the old man said softly, and then belched. He was in the kind of worn and lumpy clothing the bartender knew had been given to him by a charitable institution. He probably had another thirty or forty cents to spend for beer, money he'd gotten by begging, most likely.

"It's the third day after Christmas," the old man went on. "It's not so long after Christmas any of us has got a right to forget trying to help a small boy home."

"Ah, what's the matter?" another drinker asked from his chair.

"Nothing's the matter," the bartender said. "This boy's father asked him to wait for him outside, that's all." The bartender turned to Donald Efaw. "If you don't know how to get home, just wait outside like your father told you to, and pretty soon he'll be back and he'll take you home. Now, go on and get out of here."

The boy left the place and began standing where he had already stood more than an hour. The old man began to follow the boy. The bartender swung himself over the bar, caught the old man by the shoulders at the swinging doors, twisted him around and walked him back to his chair.

"Now sit down," he said softly. "It's not your place to worry about the boy. Keep your worry for yourself. I'll see that nothing happens to him."

"What do you take me for, anyway?" the old man said again.

At the swinging doors for a look up and down the street the bartender, a short, heavy Irishman in his early fifties, turned and said, "Have you had a look at yourself in a mirror lately? You wouldn't get to the next corner holding the hand of a small boy."

"Why not?" the old man demanded.

The Third Day After Christmas

"Because you don't look like any small boy's father or grandfather or friend or anything else."

"I've had children of my own," the old man said feebly.

"I know," the bartender said. "But just sit still. Some people are allowed to be kind to children and some aren't, that's all."

He took a bottle of beer to the old man's table and set it down by the old man's empty glass.

"Here's a bottle on me," he said. "I'm allowed to be kind to old men like yourself once in awhile, and you're allowed to be kind to bartenders like me once in awhile, but you're not allowed to be kind to a small boy whose father is some place in the neighbourhood, most likely. Just sit still and drink your beer."

"I don't want your dirty beer," the old man said. "You can't hold *me* prisoner in your dirty saloon."

"Just sit still until the boy's father comes and takes him home, and then you can get out of here as fast as you like."

"I want to get out of here *now*," the old man said. "I don't have to take insults from anybody in this whole world. If I told you a few things about who I am I guess you wouldn't talk to me the way you've been talking."

"All right," the bartender said. He wanted to keep things from getting out of hand, he didn't want a fuss, and he felt he might be able to humour the old man out of his wish to be helpful to the boy. "Tell me a few things about who you are and maybe I won't talk to you the way I've been talking."

"I'll say you won't," the old man said.

The bartender was glad to notice that the old man was pouring beer into his glass. He watched the old man drink the top third of the glass, and then the old man said, "My name is Algayler, that's what it is."

He drank some more of his beer and the bartender waited for him to go on. He was standing at the end of the bar now, so he could keep his eye on the boy in the street. The boy was rubbing his hands together, but it was all right. He was a boy who had been toughened by hard times of all kinds, and this waiting in the street for his father wasn't going to be too much for him.

"Algayler," the old man said again, and he went on softly. The bartender couldn't hear what he was saying now, but that didn't matter because he knew the old man would be all right from now on. He was back in himself altogether again where he belonged.

A woman who had been coming to the saloon every day now around noon for a week or so came in with a fox-terrier on a leash and said, "There's a small boy standing out front in the cold. Now, whose boy is he?"

The woman clamped her false teeth together as she looked over the drinkers, and her dog danced around her feet getting used to the warmth of the place.

"He's all right," the bartender said. "His father's gone on an errand. He'll be back in a minute."

"Well, he'd *better* be back in a minute," the woman said. "If there's one thing I can't stand it's a father who leaves a boy standing in the street."

"Algayler," the old man turned and said in a very loud voice.

"What did you say to me, you drunken old bum?" the woman said. Her dog moved toward the old man, tightening the leash, and barked several times.

"It's all right," the bartender said politely. "He only said his name."

"Well, it's a good thing he didn't say something else," the woman said, clamping down on her false teeth again.

The dog calmed down a little, too, but still had to

212

dance about because of the warmth. He was wearing the coat she always strapped on him in the cold weather, but it never did his feet any good, and it was his feet that felt the cold the most.

The bartender poured beer into a glass for the woman and she began to drink, standing at the bar. Finally, she got up on a stool to take things easy, and the dog stopped dancing to look around the place.

The bartender took Algayler another bottle of free beer and without a word, or even a glance, they were agreed that they could get along on this basis.

A man of thirty-five or so whose face and neatly trimmed moustache seemed faintly familiar came in from the 37th Street entrance and asked for a shot of bourbon, and after the drink had been poured, the bartender said very quietly so that no one else would hear him, "That wouldn't be your son standing outside, would it?"

The man had lifted the small glass to his lips, looking at it, but now, having heard the question, he looked away from the glass to the bartender, then swallowed the drink quickly, and without a word moved to the front window to have a look at the boy. At last he turned to the bartender and shook his head. He wanted another and had it, and then went out and walked past the boy, hardly noticing him.

After finishing the second free bottle of beer Algayler began to doze in his chair, and the woman with the fox-terrier began to tell the bartender something about her dog.

"I've had Tippy all his life," she said, "and we've been together the whole time. Every minute of it."

A fellow under thirty in pretty good clothes came in at a quarter after twelve and asked for Johnny Walker Black Label over ice with a water chaser, but quickly settled for

Red Label, and after finishing the drink said, "Where's the television?"

"We don't have any."

"No television?" the man said cheerfully. "What kind of a bar is this, anyway? I didn't know there was a bar in New York that didn't have a television. What do people look at in here, anyway?"

"All we've got is the phonograph."

"Well, O.K., then," the man said. "If that's all you've got, that's all you've got. What would you like to hear?"

"Suit yourself."

The man studied the titles of the various records that were in the machine and then said, "How about Benny Goodman doing *Jingle Bells*?"

"Suit yourself," the bartender said.

"O.K.," the man said, putting a nickel into the slot. "*Jingle Bells* it is."

The machine began to work as the man sat at the bar again and the bartender fixed him another Red Label over ice. The music began and after listening a moment the man said, "That ain't *Jingle Bells*, that's something else."

"You pressed the wrong number."

"Well," the man said pleasantly, "no matter. No matter at all. That ain't a bad number, either."

The boy came in again but the machine was making too much noise for the bartender to be able to tell him to get out without shouting at him, so he went to the boy and led him out to his place in the street.

"Where's my father?" Donald Efaw said.

"He'll be back in a minute. You just stay out here."

This went on until half past two when snow began to fall. The bartender chose an appropriate moment to go out and bring the boy in. He began to make trips to the kitchen fetching the boy things to eat. The boy sat on a

214

box, behind the bar, out of sight, and ate off the top of another box.

After eating, the boy began to fall asleep, so the bartender fixed him a place to stretch out on on some empty beer cases, using his overcoat for a mattress and three old aprons out of the laundry bag and his street coat for covering. He and the boy hadn't said a word since he had brought the boy in, and now, stretched out, on the verge of falling asleep, the boy almost smiled and wept at the same time.

The morning drinkers were gone now, including Algayler and the woman with the false teeth and the fox-terrier, and the trade changed once again while the boy slept.

It was a quarter to five when the boy sat up. He remembered the bartender after a moment, but again they didn't speak. He sat up, as if he were in his bed at home, and then, after dreaming with his eyes open for ten minutes, stepped down.

It was dark outside now and it was snowing the way it does in a storm. The boy watched the snow a moment and then turned and looked up at the bartender.

"Did my father come back?" he said.

"Not yet," the bartender said.

He knelt down to talk to the boy.

"I'll be through work in a few minutes, and if you can show me your house when you see it, I'll try to get you home."

"Didn't my father come back?"

"No, he didn't. Maybe he forgot where he left you."

"He left me right here," the boy said, as if that were something impossible to forget. "Right out front."

"I know."

The night bartender came out of the kitchen in his white coat and noticed the boy.

"Who's that, John? One of your kids?"

"Yeah," the bartender said because he didn't want to try to tell the other bartender what had happened.

"Where'd he get that coat?"

The boy winced and looked at the floor.

"It's one of *my* old coats," the bartender said. "He's got his own of course, but this is the coat he *likes* to wear."

The boy looked up at the bartender suddenly, amazed.

"Yeah, that's the way it is with kids, John," the night bartender said. "Always wanting to be like the old man."

"That's right," the other said.

He took off his white coat and got into his street coat and overcoat, and took the boy by the hand.

"Goodnight," he said, and the night bartender answered him and watched him step out into the street with the boy.

They walked together in silence three blocks and then stepped into a drug store and sat at the counter.

"Chocolate or vanilla?"

"I don't know."

"One chocolate, one vanilla ice cream soda," the bartender said to the soda jerk, and when the drinks were set down on the counter the bartender went to work on the vanilla. The boy did all right on the other, and then they stepped out into the snow again.

"Now, try to remember which way you live. Can you do that?"

"I don't *know* which way."

The bartender stood in the snow, trying to think what to do, but the going was tough, and he got nowhere.

"Well," he said at last, "do you think you could spend

the night at my house with my kids? I've got two boys and a little girl. We'll make a place for you to sleep, and tomorrow your father will come and get you."

"Will he?"

"Sure he will."

They walked along in the silent snow and then the bartender heard the boy begin to cry softly. He didn't try to comfort the boy because he knew there was no comforting him. The boy didn't let himself go, though, he just cried softly, and moved along with his friend. He had heard about strangers and he had heard about enemies and he had come to believe that they were the same thing, but here was somebody he had never seen before who was neither a stranger nor an enemy. All the same it was awful lonesome without his angry father.

They began to go up some steps that were covered with snow and the boy's friend said, "This is where we live. We'll have some hot food and then you can go to bed until tomorrow when your father will come and get you."

"When will he come?" the boy said.

"In the morning," his friend said.

When they stepped into the light of the house the bartender saw that the boy was finished crying, perhaps for the rest of his life.

THE PHEASANT HUNTER

Mayo Maloney at eleven was a little runt of a fellow who was not rude so much as he was rudeness itself, for he couldn't even step inside a church, for instance, without giving everybody who happened to see him an uncomfortable feeling that he, Mayo, despised the place and its purpose.

It was much the same everywhere else that Mayo went: school, library, theatre, home. Only his mother felt that Mayo was not a rude boy, but his father frequently asked Mayo to get down off his high horse and act like everybody else. By this, Michael Maloney meant that Mayo ought to take things easy and stop finding so much fault with everything.

Mayo was the most self-confident boy in the world, and he found fault with everything, or so at least it seemed. He found fault with his mother's church activities. He found fault with his father's interest in Shakespeare and Mozart. He found fault with the public-school system, the Government, the United Nations, the entire population of the world. And he did all this fault-finding without so much as going into detail about anything. He did it by being alive, by being on hand at all. He did it by being nervous, irritable, swift, wise and bored. In short, he was a perfectly normal boy. He had contempt for everything and everybody, and he couldn't help it. His contempt was unspoken but unmistakable. He was slight of body, dark of face and hair, and he went at everything in a hurry because everything was slow and stupid and weak.

The only thing that didn't bore him was the idea of hunting, but his father wouldn't buy him a gun, not even a .22-calibre single-shot rifle. Michael Maloney told Mayo that as soon as he was sure that Mayo had calmed down a little, he would think about buying him a gun. Mayo tried to calm down a little, so he could have his gun, but he gave it up after a day and a half.

"O.K.," his father said, "if you don't want your gun, you don't have to try to earn it."

"I did try to earn it," Mayo said.

"When?"

"Yesterday and today."

"I had in mind," his father said, "a trial covering a period of at least a month."

" A month?" Mayo said. " How do you expect a fellow to stay calm all through October with pheasant to shoot in the country?"

"I don't know how," Mike Mayo said, "but if you want a gun, you've got to calm down enough so I can believe you won't shoot the neighbours with it. Do you think my father so much as let me sit down to my dinner if I hadn't done something to earn it? He didn't invite me to earn any gun to shoot pheasant with. He told me to earn my food, and he didn't wait until I was eleven, either. I started earning it when I was no more than eight. The whole trouble with you is you're too pent-up from not doing any kind of work at all for your food or shelter or clothing to be decently tired and ordinary like everybody else. You're not human, almost. Nobody's human who doesn't know how hard it is to earn his food and the other basic things. It's the fault of your mother and father that you're such a sarcastic and fault-finding man instead of a calm, handsome one. Everybody in this whole town is talking about how your mother and father have turned you into an arrogant ignoramus of a man by not making you earn your right to judge things."

Mr. Maloney spoke as much to the boy's mother as to the boy himself, and he spoke as well to the boy's younger brother and younger sister, for he had left his office at half past four, as he did once a week, to sit down with the whole family for early supper, and it was his intention to make these mid-week gatherings at the table memorable to everyone, including himself.

"Now, Mike," Mrs. Maloney said. "Mayo's not as bad as all that. He just wants a gun to hunt pheasant with."

Mike Mayo laid down his fork that was loaded with macaroni baked with tomatoes and cheese, and he stared at his wife a long time, rejecting one by one two dozen angry remarks he knew would do no one present any good at all to hear, and only make the gathering *unpleasantly* memorable.

At last he said, "I suppose you think I ought to get him a gun, just like that?"

"Mayo isn't really rude or anything like that," the boy's mother said. "It's just that he's restless, the way every human being's got to be once in his lifetime for awhile."

Mayo didn't receive this defence of himself with anything like gratitude. If anything, it appeared as if he were sick and tired of having so much made of a simple little matter like furnishing him with an inexpensive .22-calibre single-shot rifle.

"Now don't you go to work and try to speak up for him," Mike Maloney said to his wife, "because, as you can see for yourself, he doesn't like it. He doesn't enjoy being spoken up for, not even by his mother, poor woman, and you can see how much he thinks of what his father's saying this minute."

"What did I say?" Mayo asked.

"You didn't say anything," his father said. "You didn't need to." He turned to Mrs. Maloney. "Is it a gun I must buy for him now?" he said.

Mrs. Maloney didn't quite know how to say that it was. She remained silent and tried not to look at either her husband or her son.

"O.K.," Mike Maloney said to both his wife and his son. "I have to go back to the office a minute, so if you'll come along with me I'll drop into Archie Cannon's and buy you a gun."

He got up from the table and turned to Mrs. Maloney.

"Provided, of course," he said, "that that meets with your approval."

"Aren't you going to finish your food?" Mrs. Maloney said.

"No, I'm not," Mike Maloney said. "And I'll tell you why, too. I don't want him to be denied anything he wants or anything his mother wants him to have, without earning it, for one unnecessary moment, and as you can see, his cap's on his head, he's at the door, and every moment I stand here explaining is unnecessary."

"Couldn't you both finish your food first?" Mrs. Maloney said.

"Who wants to waste time eating," Mike Maloney said, "when it's time to buy a gun?"

"Well," Mrs. Maloney said, "perhaps you'll have something after you buy the gun."

"We should have been poor," Mike Maloney said. "Being poor would have helped us in this problem."

Mike Maloney went to the door where his nervous son was standing waiting for him to shut up and get going.

He turned to his wife and said, "I won't be able to account for him after I turn the gun over to him, but I'll be gone no more than an hour. If we'd been poor and couldn't afford it, he'd know the sinfulness of provoking me into this sort of bitter kindness."

When he stepped out of the house onto the front porch, he saw that his son was at the corner, trying his best not to run. He moved quickly and caught up with him, and he moved along as swiftly as his son did.

At last he said, "Now, I'm willing to walk the half mile to Archie Cannon's, but I'm not going to run, so if you've got to run, go ahead, and I'll meet you outside the place as soon as I get there."

He saw the boy break loose and disappear far down the street. When he got to Archie Cannon's the boy was waiting for him. They went in and Mike Maloney asked Archie to show him the guns.

"What kind of a gun do you want, Mike?" Archie said. "I didn't know you were interested in hunting."

"It's not for myself," Mike Maloney said. "It's for Mayo here, and it ought to be suitable for pheasant shooting."

"That would be a shotgun," Archie said.

"Would that be what it would be?" Mike Maloney asked his son, and although the boy hadn't expected anything so precisely suitable for pheasant shooting, he said that a shotgun would be what it would be.

"O.K., Archie," Mike Malony said. "A shotgun."

"Well, Mike," Archie said, "I wouldn't like to think a shotgun would be the proper gun to turn over to a boy."

"Careful," Mike Maloney said. "He's right here with us, you know. Let's not take any unnecessary liberties. I believe he indicated the gun ought to be a shotgun."

"Well, anyway," Archie said, "it's going to have a powerful kick."

"A powerful kick," Mike Maloney repeated, addressing

the three words to his son, who received them with disdain.

"That is no matter to him," Mike Maloney said to Archie Cannon.

"Well, then," Archie Cannon said, "this here's a fine double-barrel twelve-gauge shotgun and it's just about the best bargain in the store."

"You shouldn't have said that, Archie," Mike Maloney said. "This man's not interested in bargains. What he wants is the best shotgun you've got that's suitable for pheasant shooting."

"That would be this twelve-gauge repeater," Archie Cannon said, "that sells for ninety-eight fifty, plus tax of course. It's the best gun of its kind."

"Anybody can see it's a better gun," Mike Maloney said. "No need to waste time with inferior firearms."

He handed the gun to Mayo Maloney, who held it barrel down, resting over his right arm, precisely as a gun, loaded or not, ought to be held.

"I'll show you how it works," Archie Cannon made the mistake of saying to Mayo Maloney. The boy glanced at Archie in a way that encouraged him to say quickly, "Anything else, then? Fishing tackle, hooks, boxing gloves, rowing machines, tennis rackets?"

"Anything else?" Mike Maloney said to his son, who said nothing, but with such irritation that Mike quickly said to Archie Cannon, "Shells, of course. What good is a shotgun without shells?"

Archie Cannon jumped to get three boxes of his best shotgun shells, and as he turned them over to Mike Maloney, who turned them over to Mayo, Archie said, "A hunting coat in which to carry the shells? A red hunting cap?"

Mayo Maloney was gone, however.

"He didn't want those things," Mike Maloney said.

"Some hunters go to a lot of trouble about costume," Archie Cannon said.

"He doesn't," Mike Maloney said. "What do I owe you?"

"One hundred and five dollars and sixty-nine cents, including tax," Archie said. "Has he got a licence?"

"To hunt?" Mike Maloney said. "He hasn't got a licence to eat, but damned if I don't halfway admire him sometimes. He must know something to be so sure of himself and so contemptuous of everybody else."

"To tell you the truth," Archie Cannon said, "I thought you were kidding, Mike. I thought you were kidding the way you sometimes do in court when you're helping a small man fight a big company. I didn't expect you to actually buy a gun and turn it over to an eleven-year-old boy. Are you sure it's all right?"

"Of course it's all right," Mike Maloney said. "You saw for yourself the way he held the gun." He began to write a cheque. "Now, what did you say it came to?"

"A hundred and five sixty-nine," Archie Cannon said. "I hope you know there's no pheasant to speak of anywhere near here. The Sacramento Valley is where the pheasant shooting is."

"Where you going to be around ten o'clock tonight?" Mike Maloney said.

"Home, most likely," Archie Cannon said. "Why?"

"Will you be up?"

"Oh, yes," Archie said. "I never go to bed before midnight. Why?"

"Would you like to drop over to my house for a couple of bottles of beer around ten?" Mike said.

"I'd like that very much," Archie said. "Why?"

"Well," Mike said, "the way I figure is this: It's a quarter after five now. It'll take him about three minutes to hitch a ride with somebody going out to Riverdale, which is about twenty-five miles from here. That would take an average driver forty or forty-five minutes to make, but he'll get the driver, whoever he is, or she is, for that matter, to make it in about half an hour or a little under. He'll do it by being excited, not by saying anything. He'll get the driver to go out of his or her way to let him off where the hunting is, too, so he'll start hunting right away, or a little before six. He'll hunt until after dark, walking a lot in the meantime. He won't get lost or anything like that, but he'll have to walk back to a road with a little traffic. He'll hitch a ride back, and he'll be home a little before or after ten."

"How do you know?" Archie said. "How do you even know he's going hunting at all tonight? He just got the gun, and he may not even know how to work it."

"You saw him take off, didn't you?" Mike Maloney said. "He took off to go hunting. And you can be sure he either knows how to work the gun or will find out by himself in a few minutes."

"Well," Archie said, "I certainly would like to drop by for some beer, Mike, if you're serious."

"Of course I'm serious," Mike said.

"I suppose you want to have somebody to share your amusement with when he gets back with nothing shot and his body all sore from the powerful kick of the gun," Archie said.

"Yes," Mike said. "I want to have somebody to share my amusement with but not for those reasons. He may be a little sore from the powerful kick of the gun, but I think he'll come back with something."

"I've never heard of anybody shooting any pheasant

around Riverdale," Archie said. "There's a little duck shooting out there in season, and jack rabbits of course."

"He said pheasants," Mike Maloney said. "Here's my cheque. Better make it a little before ten, just in case."

"I thought you were only kidding about the gun," Archie said. "Are you sure you did the right thing? I mean, considering he's only eleven years old, hasn't got a hunting licence and the pheasant-shooting season doesn't open for almost a month?"

"That's one of the reasons I want you to come by for some beer," Mike said.

"I don't get it," Archie said.

"You're game warden of this area, aren't you?"

"I am."

"O.K.," Mike said. "If it turns out that he's broken the law, I want you to know it."

"Well," Archie said, "I wouldn't want to bother about a small boy shooting a few days out of season or without a licence."

"I'll pay his fine," Mike Maloney said.

"I don't think he'll get anything," Archie said, "so of course there won't be any fine to be paid."

"I'll see you a little before ten, then," Mike Maloney said.

He spent a half hour at his office, then walked home slowly, to find the house quiet and peaceful, the kids in bed and his wife doing the dishes. He took the dish towel and began to dry and put the clean dishes into the cupboard.

"I bought him the best shotgun Archie Cannon had for pheasant shooting," he said.

"I hope he didn't make you too angry," Mrs. Maloney said.

"He did for a while," Mike said, "but all of a sudden he didn't, if you know what I mean."

"I don't know what you mean," Mrs. Maloney said.

"I mean," Mike said, "it's all right not being poor."

"What's being poor got to do with it?" Mrs. Maloney said.

"I mean it's all right, that's all," Mike said.

"Well, that's fine," Mrs. Maloney said. "But where is he?"

"Hunting, of course," Mike said. "You don't think he wanted a gun to look at."

"I don't know what I think now," Mrs. Maloney said. "You've had so much trouble with him all along, and now all of a sudden you buy him an expensive gun and believe it's perfectly all right for him to go off hunting in the middle of the night on the third day of October. Why?"

"Well," Mike Maloney said, "it's because while I was preaching to him at the table something began to happen. It was as if my own father were preaching to me thirty years ago when I was Mayo's age. Oh, I did earn my food, as I said, and I wanted a gun, too, just as he's been wanting one. Well, my father preached to me, and I didn't get the gun. I mean, I didn't get it until almost five years later, when it didn't mean very much to me any more. Well, while I was preaching to him this afternoon I remembered that when my father preached to me I was sure he was mistaken to belittle me so, and I even believed that somehow—somehow or other, perhaps because we were so poor, if that makes sense—he would suddenly stop preaching and take me along without any fuss of any kind and buy me a gun. But of course he didn't. And I *remembered* that he didn't, and I decided that perhaps I'd do for my son what my father had not done for me, if you know what I mean."

228

"Do you mean you and Mayo are alike?" Mrs. Maloney said.

"I do," Mike said. "I do indeed."

"Very much alike?"

"Almost precisely," Mike said. "Oh, he'll not be the great man he is now for long, and I don't want to be the one to cheat him out of a single moment of his greatness."

"You must be joking," Mrs. Maloney said.

"I couldn't be more serious," Mike said. "Archie Cannon thought I was joking, too, but why would I be joking? I bought him the gun and shells, and off he went to hunt, didn't he?"

"Well, I hope he doesn't hurt himself," Mrs. Maloney said.

"We'll never know if he does," Mike said. "I've asked Archie to come by around ten for some beer because I figure he'll be back by then."

"Is Mrs. Cannon coming with Archie?"

"I don't think so," Mike said. "Her name wasn't mentioned."

"Then I suppose you don't want me to sit up with you," Mrs. Maloney said.

"I don't know why not, if you want to," Mike said.

But Mrs. Maloney knew it wouldn't do to sit up, so she said, "No, I'll be getting to bed long before ten."

Mike Maloney went out on the front porch with his wife, and they sat and talked about their son Mayo and their other kids until a little after nine, and then Mrs. Maloney went inside to see if the beer was in the ice box and to put some stuff out on the kitchen table, to go with the beer. Then she went to bed.

Around a quarter to ten Archie Cannon came walking up the street and sat down in the rocker on the front porch.

"I've been thinking about what you did," he said, "and I still don't know if you did right."

"I did right all right," Mike Maloney said. "Let's go inside and have some beer. He'll be along pretty soon."

They went inside and sat down at the kitchen table. Mike lifted the caps off two bottles of cold beer, filled two tall glasses, and they began to drink. There was a plate loaded with cold roast beef, ham, Bologna and sliced store cheese, and another plate with rye bread on it, already buttered.

When it was almost twelve and Mayo Maloney hadn't come home, Archie Cannon wondered if he shouldn't offer to get up and go home or maybe even offer to get his car and go looking for the boy, but he decided he'd better not. Mike Maloney seemed excited and angry at himself for having done such a foolish thing, and he might not like Archie to rub it in. They had stopped talking about Mayo Maloney around eleven, and Archie knew Mike wanted the situation to remain that way indefinitely.

A little before one in the morning, after they had finished a half dozen bottles of beer apiece and all the food Mrs. Maloney had set out for them, and talked about everything in the world excepting Mayo Maloney, they heard footsteps on the back stairs, and then on the porch, and after a moment he came into the kitchen.

He was a tired man. His face was dirty and flushed, and his clothes were dusty and covered with prickly burs of several kinds. His hands were scratched and almost black with dirt. His gun was slung over his right arm, and nested in his left arm were two beautiful pheasants.

He set the birds on the kitchen table, and then broke his gun for cleaning. He wrapped a dry dish towel around the pieces and put the bundle in the drawer in which he kept his junk. He then brought six unused shells out of his pockets and placed them in the drawer too, locked the drawer with his key and put the key back into his pocket. Then he went to the kitchen sink and rolled up his sleeves and washed his hands and arms and face and neck, and after he'd dried himself, he looked into the refrigerator and brought out some Bologna wrapped in butcher paper, and began to eat it without bread while he fetched bread and butter and a chair. He sat down and began to put three thick slices of Bologna between two slices of buttered bread. Mike Maloney had never before seen him eat so heartily.

He didn't look restless and mean any more, either.

Mike Maloney got up with Archie Cannon, and they left the house by the back door in order not to disturb Mrs. Maloney and the sleeping kids.

When they were in the back yard, Archie Cannon said, "Well, aren't you going to ask him where he got them?"

"He's not ready to talk about it just yet," Mike said. "What's the fine?"

"Well," Archie said, "there won't be any fine because there's not supposed to be any pheasants in the whole area of which I'm game warden. I didn't believe he'd get anything, let alone pheasants, and both of them cocks, too. Damned if I don't admire him a little myself."

"I'll walk you home," Mike said.

In the kitchen, the boy finished his sandwich, drank a glass of milk and rubbed his shoulder.

The whole evening and night had been unbelievable. Suddenly at the table, when his father had been preaching to him, he'd begun to understand his father a little better, and himself, too, but he'd known he couldn't immediately stop being the way he had been for so long, the way that was making everybody so uncomfortable. He'd known he'd have to go on for a while longer and see the thing

231

through. He'd have to go along with his father. He'd
known all this very clearly, because his father had suddenly stopped being a certain way—the way everybody
believed a father ought to be—and Mayo had known it
was going to be necessary for him to stop being a certain
way, too—the way he had believed he had to be. But he'd
known he couldn't stop until he had seen the thing
through.

In the kitchen, almost asleep from weariness, he decided he'd tell his father exactly what he'd done, but he'd
wait awhile first, maybe ten years.

He'd had a devil of a time finding out how the gun
worked, and he hadn't been able to hitch a ride at all, so
he'd walked and run six miles to the countryside around
Clovis, and there he'd loaded the gun and aimed it at a
blackbird in a tree leaning over Clovis Creek, and pressed
the trigger.

The kick had knocked him down and he had missed the
bird by a mile. He'd had to walk a long way through tall
dry grass and shrubs for something else to shoot at, but
all it was was another blackbird, and again the kick had
knocked him down and he'd missed it by a mile.

It was getting dark fast by then and there didn't seem
to be anything alive around at all, so he began to shoot the
gun just to get used to it. Pretty soon he could shoot it
and not get knocked down. He kept shooting and walking,
and finally it was dark and it seemed he was lost. He
stumbled over a big rock and fell and shot the gun by
accident and got a lot of dirt in his eyes. He got up and
almost cried, but he managed not to, and then he found a
road, but he had no idea where it went to or which direction to take. He was scratched and sore all over, and not
very happy about the way he'd shot the gun by accident.
That should never have happened. He was scared, too,

The Pheasant Hunter

and he said a prayer a minute and meant every word of what he said. And he understood for the first time in his life why people liked to go to church.

"Please don't let me make a fool of myself," he prayed. "Please let me start walking in the right direction on this road."

He started walking down the road, hoping he was getting nearer home, or at least to a house with a light in it, or a store or something that would be open. He felt a lot of alive things in the dark that he knew must be imaginary and he said, "Please don't let me get so scared." And pretty soon he felt so tired and small and lost and hopeless and foolish that he could barely keep from crying, and he said, "Please don't let me cry."

He walked a long time, and then far down the road he saw a small light, and he began to walk faster. It was a country store with a gasoline pump out front and a new pick-up truck beside the pump. Inside the store was the driver of the truck and the storekeeper, and he saw that it was twenty minutes to twelve. The storekeeper was an old man with a thick white moustache who was sitting on a box talking to the driver of the truck, who was about as old as the boy's father.

He saw the younger man wink at the older one, and he thanked God for both of them, and for the wink, because he didn't think people who could wink could be unfriendly.

He told them exactly what he had done, and why, and the men looked at him and at each other until he was all through talking. They both examined the brand-new gun, too. Then the storekeeper handed the gun back to the boy and said to the younger man, "I'll be much obliged to you, Ed, if you'll get this man home in our truck."

They were a father and a son, too, apparently, and

233

good friends, besides. Mayo Maloney admired them very much, and on account of them, he began to like people in general, too.

"Not at all," the younger man said.

"And I'd like to think we might rustle up a couple of pheasant for him to take home, too."

"That might not be easy to do this hour of the night," the younger man said, "but we could try."

"Isn't there an all-night Chinese restaurant in town that serves pheasant in and out of season?" the old man said. "Commercial pheasant, that is?"

"I don't know," the younger man said, "but we could phone and find out."

"No," the older man said. "No use phoning. They wouldn't be apt to understand what we were talking about. Better just drive up to it and go in and find out. It's on Kern Street between F and G, but I forget the name. Anyhow, it's open all night, and I've heard you can get pheasant there any time you like."

"It certainly is worth looking into," the younger man said.

The younger man got up, and Mayo Maloney, speechless with amazement, got up, too. He tried to say something courteous to the older man, but nothing seemed to want to come out of his dry mouth. He picked up his gun and went out to the truck and got in beside the younger man, and they went off. He saw the older man standing in the doorway of the store, watching.

The younger man drove all the way to town in silence, and when the boy saw familiar places, he thought in prayer again, saying, *I certainly don't deserve this, and I'm never going to forget it.*

The truck crossed the Southern Pacific tracks to China-town, and the driver parked in front of Willie Fong's, which was, in fact, open, although nobody was inside eating. The driver stepped out of the truck and went into the restaurant, and the boy saw him talking to a waiter. The waiter disappeared and soon came back with a man in a business suit. This man and the driver of the truck talked a few minutes, and then they both disappeared into the back of the restaurant, and after a few minutes the driver of the truck came back, and he was holding something that was wrapped in newspaper. He came out of the restaurant and got back into the truck, and they drove off again.

"How's your father?" the man said suddenly.

"He's fine," Mayo managed to say.

"I mean," the man said, "you *are* Mike Maloney's boy, aren't you?"

"Yes, I am," Mayo Maloney said.

"I thought you were," the man said. "You look alike and have a lot in common. You don't have to tell me where you live. I know where it is. And I know you want to know who I am, but don't you think it would be better if I didn't tell you? I've had dealings with your father, and he lent me some money when I needed it badly and we both weren't sure I'd ever be able to pay him back. So it's all right. I mean, nobody's going to know anything about this from me."

"Did they have any pheasants?" the boy said.

"Oh, yes," the man said. "I'm sorry I forgot to tell you. They're in that newspaper. Just throw the paper out the window."

The boy removed the paper from around the birds and looked at them. They were just about the most wonderful-looking things in the whole world.

"Do they have any shot in them?" he asked. "Because they ought to."

"No, I'm afraid they don't," the driver said, "but we'll

drive out here a little where it's quiet and we won't disturb too many sleeping farmers, and between the two of us we'll get some shot into them. You can do the shooting, if you like."

"I might spoil them," the boy said.

"I'll be glad to attend to it, then," the driver said.

They drove along in silence a few minutes, and then the truck turned into a lonely road and stopped. The driver got out and placed the two birds on some grass by the side of the road in the light of the truck's lights about twenty yards off. Then he took the gun, examined it, aimed, fired once, unloaded the gun, fetched the birds, got back into the truck and they drove off again.

"They're just right now," he said.

"Thanks," the boy said.

When the truck got into his neighbourhood Mayo said, "Could I get off a couple of blocks from my house, so nobody will see this truck accidentally?"

"Yes, that's a good idea," the driver said.

The truck stopped. The boy carefully nested the two birds in his left arm, then got out, and the driver helped him get the gun slung over his right arm.

"I never expected anything like this to happen," the boy said.

"No, I suppose not," the man said. "I never expected to find a man like your father when I needed him, either, but I guess things like that happen just the same. Well, good night."

"Good night," the boy said.

The man got into the truck and drove off, and the boy hurried home and into the house.

When Mike Maloney got back from walking Archie Cannon home, he was surprised to find the boy asleep on his folded arms on the kitchen table. He shook the boy gently, and Mayo Maloney sat up with a start, his eyes bloodshot and his ears red.

"You better get to bed," Mike said.

"I didn't want to go," the boy said, "until you got back, so I could thank you for the gun."

"That wasn't necessary," the man said. "That wasn't necessary at all."

The boy got up and barely managed to drag himself out of the room without falling.

Alone in the kitchen, the father picked up the birds and examined them, smiling because he knew whatever was behind their presence in the house, it was certainly something as handsome as the birds themselves.

THE CORNET PLAYERS

The town of Sanger, California, sits serenely around its Court House Park eleven miles east of the city of Fresno (population 65,000). Sanger's population is not great as populations go, a mere 5,332, but it is lively, and in one or two things unique. The town is noted among amateur observers, including the writer, for the alacrity, energy, and earnestness with which it creates and follows trends, for instance.

From 1919 to 1949 a rich variety of trends overwhelmed the population of Sanger, but the trend with which the writer is concerned is the trend of 1939.

This was the cornet-playing trend.

Early in that year a farmer named Khook Jenj gave his eighteen-year-old son a cornet for a birthday present, and this boy, named John, soon revealed that it was not impossible to learn to play the cornet without taking lessons. Of course John had received with the cornet a pamphlet entitled *Cornet Self-Taught* to which during the winter months he had applied himself assiduously, so that early in March his rendering of the song, *It's a Sin to Tell a Lie*, was accepted by everyone who heard it, and everyone heard it, for John Jenj frequently stood alone in the Court House Park and played it. As it was well-known from his record at Sanger High School, and from his performances in other trends, that John Jenj was not an exceptional boy in any way, a thought occurred to a great many people of Sanger, and this thought was that they too could learn to play *It's a Sin to Tell a Lie* on the cornet.

239

Thus, the trend came into being.

One day in April as John stood in the Court House Park playing the song, he was joined by a boy of eleven playing the same song equally effectively on a second-hand cornet.

This boy's name was Peter Garifiola, although he was generally known as Pete or Petey Boy. John Jenj was a little scornful at first of Petey Boy's presumption, but after a while he condescended to chat with him about the art of playing the cornet, and a week later when Pete demonstrated unmistakably that he could do a thing or two on the horn that probably had never before been done by anybody in the world, John Jenj wisely decided to accept Pete as his partner.

They gave themselves the professional name of *Jenj and Garifiola, Cornetists Par Excellence, Suitable for Picnics, Weddings, and Funerals, Telephone Sanger 33 Ring 5.*

Sanger 33 ring 5 was the Jenj family telephone. Whenever John was at home and the telephone bell happened to ring five times he would lift the receiver and in a very business-like tone of voice say, *Jenj and Garifiola.* Now, it happened that the Garifiola family's telephone was on the same line, ring 7, so that if the ring happened to be either 5 or 7 and both boys happened to be at home, both boys would get on the line. If the ring was 5, Petey Boy would listen to John Jenj, to see if it was a job to play at a wedding or a funeral, and if the ring was 7, John Jenj would listen to Pete. At the same time, everybody else on the line would listen, so that if it was actually an assignment very nearly the whole town would know about it.

Their fee to play was a dollar apiece, with refreshments provided by the client according to his personal inclination.

Jenj and Garifiola played *It's a Sin to Tell a Lie* at the

wedding of Alice Mendoza to Ifton Slake, a part-Indian, and they made the marriage more memorable than anyone had imagined might be likely. They played the song eleven times. They played it at the church with what they called "the religious feeling", and riding in the truck from the church to the house in which Ifton Slake lived on Sam Bogley's vineyard they played it with what they called "the rollicking, devil-may-care feeling". Jenj and Garifiola, in fact, had eleven accurately identified feelings with which they could play the song. After using up these eleven feelings, they reverted to a favourite feeling, or played the song with requested feelings.

They played the song with "the funeral march feeling", for instance, as they led the procession four blocks from the church to the graveyard when Eva Flange, aged three days, passed away, bringing the number of feelings up to a grand total of twelve.

In the meantime, the trend had acquired momentum, and competition was great. There had come into existence by the first of August a dozen more teams of cornetists, including a father and son, a mother and daughter, a husband and wife, a brother and sister, full brothers, step-brothers, a full-blooded Tule Indian in costume and a real East Indian in turban, and two or three other odd combinations. Each team was in business in earnest. Each team handed out cards to the people in the streets or distributed descriptive pamphlets to every house in town as well as to a great many farm houses. Each team had at least one telephone number. And the free concerts in the Court House Park started early in the morning and continued late into the night.

Business for Jenj and Garifiola fell off a little with so much competition, but the boys were on their toes and they could always be counted on to offer—and what's more deliver—something extra, something no other team could offer. They were the avant garde of the cornet-playing trend, and the others were imitators. Still, some of the imitators were quick to pick up an innovation and perhaps improve or extend it, so that Jenj and Garifiola had to have a reserve of ideas.

The printing of new cards and pamphlets became so necessary a part of the business that they sent away to Chicago for a very simple press, and unlike their competitors did not limit their ink to black but used red and green as well, and finally blue. They also went in for pamphlets that told a story : how and when the team had come into being ; how many hours per day they played ; how many occasions they had played for ; the names and addresses of satisfied customers ; and the actual spoken or written remarks of many well-known people in Sanger who had heard them :

"You boys certainly brought something to Sanger nobody ever thought," Mr. Ed Hurling, assistant manager of Apperson's Notion Store, 909 Broadway.

"I could listen to Jenj and Garifiola the rest of my life," Mrs. Emma Stain, fancy laundry work, 307 Malaga Avenue, telephone 44 ring 4.

"Marvellous is the word for Jenj and Garifiola's cornet wizardry and musical statesmanship," Mr. Arthur F. Frogging, coloured, Ace Shoe Shine Parlour, next door to the Post Office, across the street from the Court House Park, the best shine in Sanger at any cost.

"I want Jenj and Garifiola to play at my funeral," Miss Constance Askler, plain housework at reasonable prices, cleaning, cooking, minor carpentry or gardening, families only, no bachelors, 411 Alberta Street, telephone 51, ring 2, make a note of it and put it by your telephone : 51 ring 2.

The Cornet Players

And so on.

Of course the boys solicited these testimonials in a friendly, co-operative manner, playing in front of the testifier's home or place of business, or directly in front of him or her in the street, and attracting a crowd.

Jenj and Garifiola, once they got going in earnest—which was early in May before the competition got tough—began to make a modest living through their art, earning frequently as much as eighteen dollars apiece a week; and one week during which there were a great many burials, weddings, and a wide variety of other occasions requiring cornet-playing they earned twenty-two dollars apiece. At the same time they kept learning more and more about what could be done in the cornet-playing business, and finally Peter Garifiola evolved what he generously called "The Jenj and Garifiola cornet-playing style".

This consisted of a rather tricky employment of John Jenj's cornet as any number of other instruments—the violin, the clarinet, the saxophone, the tuba, the flute, the drum, and so on—while Peter Garifiola exploited the melody. Still, not satisfied with this strange but effective innovation, the team worked out an even more clever idea: the employment of the human voice, generally in what might best be identified as the shout, as counterpoint to the melody. In this case, determined to be fair and square through and through, the partners agreed that John Jenj should play the melody and Peter Garifiola do the shouting.

This was very nearly their most magnificent achievement, and it impressed everybody in town the first time it was tried. That was in the middle of May, as the smell of summer was coming back to Sanger, and it happened at half past nine at night when everybody still alive somehow felt like shouting, too. The song was still *It's a Sin to Tell a Lie*, but Peter Garifiola's shouting was creative, so that a half dozen people gave the team a brand new idea by asking, "What's the name of *that* song?"

Without thinking, and knowing little about patent infringements or copyright laws, Peter Garifiola stopped shouting to say, "The Jenj and Garifiola Special."

"The Jenj and Garifiola Special" was frequently in demand thereafter, and one thing leading to another, John Jenj, with the full support and assistance of his partner of course—who had grown considerably in the meantime —took up composing, and in only three hours of a warm afternoon came forward with a ballad, "Sanger, Sanger, Heaven on Earth".

This song caught hold like wildfire and was soon being played and sung by the imitators. The melody was the melody of *It's a Sin to Tell a Lie* of course, rendered, however, in the Jenj and Garifiola style, but with something new added: *the hymn-quality*, for some of the words of the song had to do with a man's going away from Sanger, or *thinking* of doing so, and then feeling bitterly sorry that he ever did, or thought of doing, such a foolish thing.

The actual lines were:

> *When next you hear of me,*
> *In old New York I'll be,*
> *Alone and far from thee,*
> *Sanger, my heaven on earth.*

Children, who are deeply moved by these notions of far travel, upon hearing the song, invariably wept.

The beginning of World War II somewhat coincided with the cornet-playing business of Sanger when it was at its peak, but it was not the beginning of the war that put

244

the business out of commission, it was the experience John Jenj had in concert, so to say, out of town, in Fresno, the evening of the first Sunday in October.

This came about as follows :

News of the cornet-playing fever spread from Sanger to the still smaller towns nearby, and then it reached the city of Fresno itself. *The Bee* decided to have a reporter pay a visit to Sanger and get to the bottom of the trend. This man, recently graduated from the College in Fresno and planning to write a novel at the next opportunity, had a touch of the poet in him. His name was Wallace Asfanasia, and he was nothing if not earnest in his ambition to find material for writing at home in Fresno rather than in the Latin Quarter of Paris. Wallace was a hard-working reporter but as he was paid by the line and as he was willing to work on speculation, the story of the Sanger cornet-playing trend was offered to him because it was cheaper that way. He would have to gamble on whether or not the managing editor of *The Bee* would want to use his story, and of course he would be required to pay his travelling and food expenses out of his own pocket. He was given carte blanche, however, to write the story any way that pleased him, and to make it as long as he cared to.

One entire day in Sanger was not enough for Wallace Asfanasia, however, so he went back to the town five days in a row, talking to John Jenj and Peter Garifiola, hearing them play, listening to Jenj's own ballad about Sanger, and asking them all kinds of questions. Some of these questions had to do with the cornet, with the cornet-playing business, with music in general, with the Jenj and Garifiola conception of music, and every now and then the questions had to do with what was happening in Europe. Jenj, older and more reserved than his partner, modestly

answered the question about what was happening in
Europe by admitting that he was not abreast of anything
outside the musical world ; but Peter Garifiola, younger
and more confident about all things, said he didn't care
what happened in Europe ; Europe's affairs were Europe's
affairs, and if the people of Europe would rather kill each
other than take up art and music, well, that was no skin
off his elbow.

"Do you think America will be drawn into the war?"
Wallace Asfanasia asked the team, and Petey Boy said,
"No. What the hell for?"

Two years later Wallace's conscription number was one
of the first to come up, and the novel he was working on
at that time was interrupted for five years. Hence, it may
be presumed that he'd had a feeling all along that America
was going to get into the war, and as it turned out his
feeling was right.

After interviewing and listening to Jenj and Garifiola,
the reporter moved on to their competitors, so that the
trend would be thoroughly understood.

It was.

And Wallace Asfanasia made it perfectly clear in the
brilliant story he wrote about it for *The Sunday Bee*. The
piece was spread over two pages of the magazine section,
and quite understandably concerned itself mainly with the
creators of the trend, John Jenj and Peter Garifiola.

"In Europe," Wallace Asfanasia concluded his story,
"the common people are not permitted by corrupt and
selfish politicians and political systems to express themselves artistically, but in America they are. And only
eleven miles from Fresno, the good people of Sanger—
most of them from roots in Germany, Italy, France, Den-
mark, Finland, Greece, Syria, Armenia, Egypt, and
Portugal, as well as a sprinkling of native American

Indian stock—are a living demonstration of the power of democracy to guide the energies of the masses into expressive and creative channels. More power to you in the arts, Sanger! And more power to the leading lights of this musical renaissance, Jenj and Garifiola, the first a first-generation Syrian, the other a first-generation Italian! May our country never forget them, in war or peace!"

The story was a sensation and Wallace Asfanasia's name as a reporter with poetic undertones was instantaneously established. In addition to this, which was not his intention in the first place—largely he hoped America would not go to war and he felt his story might help America keep out of war—a great many Sunday pleasure-drivers motored out to Sanger that very Sunday, parked their cars, and got out to listen to Jenj and Garifiola, as well as to some of their imitators and competitors.

Among these travellers was the leader of the summer Sunday afternoon band concerts in Roeding Park, in Fresno, a Finn with a real musical education whose name was Lars Harling. This man immediately sought out the famous team and, having been deeply moved by the sweep of Asfanasia's story and believing it was the generous thing to do, invited the team to appear as soloists at the open-air concert the following Sunday.

"You boys will be paid five dollars apiece," Mr. Harling told the boys, "but you will be expected to take care of transportation, lodging and food."

Jenj and Garifiola accepted the offer and Mr. Harling drove back to Fresno just in time to lead that afternoon's band concert. *The Bee* was informed by Mr. Harling himself of what he had done to encourage the Sanger cornet-players, and variations of the invitation appeared in every issue of the paper the following week.

Wallace Asfanasia wrote an inspiring editorial about

Mr. Harling's act, but the managing editor could not break the rule of not having editorials run with a by-line. Still, a number of astute people guessed that the author of the editorial was Wallace, but he wasn't after glory. All he wanted was for this sort of thing to get the same kind of attention as embezzling, bribery, fire, rape and murder, and for America to stay out of the war. He did his share and then some, but of course it wasn't quite enough, and his sense of personal failure harassed him considerably all the years he spent in Australia and the Islands of the Pacific.

As for Sanger itself, the town was beside itself with pride, even though Sanger had been acclaimed for its illustrious sons at the height of the fruit-picking-and-packing season when ordinarily nobody had any time for anything except work. Time was somehow found by the people of Sanger to take pride in themselves, however, and everybody felt that this invitation for Jenj and Garifiola to appear with The Fresno Band was only the beginning of much greater things for them. Only a handful of people were going to be able to travel to Fresno and attend the concert, but the good wishes of everybody—busy working that Sunday in the vineyards and orchards and in the packing-houses—would go with the boys.

The excitement grew day by day, but no one's excitement equalled Peter Garifiola's. In the end it got out of hand and turned to pneumonia, and a serious problem arose.

Should John Jenj appear at the concert alone? Should he postpone the event until Peter Garifiola recuperated? Or should he select another partner from among the many other cornet stylists of Sanger?

Opinions varied of course, and Wallace Asfanasia, having gotten wind of Peter's illness, rushed to the boy's

248

bedside and interviewed him. Sick as he was, Peter Garifiola said the people of Europe could kill each other all they wanted to; the American way of life was not like that.

The reporter then talked to John Jenj who was rather unreasonable about the whole thing, almost implying that Peter Garifiola had gotten cold feet and come down with pneumonia on purpose.

"I think I'll go it solo," John Jenj said, and this was mentioned in the reporter's Sunday morning story in *The Bee.*

"Unwilling to let Sanger down," Wallace Asfanasia wrote, "John Jenj stood as straight as he does when he plays the cornet, and he said, 'God willing, I'll do the best I can alone.'"

By now the cornet-playing business of Sanger, California was swiftly deteriorating, although no one suspected it at the time.

The concert began on schedule at half-past two that Sunday afternoon with John Jenj occupying the guest soloist's chair on the bandstand, a cane and rattan chair of the same quality occupied by each of the other musicians. John was neatly dressed and reasonably calm. The concert had attracted an unusually large crowd which was spread out on the lawn, under the shade trees, most of them young men and women with nothing better to do than fool around. The day was hot, serene and peaceful, and to Wallace Asfanasia, sitting beside John Jenj on the bandstand, the war in Europe seemed far away indeed. The concert moved gracefully through the first three numbers, and then it was time at last for John Jenj to be introduced.

Wallace Asfanasia stepped to the front of the bandstand to introduce him. He said some things that brought tears to John's eyes, but these things didn't do anything like that to anybody stretched out on the lawn, or to any of the musicians on the bandstand. What it did to the musicians was make them bring funny papers out of their pockets which they began to read. What it did to the people lying around on the lawn was make them laugh out loud. But Wallace went right ahead with the speech he had prepared.

Some of the musicians began to whistle softly about some of Wallace's remarks about John Jenj. Still, Wallace knew he was right, so he went ahead fearlessly with his speech, talking better than he had talked when he had been valedictorian for the graduating class at Fresno High School in 1933, and still more tears came to John Jenj's eyes.

Now, however, a number of the young men who had nothing better to do than fool around on a Sunday afternoon at a serious band concert, began to make noises at Wallace Asfanasia, and John Jenj began to feel a little angry.

One thing about fellows from Sanger, they didn't take that kind of stuff from anybody anywhere, let alone an artist from Sanger who had been hired at considerable expense to appear with the band.

The next thing John Jenj knew almost every young man lying on the lawn was making vulgar noises, and they were making them loudly. As he talked on, Wallace Asfanasia reasoned that these noises were the direct consequence of the let-down of moral values in every part of the world when a major war begins. He felt sympathy rather than anger toward the makers of the noises. It was not their fault. Most of them probably felt, as he did, that pretty soon they *might* be in the army and in the war, and even if their apprehensions proved to be un-

250

founded, as Wallace certainly felt at that time they would be, the young men could not be blamed for letting off a little steam. It was American to do that, and Wallace was all for it, in a way.

But John Jenj, about whom Wallace Asfanasia was now desperately trying to get an eloquent word in edgewise, did not feel so charitable about the rudeness of the young men and young women who were making the vulgar noises.

No fellow from Sanger took that kind of stuff from anybody anywhere, that's all.

Now, to make matters worse, the young men stopped making vulgar noises and began to *shout* at Wallace Asfanasia.

"Come on, come on, let the hick play his solo and sit down."

John Jenj heard this remark very clearly, and then he refused to take any more of it. He jumped to his feet and stepped forward. He was holding his cornet, and Lars Harling, who had been half-asleep in his chair, jumped to his feet, too, under the impression that John was ready to render his solo. He rattled his baton on the tin music stand and all the musicians in the band dropped their funny papers and got all set with their musical instruments, to be ready to go with *It's a Sin to Tell a Lie* when Lars gave them the sign.

But John Jenj didn't lift the horn to his lips. Instead, he began to shout back at the young men and young women lying around on the lawn under the shade trees fooling around in the afternoon.

"We don't take that kind of stuff in Sanger," John shouted.

The young men and young women laughed and shouted back at him.

251

"We just don't take that kind of stuff where I come from," John shouted.

Lars Harling rattled the tin music stand again, hoping to get John set for the solo, but John just didn't take that kind of stuff.

As the matter got out of hand, Wallace Asfanasia made his way to the edge of the platform, jumped down, and wandered off to a tree near which no one was lying, and from this point in the park he watched and listened to John Jenj and the people who had come to the band concert.

The worst of it was that even adults, husbands and wives with kids, were not in sympathy with John. Their kids weren't, either. Everybody was completely in accord with the young men and young women who were heckling John Jenj.

"People like you," John shouted, "ain't going to hear *me* play the cornet. I'll go back to Sanger where people appreciate music."

"Get going, get going!" the crowd shouted back at John Jenj.

Wallace Asfanasia decided to walk through the park and think about the novel he was going to start writing just as soon as he was sure he had gathered together enough material for something major rather than something minor. He walked swiftly for a young man with an ambition like that, and a fellow lying on the lawn remarked to his girl, "That guy looks like he's in a walking race, don't he?"

Wallace didn't know it at the time but he had literally turned his back on the people, and he had always believed that that was something he would never do. He had gone about two hundred yards when the shouting and laughing became louder than ever, and he believed he heard John

Jenj's voice above all the others saying, "In Sanger we don't take that kind of stuff."

But now John's voice was more like a scream, and it occurred to Wallace Asfanasia that in all probability John had leaped down from the bandstand and was using his cornet as a weapon, but probably not effectively.

Then the band began to play *It's a Sin to Tell a Lie*, and without intending to do so Wallace Asfanasia began to say the words of the song to himself, although he was not by any means singing. Strange words they were, too, very strange indeed, and in some way connected with the war in Europe, no doubt.

Thus it was that the cornet-playing trend of Sanger came to an end, and was swiftly supplanted by a trend not nearly so local: a trend much more popular but not very much more reasonable than the cornet-playing one, but one the writer need not go into in detail, since so many others have already done so.

THE COCKTAIL PARTY

The water around Manhatten Island was stinking worse than ever, and enough of the smell had gotten into the warm moist haze over the city to make breathing and walking unpleasant, so a very lazy man in his early forties —named Andrew Loring—abandoned his plan to stroll to the cocktail party his first wife was giving.

He abandoned the plan as if doing so were accidental. He simply stepped into one of the many art galleries on 57th Street between 5th and 6th Avenues.

He was not interested in painting especially, it was simply that he knew he would not enjoy his walk and there was an hour or so to kill. He had no wish to be the first to arrive at the party, for he had not seen his first wife in six years. She had telephoned much too early that morning, about ten it must have been, when he had been half-asleep.

"Andy," she had said, "I'm giving a cocktail party tonight for a few old friends and of course you've got to come. I don't care how you've changed. I've heard you're very fat these days, but I know it's nothing serious, and anyhow I don't care what happens to people's bodies, just so the rest of them is O.K. Your last book was very bad, I hear, but every writer is entitled to at least two or three miserable performances."

At first he had only guessed it might be Clara Phipps, but very soon there was no doubt about it.

"I'm sure I've interrupted your work," she had gone on, "but I know nothing can really interrupt *you*, so I'm sure it's all right. There'll be only a dozen or so, and I think you will like them all. I must see you at least once every six years."

He had yawned noisily.

"What, darling? Surely I didn't wake you up? Well, anyhow, write this down." She had given him the address and then, "Any time after six, although it would be fun if you were to make it around half-past five. You must be asleep, so don't bother to talk. I'll just hang up and expect you."

She had hung up and he had taken the top book off a pile on the night table and had opened it and read eight or nine pages before he remembered that he had read the book only last night, a book called *The Unburied Dead,* by a new writer named Ivan Glossip. The upshot of the novel seemed to be that the unburied dead are the people who have not yet started to hope for some sort of decent human order, or who have stopped hoping; and that took in just about everybody.

He had put the book aside and taken the next one and read around in it until he had grown sleepy again, and then he had gone back to sleep.

"Bed," he had said. "That is the name of the next book I must write. Bed. Just bed."

Around two that afternoon the ringing of the telephone bell had awakened him again and he'd heard her say, "Of course you're the only writer I've asked. Don't think I've forgotten how little you care for even the best of them. And I think you're right. Luther will be with me, though, at least for awhile, but I'm sure you won't mind that *he's* having a book published in two or three weeks. It's quite good, I hear. I always said I'd never marry again and I meant it, but I did. It was a mistake of course, so I'm glad it's over, and if you want to know the truth I'm glad you finally got that movie actress out of your system, too. I always said if you couldn't make a marriage with me, you couldn't with anybody." She had stopped a moment, waiting for him to speak, and then she'd said, "Don't tell me you're still asleep?"

"No, but I wish I were."

"But why?"

"At the risk of being tiresome," he had said slowly, "I have come to the conclusion that it is better to be asleep than to be up and about for no good reason in the world."

"But everybody *is* up and about for perfectly *good* reasons," his first wife had said. "I don't mind your having gotten a little heavy in body, but I think it would be a pity if you'd gotten heavy in mind, too. You haven't got the makings of an old man in you, so you might as well stop trying to act like an old man."

"Old men can't sleep at all," he said. "Luther's about seventeen now; isn't he?"

"He's nineteen and you know it."

"I wasn't published until I was twenty-five."

"Yes, I remember. Well, I know you don't enjoy talking over the telephone. Come at half-past five."

It had been a quarter after five when he had left his apartment at the Pierre. He had hoped all night for snow. He had been hoping for it for several weeks, but now on the last day of November the weather was still unpleasantly warm. He had walked through the edge of Central Park, stopped a moment at the bar of the St. Moritz for a glass of ginger ale, and moved on down 6th Avenue to 57th, and it was in the middle of the block that he had decided to give up the notion of walking to the party, and had stepped into the art gallery.

He'd had no idea what the name of the gallery was, although he had passed it surely three or four hundred times, but as far as he knew he had never stepped inside. There had always been one picture in the window, and he had always stopped to notice it and had always felt that having noticed *that* picture it was not required of him to notice any more by that particular painter. But this time he had not noticed the picture in the window, and so had stepped in. The place was empty except for two gallery employees in the small office off the hall and a man seated on a stool in a corner of the gallery itself. This man got to his feet when the writer appeared. It was as if he were stunned that any one at all had come to the gallery, and it was as if he wanted desperately to speak to somebody. They glanced at one another and the writer bowed slightly on the chance that he knew the other. The other smiled faintly and, after a moment's hesitation, sat back on the stool.

"He's the painter," Andrew Loring decided before he'd had a chance to look at the paintings. He had noticed straight off that apparently every painting was a portrait, but he felt quite sure that that was only an impression and that he would soon discover the usual still lifes and landscapes. In the meantime, he noticed that the painter was small, slight, and emaciated-looking and that he radiated an innocent kind of excitement, an excitement of hope, though it was difficult to imagine what the hope might be for.

He glanced at his watch and noticed that it was a quarter to six. "I'll spend a half hour here," he thought, "and then I'll be there decently late."

He believed he would not mind seeing his son after six years, now a different person from the person he had known a little, but at the same time he could not help belittling in his mind the fact that this boy, named Luther after his wife's paternal grandfather, had actually had the audacity to write a novel. As for the boy's mother, he had known her from the time he and she had been twenty, and it would be nice seeing her again, although he did not like cocktail parties.

When they had gotten married he had not felt that Clara Phipps was a mature woman, although he himself had felt extremely mature. But as he had grown to understand the depth and breadth of his ignorance, she had remained in the same very young place: a young woman thrilled by the adventure of marriage, of home, of motherhood. The appearance of Luther had been for her a personal triumph, and some of her enthusiasm had communicated itself to him for at least a half-dozen years, years during which he worked very hard and wrote what the critics called his best work, eight novels which struck everybody as being both serious and funny. His people, the critics had said, were all cockeyed themselves, and they had been noticed by a vision that was cockeyed.

The first painting held him almost a full minute, although there was little in it worthy of any special notice. It was a portrait of a boy of five or six sitting at a bare table.

"I hope you like it," he heard someone say, and of course it was the artist. He had expected to find the man very near, but when he turned he saw that he was still on the stool.

"What do you call it?" the writer asked.

"The New Man."

"Oh, yes. Who sat for you?"

"Well, no one."

"But that's not possible, is it?"

"I find it easier than the other way."

"Is it yourself, then?"

"I suppose, but that would be so even if someone had sat, wouldn't it?"

"No doubt. Still, one has the feeling one has seen any number of such fellows sitting at tables."

"I'm glad you think so."

"I'll have a look at *this* one now."

He moved to the second picture and began to examine the artist's painting of a girl of eight or nine holding a rag doll by the foot. The girl seemed a little crazy, but she seemed so in a way that was somehow both refreshing and heartbreaking. The painter apparently had no use for settings as such, and the edges of his props soon disappeared, fading into space, so that one was compelled to notice more pointedly that which the painter chose to make very clear.

"This, I am sure," the writer said, "is called The New Woman. Is that right?"

"Not quite, although I must say I *did* think of calling it that for awhile. It's called The Mother. I also thought of calling it The Old Woman. There's no need to say why, or why I finally called it what I did."

"I see the face of the rag doll is also the face of the little girl."

"Yes, I thought that that was in order, too."

"Why?"

"Well, now that you ask me, I'm afraid I don't know, although I do appreciate your asking. As a matter of fact, I'm quite pleased that you're looking at the paintings at all."

Frequently the writer had come to have doubts about his hearing, and this was such a time. He distinctly got the impression that the painter was being respectful, and he couldn't imagine why.

The Cocktail Party

"I beg your pardon?" he said.

"Well, I mean I've read your books."

"Are you sure?"

"Yes, of course," the painter laughed.

"Well, thank you."

"It never occurred to me that you would bother to come to my first show. In fact," the painter laughed, "until you arrived I was beginning to think no one would bother."

"Well, I'm glad you're amused because I owe it to you to say I've stepped in here by accident, and I'm afraid I don't even know your name."

"Well," the painter laughed, "it's George Garrett."

They shook hands and then the painter said, "I'll try not to disturb you as you look at the rest of them, but of course you may not intend to."

"I have half an hour."

The painter was older than he had thought, perhaps thirty. He was nervous and proud and terribly eager not to seem clever in the wrong way.

"And if you want to know the truth," the writer went on, "I like your work. You like it, too, I'm sure, but you have a *right* to like it. Some of my books have been liked for the wrong reasons, you know. I have resented that not because I'm not grateful that they're liked at all, but because having them liked for the wrong reasons puts me to work trying to make sure the next book will be liked, or even *disliked*, for the right reasons, and pretty soon that sort of thing makes trouble. It was a most unhappy day for me when I discovered how ignorant I am. I might have taken pride in it, but I didn't. Being ignorant is a man's most underrated virtue. I suppose this is a very important time in your life."

"Well, it's my first show, but so far none of the critics

261

have come around. I suppose they will say something or other when they *do* come around, and I suppose I shall be eager to know *what* they say, but I can't imagine what use it will be. By ignorant, do you mean indifferent to details?"

"No, I believe I mean just plain ignorant. And it *is* a virtue, a most precious one, I might say. But it is no good at all when you are bothered by it. A writer ought to be ignorant and never have time to *suspect* it, even. He should be that busy living and working. But it's easy to talk."

"Sculptors talk best, I think," the painter said. "It takes them quite long to say the very simplest sort of thing, such as, 'I guess I'll go for a walk now.' The most capable talkers, I've found, stick to simple subjects, like their troubles—getting a job, getting along with the boss and with other workers, finding a place to live, transportation complications, the cost of food, and stuff like that."

"Yes. When did you begin to paint?"

"Oh, very early. Every kid paints. I've been painting seriously, as the saying is, since I was fifteen or so."

"How much is *this* one?"

The picture was three very old men seated on a bench. They looked as if they were in a home for the aged.

"I don't know what price the gallery has decided to put on any of the pictures. In fact, I don't think they've decided yet. Do you want it?"

"Well, no, but I just wondered how a painter makes a living."

"I work Saturdays."

"What do you mean?"

"I work in a vegetable market, from six in the morning till nine at night."

The Cocktail Party

"Is that so?"

"Oh, yes. But Saturdays only. I like the work and it pays enough for the week, ten dollars."

The writer came to the end of the paintings. There had been eleven of them, all rather large, all people, not one of them ordinary.

"What do you believe?" the writer said.

"Damned if I know," the painter said without hesitation, "but what do you think of them?"

"They're very good. That one of the three old men. What's it called?"

"The Boys."

"Yes, of course."

"Well, I guess I believe *something*, before you go," the painter said. "I didn't mean not to try to answer your question, it's just that answering *that* one takes a lifetime. I suppose I could say something. Could it be this? 'Every one of us is mistaken.'"

"Very likely. And your idea in these paintings is to point out that we *are*?"

"Well, I don't think so. I think I mean it's all right."

"Yes, it might be a pity if we stopped being mistaken. It's been a pleasure."

The painter had been standing for some time. He nodded and smiled, being excited and glad, and the writer stepped into the street. It was past dusk now, but the weather still smelled and it was no pleasure being out in it. He stopped a taxi and got in.

He noticed that the face of the taxi driver in the photograph inside the cab resembled, in many ways, the painter's face. It had the same sort of sullen simplicity: a kind of controlled rage about being who he was. It seemed as if the artist had made one thing clear to him, at any rate—the human face is more revealing than human behaviour.

The taxi lurched, then plunged ahead with a burst of speed that seemed absurd because it was not required, then came to a jolting stop at 5th Avenue. The writer glanced at the people crossing the street in a body and noticed that a woman with three small children was looking up at the sky and smiling. "God knows the secret of that smile," he said to himself, for he had come over the years to write (or put in words) everything he saw and felt and did, so that if the truth were known he was the author of a new book every day. The trouble was that for almost three years he had been unwilling (or unable) to put his books into written words. They did not seem urgent or important enough for that. He had started dozens of them and had worked at them a day or two and then had given them up with a sense of relief. He had gone so far as to make a joke of it by telling friends that he felt entitled to some sort of award for not having finished any of the bad books he had started. "I have served literature better than any of my contemporaries," he'd said. Still, he knew he was eager to get going again. "I never really learned to write," he once told a critic, "but, even so, I always manage to finish something."

"Exuberance did the trick," he thought, "but now it doesn't, or maybe I haven't got any more of it. It did the trick for Thomas Wolfe as long as he lived, and for a lot of others, too, but exuberance seems to stop when a man gets past his middle thirties, or the man himself stops."

The taxi shot forward again just as he noticed that the old man on the corner, tired and dazed, was a very famous writer whose works he had read as a kid, who had not written anything good in twenty years, and whose name, even, slipped his mind for a moment. He remembered the man very well, though, for they had met one night ten years or so ago at a dinner at the Waldorf. The purpose of the dinner had been to raise money for political refugees, and the old writer had been a guest of honour. He had given the impression of having been washed like a little boy for a party. His fingernails had been cleaned, his teeth brushed, his hair combed, his nostrils cleared and dried, and he had been dressed in formal black by somebody or other. He had come to the dinner in a daze of childlike joy, his tired face bright for a moment, his eyes excited, and then when he had been introduced to the audience, he had gotten up to speak, and Andrew Loring had heard his voice for the first time.

He had expected the man to look like a giant, and to act something like one, but the old writer had looked like a bewildered child, and he had spoken like a frightened schoolboy, his voice high-pitched, his words banal and ludicrous, his very presence an embarrassment to everybody.

He'd talked about himself, making no sense at all, seeming to say only that it was a lonely thing to be a writer, it was a painful thing to be no longer the writer you were, it was a shameful thing to be an old writer, it was a heartbreaking thing to be so glad about having been invited to a free dinner whose purpose was to raise money for fellow-writers in Europe who were having political troubles with foolish governments. Worst of all, though, was the old writer's intention every now and then to seem young still, to seem powerful, witty, full-voiced, a force for righteousness in the world. And the pathetic jokes he had tried to tell were very nearly sickening.

The Cocktail Party

The old writer had talked in circles for what seemed hours, and everybody at the large table had begun to fidget and look at one another and whisper and rustle papers and try to balance spoons on glassware, and then finally someone had whispered to him—it was the young critic who had introduced him—and the old writer had smiled and said, "I have just been informed that I am taking up too much time." His face had grown suddenly aged and outraged and he had said very softly, "I suppose that that is the truth. There was something I wanted to say, but I have forgotten it." And he had sat down.

After dinner Andrew Loring had gone to the old man and introduced himself and the old man had said, "Now I remember what I had wanted to say. It was this. None of us gives a hoot about anybody else. When the money they gather here tonight brings over some of the writers of Europe, do you think any of them is going to look around for somebody worse off than himself to help? I knew I shouldn't have come to this dinner, for we are a foolish profession." The old man giggled suddenly. "Why, when I was a boy I thought God wrote books—nobody else *should* write them. We are impostors."

Now, ten years later, he had seen the old man for an instant standing on a New York street corner, and the old man had seemed to be nothing so much as a beggar.

"He might have been given the Nobel Prize at one time," the man in the taxi thought. He then remembered the old man's name and began to go over each of his books, in the order in which he had discovered and read them, and it seemed suddenly true to him that there had been nothing in any of them excepting exuberance.

His mind wandered to the time when his nineteen-year-old son had been perhaps no more than five and had broken into the small room that was called his study, and he had said to the boy, "Now, you know I'm working, so why do you come in here where you don't belong?"

"Because I want to work, too," the boy had said.

He'd had bad luck at his work that day, and he'd told the boy in irritation to please take his place at the typewriter and go to work.

"I suppose you could do better, anyway," he'd said. "Anybody could."

The boy had permitted himself to be lifted and seated at the table, but he had not permitted himself to cry. Instead, he'd begun to tap at the keys.

The father had watched a moment, and then had shouted, "Clara! For God's sake, Clara, you have got to keep him out of my study when I'm trying to work!"

"Mama's not home."

"Where is she?"

"She went to the doctor's."

"When?"

"Today."

"Why did she go to the doctor's?"

"My sister."

"Oh, for God's sake."

"Oh, for God's sake," the boy had repeated.

Suddenly the writer had become ashamed of himself and had wanted to balance his rudeness with a little decent kindness, but he hadn't known how to go about it without making fools of both of them.

"Listen," he had said. "I'm sorry I shouted at you, but writing is hard work. Just because I've got to work at home doesn't mean you can come in here any time you feel like it and stop me. If I don't work, we won't have any money, and people can't live without money."

Having felt his father's kindness and having been made vulnerable by it, the small boy had expressed his resentment by saying, "I don't like money. I don't like you. I don't like Mama." He had gotten down from the chair at the table, his face white with rage. "I don't like anybody," he had said, and then he'd run out of the room to his bed.

The writer had gone to the kitchen and sat at the table there and after five or ten minutes the boy had come and sat across the table from him.

In the taxi, the writer understood why he had looked at the first painting in the gallery for so long. His son and the boy in the painting were one and the same, and the thing that had made them the same was resignation to loneliness. The writer and the boy had sat quietly a long time, neither of them so much as smiling, and then they had heard the key in the lock and Clara had come in and hugged and kissed the boy and then the man.

"Well," she had said when they were alone, "I'm pregnant, and it's about time, too, don't you think?"

"Yes, I suppose it is. You might have told me."

"I wasn't sure."

"You might have told me you were going, I mean. He broke into my study, and I'm afraid I was rude."

"A father can't be rude to his son."

"Oh, yes he can. I know, because I was, and he let me *know* I was."

"Well, aren't you glad?"

"About his sister? Of course. We can't afford it, but what's the good of having anything you can afford?"

"My father will help."

"I'd rather he didn't."

In those days of apprenticeship he had worked at odd jobs, very much as the painter was working these days, one or two days a week, for a little money, but he had always known that his wife had been receiving small sums of money from her father, too. He had worked as a clerk in book and department stores, and once he had taken a job in a theatre as an usher. Thus, they had managed, and they had always taken his writing seriously, and believed he would finally come through.

And he had been lean and hard, high-strung and irritable, and his energy had seemed inexhaustible. He had lately come to believe that he had been rather arrogant most of the time, although he was quite sure that this arrogance had been an impression others had gotten from his behaviour because he had been so eager to escape from ineptitude and anonymity, and had had no time in which to be gracious, or even civil in a routine way. He certainly could not remember ever having *felt* arrogant or ever having been pleased that he had slighted or offended anyone. He had never felt that plain work, for very little money, was beneath him, but he had always been eager to get back to his writing. Every now and then when the going was tough he had even grown fearful that he might never break through, and that he might find himself working steadily at a common job, solely because he had to provide for his family.

He had always taken it for granted that he would work at his writing at any hour of the day or night, and he had always seemed to find this no difficulty at all. Still, he had never neglected his wife, though he had very likely neglected his son, believing at the back of his mind that to neglect his son was the proper way for a father *not* to neglect him.

"The sooner he learns to go his way alone," he had reasoned, "the better it will be for him."

He had always enjoyed his wife's company and every now and then in the midst of love he had been enchanted by her wit and laughter and boldness and innocence, and he'd believed that she was as wise as any woman could or ever ought to be. They had discovered very early that there is little humour in love, but this had seemed to both of them so odd and unseemly that by the time they had been married three years they had put a great deal of humour into it.

They had always been outspoken with one another, and very often she had confessed to him that she had been lonely for him all day and when would he please stop work? He would be pleased by the boldness of his wife and he'd hurry along as swiftly as might be, and then get up suddenly and seize her, and they would go after themselves with laughter and a kind of tenderness and generosity that was altogether animal and yet handsome and humble, too.

There would have been others besides Luther, but one was lost before the one that was to have been his sister, which was lost in the third month and put his wife to bed for a month, and after that two more were lost, and it was then that they learned there could not be another.

She had wanted others more than he had, even, but he had wanted them very badly. And so little by little the laughter had left their love, for they knew there would never again be a new life out of it, and it had been the possibility of a new life coming out of it that had given them the best pleasure of all.

They were frequently sullen, and knew why, and were even able to talk about it. She had been the one to say they might be happier separated, and he had said it might do to think of adopting a foundling or an orphan every three years or so, but that idea had been no good at all for her.

And so finally, each of them picking fights about all sorts of insignificant things, they'd laughed at themselves and ended it, and she'd gone off with Luther to her father's home in Boston.

He had missed them both at first, and had frequently telephoned and argued that she should come back. Instead, though, she took Luther to Nevada during his school vacation and there she obtained her divorce.

He was thirty-six then, so it was easy to believe that what had come to pass had had to come to pass, and he had found adventure and even refreshment in the women whose lives casually touched his own. He had believed for a day or two that he might marry each of them and take up again the pattern of family life, with children, but one after another the women had wandered off, or he had. Finally, he'd met a young woman at a party named May Macy, a moving-picture actress, who had just divorced her husband, and he'd believed that with her the pattern might be resumed, for she was young and beautiful.

They had been married two weeks when May Macy flew to Hollywood because her agent had telephoned saying several studios had looked at her screen test and were ready to give her a contract, as a starlet. He had gone to the airport with her, and they had agreed that he would join her in a month, after he had finished his new book. And then after she had finished her first picture, they would fly to Europe for a holiday.

One evening he'd read in a gossip column that his wife had been seen at Ciro's and other fashionable places in Hollywood with a producer who was past sixty, and about whom he had heard a number of lurid if not ludicrous stories. The producer entertained only very young girls who were not yet very famous. He telephoned his wife and she said the producer was a perfect gentleman.

"How can you be so suspicious?" she said. "What do

you think I am, anyway? He's one of the biggest men in the industry. The most famous stars would give *anything* to have him take them out. I can't help it if he wants me to star in his next picture, can I? It's going to be his most expensive picture, and he says I'm the girl in America for the leading feminine role."

He had been amazed at the fierceness of her protest, and he'd said, "I'll tell you what. I'll fly out tonight and see you tomorrow morning."

But his wife had protested that that was exactly what he *shouldn't* do. That would wreck her career before it had begun.

"All right," he said. "Take care of yourself, and I'll call again tomorrow."

A week later a scenario writer who had just flown to New York from Hollywood had been overheard at a party talking rather freely about his wife and the producer. It was his agent, Harry Froyland, who had overheard the scenario writer's remarks, and Froyland had said, "What I think you'd better do is this. Let me get you a ten-week assignment at Metro, and while you're straightening things out with May you can be making a little money, too. It's no good having this sort of gossip going around about your wife. I don't want to rush you into this, but I think it's the right thing to do just now, and I know the deal's all set. How about it?"

"No," the writer had said.

He had flown to Hollywood the following morning and had reached there at ten at night and gone to her apartment, but she hadn't been home. He had been nervous and hungry and had felt a little foolish about the whole thing. The very fact that he was in Hollywood at all had embarrassed him. At one time or another he had met the biggest people in the industry, as they liked to call it, and had been astounded by their preoccupations. He had always avoided the place.

He arranged for a restaurant to have some cold food sent up to the apartment, along with a bottle of whisky, but when the food and drink had come, he found that he wanted only the whisky. By half past three in the morning more than half the bottle was gone, he was drunk, and he believed nothing his wife had done could possibly change the way he felt about her. He wanted her, they were going to have a life together, and that was all there was to it. He stretched out on the sofa in the living-room and soon fell asleep.

He sat up when he heard the door open, but it was only a maid who wanted to know if she could clean up. He asked her to come back later.

About fifteen minutes later, around nine in the morning, he saw his wife. She didn't want to say anything and he couldn't. They simply looked at one another drunkenly, each of them almost exhausted, and he was just barely able to control his impulse to beat her. He felt completely stunned and degraded. At last he took her by the arm and said, "Come on." They moved out of the apartment as if they were two people in a nightmare, but in the elevator the girl collapsed. The elevator boy helped him get her back into the apartment, and the writer put her to bed. He knew she was very ill, and he pitied her so deeply he forgot completely his feeling of outrage. All he wanted to do was help her. That evening she was much better, and two days later she was up and about and busy with plans for her career again. He was too confused to know what to do, and it was at this point in his life that he began to be lazy and to grow fat.

He began courting her again, taking her from one small night club to another because she wanted to avoid the big places, and for a while he believed their marriage might still be salvaged : she herself might be salvaged, he might be, and their children together might be. After all, she was young and ambitious, and what had happened was surely meaningless. She was tense all the time, though, and she had to have a lot to drink.

She waited every day for word from the producer about the new picture, but it never came, so she began to telephone the studio. She was told he was in conference and would call her back, and then several days later she was told he had gone to Mexico and would not be back for at least a month. She visited the studio a number of times with her agent in the hope of having the contract signed, but they were told the producer had not yet made any plans for the production of the film, and might even abandon it because it was so expensive. The agent turned to other studios, then, and after a week the writer knew his wife was becoming seriously ill. He felt sorry for her, and in a way for himself, too.

Harry Froyland urged him to accept the contract at Metro because he could practically write his own ticket. He could write an original story and give the best part in it to his wife, Harry said, and the writer was now too lazy to turn the offer down. He wrote a story called "Indiana Queen," but the studio changed the title to "Passion."

Lloyd Wilkinson was borrowed from Sam Goldwyn to direct the picture because he was so good at directing women, and during the making of the picture the writer watched the director miss the irony of the story and turn it into something like a hundred other films about beautiful girls from small towns, but he was too confused and lazy to bother about getting anything straight any more.

Besides, that hadn't been the important thing anyway:

he had wanted to give his wife what she had wanted, and to restore her health.

The picture was a long time being made, and he stayed beside his wife the whole time. The money kept coming in every week, and the offensive gossip about his wife began to be replaced by predictions of sensational success. They went to a number of premières and were photographed, and his wife behaved in the only way possible for her under the circumstances. That is, as if she were the greatest actress who had ever lived. Some of this Hollywood nonsense invaded his own thinking, and he remembered one evening having felt for an instant that he had done a very brilliant thing in writing the picture.

His name began to appear in the gossip columns of Hollywood and New York, and the tone was always the derisive tone professional gossips take when they believe they have discovered the betrayal of integrity.

"Andrew Loring," one of the more famous gossips had written, "who swore only last year in an interview that he would never sell out to Hollywood, has finally sold out and written a little item called 'Passion.'"

At last the film was finished and he asked to see it in private with his wife. It was done up in a big and dramatic way, with extremely loud and embarrassing music all over the place, stolen from the best composers, and it was so preposterously bad that he was by turns sickened and amused. It was as if someone he had never known had written the story. He heard his wife sob as the story unfolded, however, and he wondered if he would ever be able to guess why she did so. After the showing of the film they went for a walk along the company streets, and his wife finally said, "It's so hard to be a real artist. I tried my best, but that fairy Wilkinson just had to have his way. Still, it's a very great picture."

The Cocktail Party

The picture was released three months later, and by that time they were back in New York. They saw the première at one of the biggest theatres on Broadway, and people fell all over his wife. After the show the studio gave a party, and practically everybody in New York piled in, and ate and drank, and told one another how wonderful they were.

His wife flew back to Hollywood three days later, but this time he knew he had gone as far as he could go with her and the marriage. He was sure she would be all right from now on, so he didn't telephone and he was not surprised that she didn't, either. Three months later she went to Reno for a divorce, charging desertion, and he let it go at that. But there was nothing he could do now about the laziness that had started in Hollywood, or the fat that kept thickening his flesh, and he had to have new clothes made to fit him. He read a number of fan magazine stories about his wife and in one of them she was quoted as saying, "It's no fun being married to a genius like Andrew Loring. A great man like that just can't stand a little competition from his wife, but it was fun while it lasted. Oh, we're still friends, and when I go to New York we'll certainly go out together because love isn't something you can get over just like that."

When she did get back to New York she telephoned and begged him to take her to El Morocco because it would do her career so much good, and he was too lazy to tell her not to bother him any more. She got the publicity she wanted, and then flew back to Hollywood again.

A month later he began to hear new stories about her, and he wondered why he still wanted to try to help her.

Her second picture was abandoned after a month of shooting because she just couldn't look the way they wanted her to look, or act the way they wanted her to act.

The Cocktail Party

The studio suspended her not long afterwards for refusing to play a secondary role, and finally her agent had her contract broken, so he could try to make a new one with another studio. But by now it was generally acknowledged that her success had been a fluke. She telephoned, asking him to do another story for her, and he was too lazy to say he couldn't, but when he tried to write a new story he discovered he was also too lazy to finish it. She flew to New York, and he was too lazy to get out of town. But he knew she couldn't be helped any more by him.

"Please go home to Indiana," he urged her.

He was not altogether surprised when she telephoned one night to say that she was going to take an overdose of sleeping pills. He told her he would be right over, and when he saw her he told her he would write the story. He tried for six weeks, but it was no use. The stuff just sickened him.

Finally, she wandered off, and once months later he saw her in a B picture. By that time she was married to a cameraman.

The taxi stopped and the writer got out.

All cocktail parties are alike in that the idea is to drink and talk, but every party is made special and unique by the combinations of people who happen to be at them. For Andrew Loring, his first wife's party was unique because his son was there.

When he entered the room in which the party was going on, he saw his son standing beside the woman who had given birth to him, and he was so pleased about them that he could not speak. It was as if a man had gone off in his youth to an adventure and had come back old and only able to nod by way of expressing what was in his heart.

"I expected you to be *very* fat, but you're not at all," his first wife said, and he nodded.

277

She then said, "I'm not going to bother to introduce anybody to you just now because Luther's going along to catch a train for Boston in a little while, so why don't you two wander off somewhere and talk about girls? Luther's been having a time with them lately, too, you know."

The writer nodded, and his first wife turned away.

"Mother's looking well, don't you think?" the writer's son said.

Andrew Loring was able to smile by now, but he was still speechless. The boy was just as high-strung as he himself had been when he was nineteen, and he knew from the laughter in his son's voice that they were certainly friends, if nothing else.

"I finally got around to reading every book you've had published," his son said, "and I hope you don't mind my talking about your writing a moment. Am I mistaken in feeling your work has been misunderstood and that what you have been saying from the very beginning is that—— Well, maybe I'd better not try to go into that just yet."

"No, please do," Andrew Loring managed to say.

"Well, hell," the younger man said quickly, "I seem to feel that what you've been saying from the beginning is that a human being does not live, but *is* lived. Is this anything like what *you* think you've been saying?"

"Yes, it is," the writer said. "We have been led to believe that being alive is a personal experience, and I do not believe it is. I believe it is absolutely impersonal. No man knows himself. No man knows another. No man decides for himself who he is or who he is to be, what he is to do, or how he is to do it. Every man belongs to matter, that's all. Matter is a large order, and every man is a small order. Matter happens to a man, and the man goes along for the ride, as the saying is. I'm delighted that you've understood my work so well. What is the name of *your* book?"

"*Yes*."

"An excellent title," the father said. "And what do you say in this book?"

" 'Yes,' " the younger writer said again, nervously and quickly. "For years I gave the matter of what to say and what not to say a great deal of thought, and for a long time it seemed to me that I *might* very well say anything, so of course I had to make a choice. At last I knew that I couldn't choose to say *no*, or even *maybe*, or yes *and* no. I knew I had to say *yes* and nothing else, so I knew I was ready to write, too. After that, it was just a matter of finding time to sit down somewhere and go to work, which is not the easiest thing in the world to do, with so many wonderful distractions all around. Still, I managed to find the time, and wrote the book. I'm sure some other new writer can say no, if he wants to, and very likely be right, too, but even so all I can say is yes, and I'm satisfied that I'm at least as right as he is."

"I understand perfectly," the older writer said, bursting into laughter because this stranger before him was his son, which was beside the point, and because the stranger was nervous and quick and might just actually be a writer, which was *not* beside the point. The stranger certainly looked and spoke as if he might be a writer. And the older man laughed because for the first time in years he no longer felt fat and lazy. He laughed because even though he had been so poorly lived, it hadn't been altogether meaningless, for here at last was a little meaning. Here was the five-year-old boy who broke into his father's study to tell him that he too wanted to write—now taller than his father, even more nervous and alive than his father had been. Here he was, proudly resigned to the loneliness which is man's lot, ready and able to write, and to say yes, with no strings attached. Here he was, as ignorant as any writer, and yet too busy living and working and learning to be bothered by that. Andrew Loring laughed *especially* because the stranger's ignorance was so great and yet so irrelevant.

The younger man laughed, too.

"When I first saw you tonight," he said, "I didn't recognize you for a moment because apart from the fact it's been a long time since I saw you, you seemed so tired."

"I *was* very tired when I arrived a few minutes ago," the older man said.

"Well, you don't seem tired now," the younger man said.

"No, it doesn't take long to stop—or start—being very tired," the older man said. "I started very suddenly, and that's how I've stopped, too."

The younger man looked at his watch.

"I've got to go now," he said. "I came from Boston especially for this party because Mother said you might be here. I've been hanging around since four o'clock. For a while, after everybody else had arrived, I felt pretty lousy because I was afraid you might not show up. But you did, and so it's been a great party for me."

"I'm enjoying the party very much myself," the older man said, "although as a rule cocktail parties depress me."

"I like them," the younger man said, "but if I don't get out of here and grab a taxi the minute I get to the street I'll miss my train."

The two men laughed, then the older one watched the younger break away, not saying goodbye to anyone, but stopping at the open door to wave thanks to his mother.

Andrew Loring quickly finished his drink, took another off a tray, and hurried to join his first wife.

The Cocktail Party

"Well," she said, "how do you like the way he's turned out?"

"I like the way he's turned out very much," he said, "and I've come to thank you for asking me to this party. It's the best cocktail party I've ever been invited to, and if you don't mind I'd like to hang around a while and meet everybody."

"I don't mind at all."

The woman took the man by the arm and they moved to a group of three people, who immediately stopped talking about how long the next war might be postponed in order to find out who the man was who seemed so pleased about something or other in a world so full of unpleasant things.

THE LEAF THIEF

The solitary walker reaches people and things quite often just in time to get all he needs of them and goes right on, but every now and then he will slow his pace down in order to get a little more, or he will even loiter. Sometimes he will stop.

Walking is as good as reading a book about which you know nothing. Or a book that's been around a long time in which you want to see how many things you failed to notice when you read it last. Or what you are going to think about while you are reading it again.

A proper walk ought to have no time limit. It should have a general destination, but not a course. A neglected street should be discovered if doing so seems to be a good idea at the time, or a favourite street should be ignored if that seems to be a good idea. Being free to walk at all is the real idea, and it doesn't matter much where.

I usually settle for the ocean in San Francisco because it's not too far off, and because once I get to where the water comes and goes I feel glad, no matter how I really feel. Most people who walk on the beach do so because they don't want to be bothered about trying to nod or smile or speak to other people, and they may come face to face with one another and not see one another and think nothing of it, for they know they are there in the first place in order not to need to go to the trouble of putting on.

283

The Leaf Thief

But every now and then a man of sixty or so fishing in the surf will stop you to say, "Well, I fished all morning at the end of Taraval and got a little six-pounder. Then I went home for some lunch and a nap and now I've been fishing here at the end of Ortega all afternoon and if I don't get anything at all I won't mind."

He won't exactly stop you, he'll meet you head-on, say all he's got to say before you've gone past him and won't care if all you do is listen seriously and nod once.

It's the ocean, no doubt.

And I suppose I walk to the ocean because it's almost always grey and foggy in San Francisco and the ocean is best of all then.

There was an August Sunday, though, that started out high, bright, warm and fine, and stayed that way one hour after another, so that you knew it was going to be a day during which to look at the city itself from the top of a hill—a day you could have a real look at it from one hill after another, and then from a valley, from streets down in a valley, and find out how the city's holding up, how it's changing, how it isn't.

So I set out for town and climbed the hills and looked and stepped up to a lot of fine things just in time to get all I wanted of them and went on, and then on my way back the best thing of the whole walk happened.

The walk was a two-and-a-half-hour one: across the street to the steps that climb Red Rock Hill, around the hill, down the valley, up a hill (an unnamed one), down through soft dirt and weeds and junk and bushes and small trees and broken branches to the street, and then up the group of hills there through Sutro Forest, down a little, up again, around to the left, and then steeply down a mile and a half or more to Market Street, and slowly up, past

The Leaf Thief

the United States Mint, and then all the way into town—
a distance of seven or eight miles, all fine, the day
high, bright and warm, about two hours of steady hard
walking, with no need to slow down or loiter or stop
anywhere.

The streetcar comes back almost before you've finished
smoking a second cigarette, and then there's a half mile
uphill and the walk's finished.

The fifth house down the hill from my own house has a
fine young gum tree in its front yard, a tree you can't
help feeling happy to see because the clear light makes
everything so easy to see and because the leaves of the
tree are so new and fresh and red and green and black
and part of the day.

When I came around the hill and started to climb this
street I saw a boy of ten or eleven walking slowly ahead
of me fifty yards or so. When he came to the tree he
plucked a leaf off of it.

That is to say, I saw him do it, and I decided to have
a look at the tree myself when I reached it. But I didn't
see the man who was standing on his brick threshold
breathing the fresh air. The boy hadn't seen him,
either.

The next thing I knew the man had stopped the boy's
walk and the two were standing there talking. That is to
say, the boy was trying not to stop and at the same time
to be half-way polite or adequate, and nothing much
seemed to be happening one way or another.

When I began to hear what the man was saying I also
began to slow down, although I was eager to get to a
shower.

"What did you say?" the man said.

"Took it," the boy said. He spoke respectfully.

"Well, that's just fine," the man said. He was very

serious and a little angry. "Do you do that everywhere you go?"

"No."

"Well, why do it here?"

"I don't know." The boy looked at the leaf, then held it out. "Do you want it back?"

"Hell, no," the man said. "What good is it now?" He looked at the leaf in the boy's fingers. "Do I want it back?" he said bitterly. "I didn't want you to take it off the tree in the first place."

"I didn't know," the boy said.

He wanted to go, but at the same time it appeared as if he was genuinely sorry about what he had done, or about the man's being so upset by it, or about a little thing like plucking one leaf off a tree meaning so much to some people, or about the way a fellow could be going along on a Sunday afternoon, thinking about things in general and then suddenly see a nice tree covered with new leaves and reach out and take one and not mean anything by it and then somebody had to stop him and make a fool of him.

He was a boy from another neighbourhood, wandering around anywhere because it was a nice day, who'd decided to climb the hill of this street and have a look. He was a boy with a nature that was either calm or was susceptible to becoming calm after idle walking on a good day, and there was no rudeness or defiance in his nature, even though he was probably the son of a working man, a boy who scarcely ever came into half a dollar unless he earned it himself, but mainly he was a stranger on this street.

As for the man, I understand he is employed by a bank. I suppose he has been called down many times for small errors. At any rate, I was scarcely walking at all, waiting for the matter to be resolved, but it seemed the man refused to drop it and the boy wasn't quite up to just walking away.

At last the man said, "Suppose everybody who came by here took a leaf off the tree?"

"There wouldn't be many on it after a while," the boy said dutifully.

"No, of course there wouldn't," the man said. "And that's just the point."

"Yes, sir," the boy said.

"O.K.," the man said. "The next time you come by here, don't let it happen again."

"Yes, sir."

The boy turned away from the man and with a sudden, almost startling, burst of energy began to get away, and then just as suddenly almost halted. He turned around and noticed that the man was standing in front of the tree, examining the place where the boy had taken the leaf.

Then the boy slowly moved on up the hill.

Well, it turned a good walk into an almost memorable one, for when the boy turned to get away I could not help thinking that *turning* is the source of all beauty and all drama. Except for turning—turning to notice a small tree covered with new leaves, turning to notice one leaf in particular, turning to take it, turning to stop because someone has called out, turning to see who it is, turning to stone from shame and humiliation, and then turning to flee—there would be little beauty and drama in the experience of living.

And suddenly, while the boy, with hanging head, with the inside of the hanging head turning hard and angry, prouder and lonelier than ever, moved past my own door, I remembered the times, again and again, all my life that someone had asked me suppose everybody did something or other that you have just done, and not once in all my life, not even when I was finally fifteen, then twenty, then thirty, not even when I was finally an old man of forty did I know how the devil to answer the question.

There is a good answer to it, I know, but it never seems to occur to me. I just stand there with my mouth open, the way the boy did.